Dear Reader,

Autumn's just around the corner—and, of course, a new month means four exciting new romances from Bouquet!

First up is Marcia Evanick, continuing her Wild Rose series with **Hand in Hand,** the story of a woman determined to reclaim the dreams she thought she lost—and who wonders if a second chance with her husband is the only one that matters. Next, Mary Schramski offers an **Angel Next Door** for an unjustly suspended cop who discovers that love can turn up in the most unlikely places.

Who can resist a cowboy? The woman in Patricia Ellis's offering, **Rodeo Hearts,** couldn't—and now love is about to take her for the most passionate ride of her life. Finally, Carol Rose explores what happens when the ultimate good girl decides to become a **Wild Woman**—and finds the one man who wants her either way.

I know you won't be able to resist even one of these fabulous romances! Enjoy—and don't forget to come back for more next month!

Kate Duffy
Editorial Director

A WALK ON THE WILD SIDE

Jake had promised his best friend he'd look after his sister. Many things could happen to a woman in a city the size of Dallas, especially a woman as sweet and innocent as Emily.

A murmur of voices drew him toward the shop showroom, a glass-fronted area that held a herd of gleaming Harleys. Jake frowned over his coffee cup as he spotted a tight circle of his employees gathered around someone who was perched on one of the motorcycles.

Curious, Jake wandered over. Nudging several guys aside, Jake moved close enough to get a better view.

And what a view it was.

The woman perched lithely astride the latest arrival could have been peeled out of one of the posters that adorned the walls. Her chin-length bob was dark mahogany, deep red highlights shimmering as she tossed her head in laughter, lips the color of a woman's passion, soft and moist. She wore a snug sweater and a skirt so tight and brief, it hardly covered her slender hips, leaving a luscious length of leg bare to the world.

Jake felt his interest stir. He cleared his throat. "I don't think the lady needs all our help. Why don't you guys get on back to work? I'll take care of her."

Turning his full attention to the babe on the Harley, Jake was glad to see her smiling broadly.

"So you'll take care of me, huh?" she said in a sultry murmur.

He moved closer. "Oh, my God. Emily?"

"Yes," she said, dropping a purring note into her voice. "Still want to take care of me?"

Jake Wolf couldn't believe sweet, decorous Emily had gone over the edge.

WILD WOMAN

Carol Rose

Zebra Books
Kensington Publishing Corp.
http://www.zebrabooks.com

ZEBRA BOOKS are published by

Kensington Publishing Corp.
850 Third Avenue
New York, NY 10022

Zebra and the Z logo Reg. U.S. Pat. & TM Off.

First Printing: September, 2000
10 9 8 7 6 5 4 3 2 1

Printed in the United States of America

*Many thanks to Shelley Bradley
for graciously making me
a gift of the idea
behind this book*

*Which is dedicated to
Hilary Sares,
the first editor
to hear my voice.*

Prologue

Emily Loughlin wanted to cry. Wanted to scream and yell as another one of her going-crazy moments threatened.

Fingers still curled tightly around the receiver, she lowered the phone carefully to its cradle. The usual office noise eddied around her. She couldn't indulge in a crying fit, not with her desk out where everyone could see and would certainly feel free to inquire into her business.

At twenty-six, she still lived within the same restraints as when she was a teenager, and she had no one but herself to blame.

It wasn't as if she'd really loved the house on Clark Street. So what if the bank had just turned down her request for a loan to buy a home? The bungalow had small windows and tiny rooms. It wasn't anything that stirred her creative blood, but it would have been her place and surely would have given her designing urges an outlet and made her feel more settled. Something had to.

She'd been feeling very unsettled lately. Unfulfilled, stifled, and frustrated. How did a grown-up woman live her own life without hurting the people she loved?

Placing her hands flat on her desktop, Emily leaned back in her chair and took a deep breath. She had to get a grip, had to subdue the urge to take her credit card and show Mr. Snotty Simms, loan officer, what a bad credit record really looked like.

She'd lived her life as steady as a rock, never failing to pay her bills, never succumbing to the urge to blow her entire paycheck on the gold sequin dress in Babcock's formal wear department. Truthfully, she never wore gold. She had her mother's word on it that the hue made her look sallow, not to mention unladylike. Which made her want to buy the dress even though she knew yellow wasn't her best color.

Staring down at her desk, Emily noted the neat piles of contracts and notes, separated into "to do" and "why wasn't this done yesterday?" categories. She usually took pride, if not comfort, in doing her job well, but now she couldn't help wondering why she worked so hard and paid her bills if doing the right thing didn't garner her any reward.

In the four years since college, she'd worked hard as one of Jim Morris's paralegals, convinced that the job was just a way of supporting herself until better things came along.

Like maybe a personal life with a man who stirred her blood with the force of a thunderstorm. Someone to inspire her with both lust and the deep contentment of a lifetime together.

Gathering a stack of files in her arms, Emily went to the file room, ruminating about the singular emptiness of her life.

She was in her prime, alone and working in a job she despised—still waiting for the payoff of years of patiently being the person everyone said she should be. Emily, the good girl.

Truthfully, she'd been following the path of least resistance for so long it took moments like these to realize she wasn't really living her life. When had she ever made choices based on what she wanted to do rather than on what was expected of her? She was a coward, too afraid to reach out and grab the life she wanted.

As a result, the going-crazy moments threatened more often now. Only six months back, she'd actually applied for an interior design internship in London. The whole time she'd been preparing her portfolio, she'd known she had no chance. Since leaving college she'd been so busy being responsible that there had been no time for her designing.

Applying for that internship had been her only real attempt to take charge of her life. Not much of an attempt since she had virtually no chance of beating out all the other applicants, but she'd even taken that slight action in complete secrecy.

She barely mentioned it to her best friend, Cassie, but she deliberately hadn't told her parents.

It wasn't so much that her parents would have disapproved. They simply wouldn't have reacted at all because it wouldn't occur to them that she could have a life beyond the small town of Middleton, Texas. A husband and children. Her proper place in society.

After carefully returning the files, each in its place, Emily went back to her desk. With a spurt of hopeful excitement, she decided to call about the volunteer job with the historical society. That, at least, held the promise of some creative release.

Her motto had recently become: "When real life sucks, find a safe diversion." She was so lacking in courage.

"Hello, Mrs. Campbell? This is Emily Loughlin."

"Oh, hello, Emily. How are you, dear?" the older woman asked, her voice stiff.

"I'm fine," Emily responded eagerly. "Have you talked with the fund-raising committee about the job?"

"Er, yes," Mrs. Campbell said. "I've been meaning to call you all week."

Emily held her breath as the other woman paused.

"I wish I had better news," Mrs. Campbell said finally. "The committee decided to go with someone else."

"What? But I'm the only one who volunteered to direct the refurbishing of your designer house this year."

"Yes," the woman allowed, "but the committee feels that even if we have to pay someone with a little more . . . style, it would be a good investment."

"But I have a degree in design," Emily protested desperately. "I have style."

"Yes, of course, dear. It's just that we're looking for *flair. . . .*"

For the second time in half an hour, Emily clutched the telephone receiver, a lump in her throat. Numbly, she stared down at the drab beige dress she wore.

"It isn't personal, Emily," Mrs. Campbell hurried to assure her as if being judged not creative enough could be anything but personal.

"We'd love your help," the woman said. "There are many smaller tasks—"

"Thank you," Emily interrupted, having heard more than enough. "Goodbye, Mrs. Campbell."

This time she slammed the phone down. To hell with what anyone thought.

The noise echoed a second in a sudden silence, her four coworkers startled out of their chatty gossip.

"Is anything wrong?" Cassie asked, pushing her glasses back up on her nose.

"No," Emily denied, too aware that the others were listening. "Nothing's wrong."

Nothing except her entire life, what there was of it. How could she have let things get so bad?

"Well, treat the phone equipment more gently," reproved Mrs. Foster, the office manager. "I don't know what Mr. Morris would say if we had to replace a phone."

"Of course," Emily murmured, very sure what Jim Morris would say, every office-related expenditure having elicited the same string of curses. The man couldn't even swear with imagination.

Despite years of ingrained restraint, Emily stalked through the next few hours of work, both angry and depressed. She couldn't even manufacture her usual smile. More and more in the last few months, it had felt tight on her lips, and today she just couldn't force her mouth to comply.

The worried looks of her coworkers bothered her some, especially Cassie's. Emily's nonexistent life wasn't their fault, but she couldn't help feeling as if the entire town were in on a conspiracy to keep Miss Emily Loughlin in a very small box of boredom and propriety. It was her own fault, she knew. She should have never returned to Middleton after college.

Some people loved small-town life, felt safe and secure in it. But then regular people like Cassie, who couldn't wait to marry her longtime sweetheart, John Robert, hadn't lived all their lives being the mayor's daughter. Middleton knew everything they did, but somehow it judged them differently from Mayor Loughlin's little girl.

Just as the clock crept toward five-thirty and Emily thought she might be able to survive the day, her boss swept in from court and called her into his office.

She'd worked for Jim Morris since shortly after graduating, and familiarity had certainly bred contempt on her part. Jim never seemed to give anyone else enough thought to even develop such hostility. Still, years of habitual paycheck-seeking carried her into his overdecorated corner office.

He stood pawing through the shuffle of briefs and papers on his desk, his thick hands crumpling phone messages she knew he'd never return. In that way, Jim was nothing more than an ordinary attorney. She'd long lost respect for the profession in general.

Still, her wearily hopeful heart reminded her, there was the matter of the raise she was due and, if life was the least bit fair, a promotion as well. Maybe the added responsibility of directing the paralegal staff would help her feel better about her situation. At least it would give her something to do.

Jim Morris looked up. "Oh, Emily. Sit down, sit down."

He walked around his desk and leaned against the corner nearest her as she perched uncomfortably on the edge of the chair. "You're certainly looking fetching today," he said, his gaze wandering over her.

Oh, gross. He was in one of his icky gallantry modes.

"Thank you," Emily murmured, reflecting to herself that she hadn't had her bangs cut in three months and the beige dress made her look sallower than the gold sequin at Babcock's ever could. Still, there was that raise and the promotion to think of.

She sat quietly waiting, her eyes focused on his maroon tie.

"So," Jim said, wandering over to push the office door shut, "I guess we have a few things to talk about."

"Yes."

Jim returned to stand behind her, the sudden placement of his hands on her shoulders making Emily start.

Great. For three years, she'd watched Jim Morris cheat on his wife with a string of bimbos, many employed in the office as "secretaries" during their brief tenures. The last one had departed two weeks ago. Apparently, Jim had some time on his hands.

"How are you doing today?" he asked in a seductive purr as his meaty hands circled on her shoulders.

Emily's body tightened to maximum stiffness. It was true. You never knew how you'd respond to sexual harassment until it happened to you.

"I'm fine, Jim." She leaned forward slightly, pulling away from his hands. "Could we talk about the raise?"

Her boss laughed, walking around to sit down behind his desk. "Sure, honey."

A breath of relief slipped out of her and she forged ahead. "I understand from Mrs. Foster that you're thinking about letting someone else direct the paralegals, so you won't have to be bothered with it."

Jim smiled across the desk. "That's right, but I'd have to work . . . very closely with her. She'd be my right-hand person, go to depositions with me, lunch together a lot. . . ."

A sick feeling started in Emily's stomach as Jim's smile widened and his gaze dropped to her chest. "You've worked with me a long time, Emily, and I've always found you . . . attractive."

"Jim, I'm not interested in having an affair with you," she blurted out, nausea and anger making the words blunter than she'd intended. The man had a temper when crossed, and four years of witnessing his rages hadn't made her immune to their effect.

His smile didn't waver. "That's such an ugly word, Emily. I'm just talking about a *working* relationship. Lots of pretty women develop feelings for the men who sign their paychecks."

"I can assure you," she said around the lump in her throat, "that I will never develop those feelings."

Jim's face hardened. "Are you very sure, Emily? Because I'm having those feelings now and it might be hard to work together if they're not shared. I'd be walking around with a constant hard-on and no relief. Surely, you wouldn't want me to go to court like that."

Emily started trembling, more frightened and disgusted than she could have imagined. "Maybe I'm not the one for the promotion."

He got up and came around to face her again. "Think about this, honey. I'm a powerful, rich man, more powerful than your daddy. Don't you think you'd like sleeping with someone more powerful than Daddy?"

Emily shot up from the chair and retreated three steps toward the door.

"I'm sorry, Jim. I'm not interested," she said breathlessly.

"I'm sorry, too," he growled, his face darkening in response to her refusal. "Because you'll just have to find another job. You're fired, Miss Too-Good Loughlin."

Emily felt as if she'd slipped into another reality. Fired?

"Go on, get out of here," he snarled. "I'll tell Foster to give you two weeks' severance. I don't need prissy, up-tight bitches working for me."

She'd never thought he'd fire her. Pass her over for the promotion, not give her a raise, and generally make her life at work miserable, but fire her? She'd worked here four years, doing darn good work in a job she'd grown to hate.

"I could sue you for this." The words slipped out, mostly just to see his reaction.

"Try it, honey." He glared at her. "I'll eat you for lunch."

Emily stood by the door, her hand on the knob as realization blossomed throughout her. He deserved to be sued and doing so was definitely her ethical responsibility, but why would she fight for a job she hated?

She never had to come back, she thought. Never again had to drag herself to the office and face another day helping clog the legal system. Never had to see Jim Morris again.

A smile spread over Emily's face. "You're scum, Jim. Real pond scum and I feel sorry for your wife. But you've just done me a big favor."

Emily opened the door and marched through it.

Turned down for the loan, rejected as a volunteer for the historical society, and fired by her boss. All in one day.

Being a good girl wasn't paying off.

Screw them all, she was out of here. There was a big, open world to be discovered and she was definitely in the mood to go exploring. Somehow, she had to find some self-respect.

One

Jake Wolf couldn't believe sweet, decorous Emily had gone over the edge.

If her brother, David, hadn't been his best friend since grade school, Jake might have suspected the entire phone call was a prank. But he'd never heard David so desperate before.

Piloting his black pickup truck through dark, dangerous streets, Jake tried to make sense of his friend's garbled words.

From what her brother had said, quiet, sedate Emily Loughlin had snapped. In a brief period of days, she'd quit her job, sold most of her belongings, and moved to the big city, claiming to be determined to try every sin the metropolis could offer.

Of course, a lot of people moved to Dallas. Nothing so strange about that. It was the sin part that put the near-hysterical note in David's voice. Emily had grown up in Middleton, Texas, the youngest child in a perfect family, wanting for nothing, sheltered in stability.

As far as Jake could remember, Emily had never done a sinful thing in her life. He didn't count the time she'd thrown rocks at him and David when they were skinny-dipping. After all, they had refused to let her join in and she'd gotten into big trouble with her mother for messing up her dress.

Jake stopped at a traffic light, hearing the lone echo of a siren through the midnight streets. Dallas was no place for Emily. She was a sweet, innocent young woman who had no idea how to manage in a place where crime lent a blood-red hue to the evening news.

The whole thing seemed unfathomable, but the scrap of paper in Jake's hand held the address of her motel and he'd promised David he'd ride to the rescue. David would have come himself if he hadn't been in the middle of a big deal for one of his father's cronies.

"Talk some sense into her," David had demanded.

Turning the pickup toward the screaming siren, Jake wondered how he'd talk sense into a woman he hardly knew. He'd left Middleton ten years ago. The grown-up Emily seemed very removed from his world.

And now he was supposed to "handle" her.

The motel looked low and gray in the glare of the dim streetlights, the ambulance's rotating red light seeming surreal.

Panic crowded in Jake's chest. He'd headed out as soon as he'd gotten David's call. Surely, the worst couldn't have happened in so short a time. She'd only arrived in town that afternoon, according to her brother.

Jake glanced again at the address he'd scribbled. Caravan Inn on Ledbetter. He sighed in relief then, noting that the police cars and emergency vehicles were clustered at the far end of the parking lot, away from the room Emily occupied.

He pulled into the lot, steering around a ragtag crowd of onlookers. A surprising number of people, considering it was past midnight on a Thursday.

The Caravan Inn consisted of eight connected rooms,

dilapidated and scrawled over with gang graffiti. Easing his truck across the pocked asphalt parking area, Jake stopped in front of number eight, wondering if Emily was inside, hiding under her bed. The noise of the city had assaulted even him when he'd first moved here from Middleton, and compared to Emily's, his life had been anything but quiet.

Jake got out and walked quickly to the door. He'd last seen Emily five years ago at Christmas when she'd been a junior in college. Slender and quiet, she'd worn a sedate green dress, her long dark hair pulled back with a bow. He remembered feeling awkward when his gaze had met her wide hazel eyes. The little girl he'd taunted and run from had somehow grown into a beautiful woman.

What was he supposed to say to her now? One o'clock in the morning at a scuzzy roach motel after she'd run away from home at the age of twenty-six.

Jake raised his hand and knocked, unable to shake the weirdness of the moment. He heard a scrabbling sound as if the room's occupant was rattling a safety chain.

"Who is it?" a muffled female voice called.

"Jake Wolf."

The door opened, framing Emily's astonished face in the crack allowed by the chain. "Jake?"

"Hi," he said, burrowing his hands in his coat pockets.

"What on earth are you doing here? How did you know I was . . ." Her voice trailed off as she brushed back a long strand of dark hair.

"David," she said, after a moment. "He called you."

"Yes," Jake acknowledged. "Can I come in?"

"Do you know what time it is?" she asked coolly, as if he were placing a social call after hours.

"Yes, Emily, I do," he said, starting to feel annoyed.

He didn't know what was going on with her, but he hadn't come into the worst neighborhood in Dallas to be kept standing at the door like a member of some annoying religious sect.

She looked at him for a long moment, the usual friendliness absent from her face. "I guess you can come in, since you're here."

"Great," Jake muttered as she closed the door to unlatch the chain. "So much for Galahad on his white horse."

The door swung wide and she stepped back to allow him entrance.

Jake looked around the room as she locked the door. Two smaller-than-full-size beds huddled against one wall, their coverlets a faded orange. On the other side of the narrow space, a single sink sat next to a small television that was bolted to the wall. The rug under their feet was stained in more places than he could count, probably with liquids he didn't want to think about.

In his mind's eye flashed a picture of the large gracious brick home Emily and David had grown up in with its fireplace and in-ground pool. There couldn't be a greater contrast.

"So," Emily said with irritation, "big brother sent in the cavalry."

"You can't really blame him for being worried." Jake looked at her with curiosity, wondering about the woman she'd become. Of average height and slender build, she had the long brown hair and fair complexion he remembered. Now her face was clouded with emotion, her graceful body seeming taut beneath a baggy T-shirt and a pair of old jeans.

It seemed strange to see her as a woman apart from her family, more than just as David's sister.

"I'm not fourteen years old, Jake." Her hazel eyes flashed with resentment.

For some reason, her hostility made it easier for him. He didn't know what he'd have done if he'd found her crying in a corner.

"Maybe not chronologically," he replied, sinking down on one of the beds without waiting for her invitation. "But it sounds like you've reverted back to something. All of a sudden, you quit your job, sell everything, and move to Dallas to stay in this roach trap of a motel?"

"It's not that bad," she protested, as if trying to convince herself.

"I know you're not deaf, so you had to have heard the sirens out there."

Her face faintly worried, Emily glanced toward the window where the regular red flash from the police cruiser still shone. "Did you see what happened?"

"Someone probably got into a fight," he said, shrugging. "Things like that happen all the time in the big city."

"Did you come here to patronize me?" she demanded, sinking onto the bed opposite him, her long hair spilling like a silken curtain over her shoulders.

"No, but what's more important is why are you here?" he asked, more gently. "Why quit a good job and leave your home?"

Emily sighed heavily. "Jake, you don't know anything about my job. And I don't have a home, just a place where everyone else has ideas about who I am and the way I should live."

"I don't understand."

"I need a new life," she said vehemently.

"What was wrong with the old one?" He didn't know why she was so upset, but he found himself wanting to help.

"Everything," Emily shot back with a hard laugh, her pale face anguished. "You don't understand because you've always done what you wanted, went where you wanted to go—even as a teenager. Footloose, hell-raising Jake Wolf."

"When I was a teenager, no one cared where I went," he said dryly, remembering all the nights when he'd come home to find his hard-drinking father passed out on the couch. "You might not believe this, but I always envied you and David for having a curfew."

"Yeah, right," Emily said, lying back on the bed, the heavy fall of hair fanning out around her. "But you made the most of it. Middleton's bad boy. Mothers, hide your daughters."

"So, I still don't get it," Jake repeated, not wanting to pursue his reputation with Middleton's daughters. "You just woke up one day and decided you hate your hometown?"

"No. I don't hate Middleton." She sat up. "It's just that life there is the same for me as when I *was* fourteen. I'm still the mayor's daughter, people still talk about me if I miss church. The ladies at the grocery warn me not to eat too much red meat, and the historical society just can't conceive of me being creative enough to direct their restoration project. Never mind the fact that I have a damned degree in fine arts. If I stay in Middleton, I'll die of suffocation. Always be sweet, little Emily Loughlin and never really myself."

"So you came here"—Jake gestured around the motel room—"to be yourself?"

"Yes," Emily said, flopping back on the bed. "I came

here to be whatever I want, to try new things, to take chances that the mayor's daughter hasn't dared to do. Experience *all* of life. I need to explore, to open myself up. My life has been so narrow."

"I came to Dallas to be like you, Jake Wolf," she continued. "For the first time in my life, I'm running wild."

"Emily," Jake said uneasily. "I'm not sure what you're fantasizing about, but running wild isn't what it's cut out to be. Believe me, I know."

"I'll tell you what I'm fantasizing about," she said, lying back on the bed with a dreamy smile on her face. "Having steamy, passionate sex with a man who drives me wild—"

Jake's breath caught so hard in his throat that he had to cough, her words conjuring up a vivid, arousing picture in his mind. Geez, he had to get a grip.

"I want to try everything, go new places, meet people who don't fit in back in Middleton. I want to take a lover because he fills me with lust, not because he fits my mother's idea of a good husband. I want to dye my hair purple, wear skintight short skirts. Do whatever *I* want to do—"

"Now wait just a damn minute," he interrupted, struggling to push away the jolting image of her lying naked amid tangled sheets, her hazel eyes filled with invitation. "Have you lost your mind?"

"Yes," she said happily. "And after I do all the wild, impossible things I want to do, I think I'll go on a talk show. 'Good Girls Who've Broadened Their Lives.' "

"Emily." Jake leaned toward her earnestly, the throbbing of his libido leaving him feeling as if he'd just run a hundred-yard dash. "What happened? Something must have happened. I mean, you quit your job. David told me you were saving for a down payment on a house."

"A house I didn't like." She tucked her hands beneath her head and smiled at the ceiling. "I thought maybe if I had a place of my own to fix up, I'd be okay in Middleton. Silly of me, and then the bank turned me down for a loan because I'm a single woman."

"They told you that?"

"No, Mr. Simms just said he was sure that when I was married and settled down in a few years, my credit record would look a lot better."

"Well, that's not fair," Jake said. "But it's no reason to act crazy. And why were you buying a house you didn't like?"

"That's just it," she said, sitting up and swinging around to face him. "I was buying that house to try and fill my empty life. I have no life, Jake. I've been waiting for something to come along, like my mother always said it would, and make me happy. But no more. I'm taking charge of my life."

"So you quit your job? How are you going to live?"

"For right now," she said airily, "I'm in this cheap motel because I'm living on my savings."

"You're *what?*"

"Living on my savings, Jake. People do it all the time."

"Not when they don't have to. Maybe if they're fired from their jobs or get laid off."

Emily's hair fell forward, concealing her face, and she stared at the floor. "Well, I'm living on my savings because I want to. I may take a job as a waitress or something if I need to—"

"A waitress? Why?"

"Because . . ." She paused. "Because I hate being a paralegal and I've stopped doing anything that I hate."

Jake surveyed her slender form, the pale pink T-shirt skimming delectable curves. "You got dumped, didn't you? You fell in love with some guy and he had a problem with commitment."

"No."

"Honey, the guy's not worth ruining your life over." He leaned forward, feeling protective enough to want to punch the guy out. "I know it hurts and you probably want to make him sorry, but—"

"Jake!" Emily yelled, glaring at him. "There was no guy. I didn't get dumped. I just didn't have a life."

"—you're only hurting yourself this way. The best revenge is being happy. I'm sure if you go back to your job and get back into the swing of things, you'll find someone else—"

"Jake, I didn't get dumped!"

He looked at her a long moment, wondering if this was a case of deep denial. Nothing she said added up. Sure, there were probably some restraints in being a politician's daughter, but nothing that would drive a sheltered, sensitive woman to spend even one night in this hellhole.

"Have you talked to your parents?" he asked finally.

Emily sighed. "Yes. Sort of. They don't understand either, and yes, David already suggested antidepressants in case I'm going through some kind of 'woman thing.' I'm not."

Jake couldn't help the reluctant grin that came to his face. "You can't blame them for being worried."

"Maybe not," she shot back. "But I can't keep living my life so everyone else is happy. They're worried about me getting hurt. I understand that. I'm not going to take risks just for the hell of it, but I want to know what life is about, and if that means taking chances, I will."

This was a side of Emily he'd never seen. Except the time in fourth grade when she'd insisted on wearing the same red sweater for two weeks. Eventually, of course, her mother's sense of propriety won out, but he'd not forgotten how shocked and upset everyone had been by the episode.

Still, this was different. She could get into real trouble here—Dallas had its rough edges and heaven knew where her "exploration" would lead her.

Unfortunately, it had fallen to him to convince her to see reason and he was failing miserably.

"I don't see why you can't make yourself happy in Middleton," Jake said. "You had a good job in an interesting field. As long as you're supporting yourself, why can't you do whatever you want with your free time?"

Although he prayed her free time wouldn't involve sex for the hell of it. Even though she wasn't at her best at this moment, with her long legs and curvaceous figure, he had no doubt she'd be able to find plenty of takers if she offered herself.

"I'm not going home, Jake. You may not understand, but Middleton is what scares me. I'm a coward there. I don't like who I've become living there, worried about everyone else's feelings until I don't feel my own. I came to Dallas because I'm determined to take chances, to live on the edge, to try everything that's out there."

"Emily—"

"No," she said fiercely, her clenched fists pressing against the bed. "Just accept it, Jake. I'm not going back."

At that moment, a knock sounded at the door.

Emily got up to open it, but Jake forestalled her, pushing aside the limp curtains to look out the window. "It's the police."

A male voice called from outside the door. "Police. Would you open the door?"

Emily went to the door, flashing an anxious glance over her shoulder at Jake as she released the chain.

"I just need to ask you folks a few questions," the officer said, his youthful face serious. "We've had a shooting and we need to know if you saw or heard anything."

"A shooting?" Emily said nervously, glancing over the officer's shoulder through the open door.

"Yes, ma'am. Have either of you been out this evening?"

"Not since I checked in about six o'clock."

"And you, sir?"

"I just got here half an hour ago," Jake told him tersely, "after you guys."

The officer nodded, giving him a sideways look. "And you, ma'am. You didn't go outside at all, look out the window? Hear any shots?"

"No, I didn't go or look out," Emily said. "And it has been so noisy outside, I couldn't really say I heard anything. Was anyone hurt?"

This was the Emily that Jake knew, the sweet person who was genuinely concerned about other people. She was an innocent who couldn't begin to conceive of the big-city evils that occurred daily.

"Yes, ma'am," the policeman said, his voice softening in the face of her earnest distress. "But we're doing our best to find out what happened. It was probably gang-related. We get a lot of that in this area. You need to be very careful around here."

"Yes, I will. Thank you, Officer."

"Good night." He left the doorway and went on to question the occupants of the next room.

Jake went to the open door and looked down toward the crime scene. With several of the police cruisers moved, he could see the area by the ambulance clearly for the first time.

A chalk outline decorated the pavement, a dark splatter of liquid beside the tracing of fallen humanity.

Emily's soft gasp drew his gaze down to where she stood next to him in the doorway, staring at the macabre scene with stricken eyes.

"This is what I mean, Emily," he said, his voice harsher than he'd intended. "People were shooting at each other while you sat in this room. What if a stray bullet had come through the window and hit you? It happens all the time."

He saw her jaw firm, despite the lingering horror in her eyes.

"I'm not going back," she whispered, the fear on her face shifting to determination. "I might never have the courage to break free again."

Turning away, Jake swore softly, damning boyhood friendship and stubborn women in one breath.

"I'm sorry," Emily said.

He knew she meant it, that she recognized his dilemma, but her sympathy didn't produce a solution.

"These people mean business," he said in his toughest voice. "They don't care who gets in their way."

"I'm not getting in anyone's way," she asserted.

Standing there in the night air, Jake realized he wasn't going to be able to budge her. Gentle, friendly Emily had suddenly turned unyielding.

"Listen," Jake said, swinging around to face her as his brain shifted into crisis-management mode. "It's late.

Maybe you won't go back to Middleton tonight, but I can't leave you *here*. Just for tonight, why don't you stay at my place."

As soon as the words were out of his mouth, Jake thought of all the reasons why it was a lousy idea. . . . *steamy, passionate sex with a man who drives me wild.* . . .

She was his best friend's sister, a woman looking for trouble.

Jake had cleaned up his life several years back. He no longer thought of himself as a magnet for a stream of women looking to lose themselves in the sweaty abandon of meaningless sex. That kind of offer didn't present much threat to his reformation.

But a woman wanting to find herself? He couldn't even imagine all the trouble she'd bring. Just being here with her brought back old feelings. She reminded him of who he used to be, the bad kid from a bad family.

Emily apparently shared his ambivalence about staying at his place. She looked up at him with eyes that held both doubt and skepticism. "Your place?"

"Yes," he said, knowing he couldn't walk away and leave her here. Promising himself that he'd get through to her somehow and get her pointed toward Middleton again in no time. He hoped.

"No, Jake," she said, shaking her head. "I didn't come here to trade one set of keepers for another."

"It isn't safe here," he said again.

"This place is just temporary," she told him. "I'll stay the night and find somewhere else as soon as I can."

Jake glanced back at the chalk outline. "Damn it, Emily. You're not staying here by yourself!"

"It's just one night," she protested.

"You're not staying here by yourself," Jake declared unequivocally.

"You can't stop me!" she shot back at him, rebellion in her pale face.

"No," he said with disgust as he turned to leave, "but I can damn well sit in my truck all night and make sure you don't get killed."

"You can't do that," Emily said, suddenly aghast. "What about stray bullets?"

Jake just smiled, so angry he wanted to shake her.

"You could be hurt," she protested. *"I'm* the one rebelling here. *I'll* take the risks."

He leaned against the door frame, saying nothing.

"Don't be so pigheaded!"

Jake stared at her, his gaze as stony as he could manage when all he wanted to do was spank her.

"Well," she said slowly after a moment. She glanced again at the crime scene. "I guess I could stay at your place one night."

"Yes, you can," he agreed, turning back into her room. "Where's your suitcase?"

Moving swiftly before she could change her mind, Jake had checked her out of the motel within minutes and was driving through the dark streets with her headlights bouncing off his rearview mirror like the reverse of a shadow. Maybe he hadn't actually accomplished what David had asked of him, but at least she wouldn't get shot at his apartment.

Of course, he couldn't guarantee that he wouldn't strangle her.

It was almost two o'clock in the morning when they pulled into the small apartment complex. Jake grabbed the luggage out of her sensible import and strode up to the door, leaving Emily to trail after.

If he hadn't been so irritated with her, Jake might have worried about dust balls in the corners of his bedroom. As it was, he concentrated on not chewing her out like a Victorian father.

As he set her things down at the foot of his king-size bed, the irony of the situation occurred to him. He couldn't remember one other situation where he'd been the parental voice. Emily's assessment of his youth rang true. He had been a hell-raiser, a bundle of testosterone determined to mow his way through the attractive females of Middleton.

Yes, he'd found his way to a measure of maturity. Owning his own business and paying taxes had a sobering effect.

Still, it felt weird to find himself in the position of trying to keep Emily's tender feet from the same path he'd heedlessly run down himself only a few years before.

The kid from the wrong side of the tracks rescuing Middleton's own princess. How unlikely was that?

"This is your room," Emily said in a breathless rush as she arrived in the doorway.

"Yes." He grabbed a fresh T-shirt and some sweatpants out of a drawer, trying not to picture her soft, naked curves sprawled invitingly across his sheets. What was he thinking, and of Emily? Such disturbing images of David's sister couldn't be allowed to form.

"I can't put you out of your bed," she protested as he turned to leave.

Jake stilled her with a look. "You've won the big battle tonight. If I were you, I'd retire from the field."

Without giving her a chance to argue, he shut the door, headed for a very uncomfortable night on the couch.

David owed him in a major way.

* * *

Emily rolled over, blinking at the sunlight streaming through a crack in the blinds. Instantly, remembrance rushed in, accompanied by the scent of Jake's sheets and the realization that she'd truly done it. She'd shed the encumbrances of her past life and leapt out into the world as naked as a newborn.

Understandably, the thought made her nervous, even terrified. But she'd had to do it, had to step out now and make a life for herself. She might be a bundle of mixed-up feelings about where to take her life, about her own ability to handle the cold, cruel world, but she knew leaving Middleton was right.

A woman couldn't really live without self-respect.

Still, lying here safe in Jake's bed, she remembered how terrified she'd been at the motel before he arrived, not that she'd have ever let him see that. The fear didn't matter, though. As scary as jumping out on her own was, staying in her old life had felt like slow suffocation. At least fear was a real feeling.

Staring up at the ceiling thinking about feelings, Emily thought about her would-be rescuer and how he must have felt when friendship dictated his late-night assignment as a social worker. She shook her head. No doubt, he saw her as a mixed-up kid, a poor shadow of a girl trying foolishly to lead a full-bodied life.

There was nothing new about Jake thinking of her as a nuisance, if he thought of her at all. She'd more or less existed on the fringes of his life all these years, David their only real link.

Emily refused to consider her youthful crush on him in days past when he wore black leather and drove his Harley down Main Street with the roar of devils. No, she didn't just want a boyfriend who was bad to the bone, she wanted—needed—to live a new, precarious life herself. She needed to be free to make her own mistakes. No longer too timid to face life.

Of course, the thought of a leather-clad lover anything like Jake couldn't help but triple her heart rate for a moment.

Looking around the bedroom, Emily reflected that it screamed "unattached macho male" from the dark plaid comforter to the dusty miniblinds at the window. How many times had she wondered about his life since he'd left Middleton?

Jumping out of Jake's bed—she couldn't think of it otherwise—Emily quickly dressed, pulling her long hair into a pony tail. From the sunlight at the window, the morning was half gone and she had some changing to do.

Minutes later, Emily quietly cracked open the bedroom door, instantly spotting Jake, still crashed on the too-short couch. Pushing back her guilt at what she knew had to have been a very uncomfortable night, she tiptoed across the small living area trying not to wake him.

He slept facedown, buried in a pillow, his dark hair rumpled. Emily swallowed. Jake had always been something like a natural wonder with his vivid blue eyes and dark hair, even back in the days before his six-foot frame had filled out.

Now he had the muscular grace of a man. The slope of his broad shoulders beneath the thin knit of his T-shirt seemed to call out for the smoothing of her touch. Emily rubbed her palm against her pant leg and reminded herself that to Jake she was as sexless as a house plant.

Turning her gaze away from the length of his powerful

legs, she searched for a piece of scratch paper to leave him a note.

"Darn it," she said softly. Here she was embracing a new liberated life, unrestricted by social niceties, and already she was automatically falling back into her old, good-girl ways.

Screw leaving him a note. She was an adult. She could go anywhere she wanted.

But he'd worry if he woke and found her gone.

Still, she hadn't asked to stay here. If he'd left her at the motel, which would probably have been perfectly safe—how many shootings could happen in one night?—then he wouldn't even have known enough to worry.

Emily took a step toward the door, then paused, glancing back to where he lay sleeping. She should just leave.

Maybe he wouldn't even care that she was gone, but just be relieved. David couldn't expect him to keep her shackled to his side. Not really.

Shifting from one foot to another, Emily dithered for another two minutes and then, with a muffled mutter of irritation, found a piece of paper.

She settled her conflict by leaving him a very brief note and being completely nonspecific. She had gone out, she'd be back later. Thanks for the bed.

The last line scrawled itself out before she realized it, but Emily refused to rewrite the whole thing. Propping the note on the table by the couch, she scurried out of the apartment.

Jake left the shop area and walked through the deserted office, his eyes gritty with fatigue, despite sleeping in until nine-thirty. He felt old. Who would have guessed that by the age of thirty, two o'clock in the morning would seem late?

Of course, dealing with a woman who'd gone off her rocker hadn't helped his stress. He'd been wondering where she was all day. Many things could happen to a woman in a city the size of Dallas, especially a woman as sweet and innocent as Emily.

Had she even had a lover? Jake shoved the errant thought aside. Emily's sex life wasn't his concern.

Pouring himself another cup of coffee, he wondered where his sales staff was. Now that he thought about it, even the shop had been empty, despite the fact that it was only three in the afternoon.

A murmur of voices drew him toward the showroom, a glass-fronted area that held a herd of gleaming Harleys, otherwise known as hogs by their besotted fans.

Jake frowned over his coffee cup as he spotted a tight circle of his employees gathered around someone who was perched on one of the motorcycles. He employed two sales guys and half a dozen mechanics, most of whom appeared to be in the cluster.

Curious about who could hold the attention of his rowdy bunch, Jake wandered over.

As he grew closer, he could see over Mark's shoulder. A woman.

That fit. Only two things secured his head mechanic's attention—hogs and women, in that order.

Still, she'd have to be a babe to gain this much notice, even in this testosterone-rich environment.

Nudging several guys aside, Jake moved close enough to get a better view.

And what a view it was.

The woman perched lithely astride the latest arrival could have been peeled out of one of the posters that adorned the walls. Her chin-length bob was dark mahogany, deep red highlights shimmering as she tossed her head in laughter. Lips the color of a woman's passion, soft and moist, beckoned with each word.

Jake felt his interest stir. A snug sweater cupped full breasts, tightening with each graceful lift of her arms. And she wore a skirt that could be measured with a child's school ruler.

Tight and brief, it hardly covered her slender hips, leaving a luscious length of leg bare to the world.

At that moment, Jake would have given anything to have been there when she mounted that cycle.

Oh, yes.

When one of his mechanics jostled him, trying to get closer, Jake snapped out of his trance.

He cleared his throat and said, loudly enough to get their attention. "I don't think the lady needs all our help. Why don't you guys get on back to work."

With obvious reluctance, the group began to disperse.

"Just give me a call if you want to ride," Mark said seductively to the woman. "I'd love to teach you."

"We're sure of that," Jake said dryly as the mechanic headed back to the shop.

"I'll, uh, help the lady," offered Jim Bermen, one of his salesmen.

"That's all right," Jake said, dismissing him with a glance. "I'll take care of her."

Being the boss had some perks, after all.

Turning his full attention to the babe on the Harley, Jake was glad to see her smiling broadly.

"So you'll take care of me, huh?" she said in a sultry murmur.

He moved closer, snared by the husky note in her voice. "Oh, yeah."

"I'm sure David would appreciate that," she said, her skirt sliding up as she leaned forward and swung herself off the cycle.

Jake got an eyeful of firm, sleek thigh before he closed his eyes. "Oh, my God."

Two

The look on his face was priceless. A giggle escaped Emily as she straightened, tugging at her abbreviated skirt. In that instant, she rejoiced in the outfit she'd impulsively purchased at the slutty shop next door to the hair salon.

The moment was sweeter than she'd ever imagined.

"My God," Jake said again with growing censure. "Emily?"

"Yes," she said, dropping a purring note into her voice. "Still want to take care of me?"

Apparently in shock, Jake stared at her a moment before snarling, "You definitely need a keeper. Is this what you came to Dallas for? To . . . to . . ."

"What?" she asked sweetly, leaning back against the motorcycle and crossing her legs.

Jake's gaze followed her movements before he jerked his attention back to her face. "This is your new life? Turning yourself into a walking advertisement for sex?"

"Suddenly that's a bad thing?" she shot back, angered by the disapproval in his voice. "It's wrong for *me*, sweet little Emily, to be sexy. But you were certainly interested in my 'advertisement' right up until you realized who I was."

"Don't be ridiculous." Jake glanced over his shoulder

to where several of his employees were clustered interestedly by the office door.

Reaching out, he snagged her hand and started walking swiftly out of the showroom, tugging her with him. "We'll talk about this in my office."

"I don't think we have anything to talk about," Emily protested, hating the sting of tears behind her eyes. Why did it matter that Jake thought of her as a virgin turned strumpet just because she wore a short skirt? She hadn't started this new phase of her life to please him or anyone but herself.

All her life she'd been shy around men, hesitant to draw their attention, too cowardly to reach out and flag down a man who might actually interest her. No more. Heck, wearing this skirt was like sending up flares.

"We have a lot to talk about," he said grimly as he towed her into a small, cluttered office and shut the door. "What on earth possessed you to come here dressed like that? You know what every one of those guys was thinking."

"The same exact thing you were thinking." She stabbed a forefinger in his direction, annoyed that his disapproval bothered her. "You just have a major double standard when it comes to me."

"That's not true," he said, his irritation evident.

"Hah! Can you deny your reaction? You weren't thinking about my intellect or my impeccable character," she ranted. "It was sex all the way. And I'm nowhere close to the sexiest woman you've ever seen. So what's wrong with me wanting to be sexual, too?"

"I wasn't thinking anything and I don't have a double standard," Jake said in a calmer voice. He walked around and sat down behind the desk. "I'm not going to deny that I went through a wild stage in my life, but I learned that ultimately that kind of thing is too risky."

Deflated by his matter-of-fact attitude, Emily subsided into a chair opposite Jake. The tight little skirt slid up her thighs, but she resisted the urge to tug at it.

Could she have been wrong about his reaction to her transformed self? He'd certainly seemed interested. But maybe he hadn't been. After all, her sexual experience was limited to one embarrassing backseat encounter with her high school boyfriend and half a dozen disappointing interludes with Stan in college.

"Listen, Emily. You and David have always had what matters. A home and people who care for you. A good name and the respect of the community. When I was a kid, I didn't have those things. Being wild seemed like my best option." He leaned forward, his dark eyes serious.

She stared back at him, remembering Jake's mother had died when he was small and that the whole town knew his father was a drunk.

"I survived some stupid choices," he said, "but it scares the hell out of me to think of you out there, running into God knows what. It's a crummy world sometimes, with really crummy people."

Not only did he not understand her need to take charge of her life, he saw her as helpless and unable to take care of herself. Someone to be sheltered as her parents and her brother had all her life.

Emily took a deep breath, aware of a foolish urge to cry. "I appreciate your concern, Jake. But I can't take your word for it. I'd rather take my chances with the crummy world than sit home in Middleton while my life ticks away."

"So this is how you get a life? By looking like this?"

"Yes," she said, getting really irritated with him. "It's a start anyway."

Jake shrugged. "I always thought you dressed nice before."

"You never even noticed me when I looked like Rebecca of Sunnybrook Farm," Emily said with an edge.

He laughed, his face filling with unconscious masculine allure. "It wasn't that bad."

She looked down, startled. Such a simple thing, only laughter. But in that moment he looked so confident and appealing and a response blossomed in her that she knew was hopeless. Damned useless adolescent crushes. To Jake she would always be David's little sister, up on a pedestal and off-limits. For anything to happen between them would be impossible, even if he wanted her, which didn't seem likely now.

"So what did you do to yourself?" he asked, considering her with his head cocked to one side.

Emily shrugged. "I tried something new. Had my hair cut and colored. Bought some new clothes."

"It is a different color," Jake murmured, looking at her hair. "Darker and with some red in it?"

"Yes," she said, struggling against a wave of self-consciousness. "I thought about blond, but that seems almost as ordinary as my own color."

He shook his head. "Not blond. You're just not a blonde."

Exasperation surged in her. What did she have to do to break out of the "Emily" mold? "I'm thinking of having them do me purple next week."

"Well, you wouldn't be ordinary Emily then," Jake said dryly.

"Actually, I'm thinking of not being Emily at all," she said, partly just to tease him.

"What?"

"I'm considering changing my name," she said, scooting down in the chair till she lay draped over it in a way that would have drawn her mother's reproach. Of course, Mother wouldn't have approved of anything she was doing now. That was part of the reason she'd come to Dallas, to spare her mother having to watch her throwing off the constraints bred by twenty-six years of living in Middleton.

"Why would you want to change your name?"

"Think about it," she recommended. "What image does the name 'Emily' trigger. What do you think of?"

"You," he said with a baffled frown.

"No, I mean generically what does the name make you think of?"

Jake shook his head. "I don't know."

"Then I'll tell you. Hair bows."

"What?"

"A little girl in a frilly dress with a big bow in her hair. Or someone's grandmother who happens to be a librarian."

He laughed then, shaking his head again. "You're nuts."

"No, I'm not." Emily stared dreamily into space. "I'm thinking of something like 'Bianca.' Something sexy and exotic."

"Like the ex-wife of an aging rock star?"

"Well, maybe a symbolic name like 'Freedom' or 'Rainbow,' " she said, propping her feet up on his desk.

Jake struggled to keep his gaze on her face, rather than follow the slender length of her bare legs now adorning his desk. "Don't you think those are a little too sixties?"

"I guess so," Emily said, seeming unconscious of the

extent of her exposure. "I've also thought of Kayla or maybe Celeste. They sound independent and unfettered."

He was a total sleaze-bag, Jake acknowledged to himself, still trying not to look at her long, slender legs or the rounded slope of her thigh. This was *Emily*. He'd known her most of her life, and now when she was going through a rough patch, it was all he could do to keep from drooling on her.

He was as bad as Mark, the mechanic. Worse maybe, since he had an obligation to behave himself.

They were from two different worlds, even if she was currently rebelling against her upper-crust background.

But when had Emily grown into such a sexy woman? Sure she'd only been about twenty when he saw her last, still in college and quiet. And last night, he'd been too worried about possible risks to her survival to notice very much. But now here she was, slender and tall with full breasts and kissable lips, and he was suddenly wrestling urges he'd never before connected with his best friend's kid sister.

"Uh, you just don't seem like a Kayla," Jake said, realizing he'd let the conversation lapse.

"What about Bambi?" Emily's lips curled in playful suggestiveness.

"No. Not unless you're considering a career in topless dancing." He knew he was glowering at her, but couldn't seem to stop it.

Emily tilted her head back, stretching her lithe body. "Working in a bar doesn't appeal to me."

"Good," Jake said in a rough voice, his gaze drawn to her upper body. Geez, he was staring at Emily's breasts. He had to get a grip.

This whole transformation thing had thrown him for a loop. It wasn't as if he hadn't known Emily had breasts before. Most women did. But now, they were right there, round and lush, covered in thin stretchy knit.

"I've actually thought about my middle name," she said, pursing her lips reflectively. "McKinnon."

"Your middle name is McKinnon?" he asked, shifting uncomfortably in his chair.

"Yes, it was my mother's maiden name," Emily said. "Kind of a British thing."

"I guess we could call you 'Mac' for short," Jake suggested, wishing she'd at least sit up straight.

"I don't think so," Emily retorted. "McKinnon sounds unusual and independent. Mac is more of a truck driver."

"You could drive trucks," he pointed out with a hint of sarcasm. "After all, you want to change careers."

She made a face at him, dropping her feet from the desk and scooting up in her chair.

"You know, Emily, I can understand if you want to make some changes in your life," he said, his brain freed somewhat from the seductive influence of her body on display. "But there are better ways to do it."

"Such as?"

"If you want to move, send out a résumé and get a good job as a paralegal here in Dallas. You'd probably earn more here and could afford a nice apartment." He paused, noting the resistant set of her jaw. "But I still don't understand why you'd want to live in a big city. I know you don't think it's important now, but you have a place in Middleton. You belong."

"You can have my place. Anyone can have it, for all I care," she said. "Although if it's such a nice town, why aren't you living there?"

"Not much call for Harleys in Middleton, unfortunately." Jake knew she couldn't argue with that one. Truthfully, his past wasn't anything he was in a hurry to revisit. Would people still stare and whisper that he was as no good as his daddy?

"There's not much call there for anything I want to do, either."

"But you had a job."

"Yes, as a glorified secretary working for a jerk. I'm not going back."

"So, if you don't like working for an attorney, you could go back to school to be one yourself. You're a bright, intelligent woman."

"Yuck. I hate the legal field. All the constant fighting and maneuvering. Deal-making and back-scratching."

"So what do you want to do?" This was looking more and more like a career crisis, to Jake's great relief. That at least was concrete and, surely, easily remedied.

She hesitated, her face seeming vulnerable all of a sudden. "I have a degree in fine arts."

"Fine arts?"

"I think I'm a Bohemian at heart," Emily said, lifting her chin. "I want to be creative. To paint and draw. Maybe sculpt. I want to try everything. That's one of the reasons I thought about buying a house. If I had a place of my own, I could create my own space. I love designing environments. Maybe I'll buy a historic home and renovate it from the ground up. Homes are so emotionally linked, so integral to our lives."

Jake sat staring at her, trying to piece together what he knew of Emily Loughlin and the woman sitting across from him. None of it fit. Emily had always been sweet and quiet. Now there were opinions and declarations spilling out of her.

"Maybe I'll do some design work. Furniture and stuff. I want to try everything, do everything," she said, throwing her arms wide open. "Experience life to its fullest and come back for more. Take chances. Think of all the great artists. They didn't worry about what their mothers would think if they quit their jobs or took a lover."

"Yeah, and most of them died in poverty and disgrace," Jake pointed out, cursing himself for noticing the way her breasts jiggled when she flung her arms open.

"But they'd *lived*," Emily said with intensity. "They had seen it all and done everything, no holds barred. No hanging back because they were afraid."

He looked at her, a trickle of uneasiness shivering down his spine. She was very serious about all this.

"Emily—"

Much to Jake's frustration, the phone on his desk rang. He picked up the receiver and soon became engrossed in soothing the irate caller, one of his best customers, who had his brand new Harley in the shop for the third time this month.

Recognizing the validity of the guy's complaints, Jake listened for a few minutes and then assured his customer that he'd stand by the cycle and make sure it was taken care of as quickly as possible.

When Jake looked up twenty minutes later, he saw that Emily had taken advantage of his preoccupation and left.

She wasn't in the showroom, so Jake checked the rest of the offices and the parts room. No Emily.

"Have you seen the young woman who was here earlier?" he asked Betty, his office manager.

"She wandered back to the shop a few minutes ago," Betty replied, smiling broadly. "You better find her. The guys won't be concentrating on their work with a honey like her back there."

Jake didn't want to think about what his mechanics were concentrating on with Emily dressed like that.

He opened the door to the shop, but found it empty except for Clarence.

"Have you seen the woman who was in the showroom earlier?" Jake asked, his words unintentionally short.

Clarence looked up. "She just left with Mark."

"What?" The word came out like a shot.

"I think he asked her if she wanted a drink," the older mechanic said, staring at his boss with puzzlement. "He clocked out."

"Did he say where they were going?" Jake asked, anger and apprehension clamoring in his head. Emily was out with one of the biggest womanizing dirt bags in Dallas. And she went voluntarily, probably just to piss him off.

He didn't know who he wanted to get his hands on first, Mark for making a move on her or Emily for going out with him.

"The Skull and Crossbones, I think." Clarence wiped a last smudge of oil off the bike he'd been working on.

"The Skull and Crossbones? Hell!" Instantly, Jake remembered the place, a dark, rough, noisy roadhouse with the worst kind of wildlife.

Without hesitation, Jake stalked out of the shop and headed toward his pickup. Mark had taken sweet, little sexy Emily to the scummiest, most infamous biker bar in town.

If she wanted trouble, she'd found it.

The bar occupied a mean little cement-block building that huddled in the midst of a dirt and gravel parking lot, a cluster of hogs always at the door.

Jake felt the beat of the music before he even opened his pickup door. The only thing worse than finding

Emily here was *not* finding her here. If she was at Mark's apartment, Jake would need a lawyer.

Muttering a string of curses under his breath, he tried not to think what he'd actually do to the guy if Mark had managed to touch Emily Loughlin in any sexual way.

Any jail term would be worth it.

Stepping through the doorway, Jake scanned the dark, smoky room, fully prepared to fight every man in the place if he had to. And a fight was always a strong possibility. Bars like the Skull and Crossbones existed for men—and women—who expressed themselves with their fists. Any excuse would do, even another man's fight.

"Hey," the bartender greeted him. "What'll it be?"

"I'm looking for someone," Jake said, barely glancing at the man.

"Take your pick," the barkeep invited. "We got a big crowd."

Jake felt a surge of relief, spotting Mark at the far end of the bar apparently getting drinks from another bartender. Emily had to be here somewhere.

"Hey, Jake, ol' buddy," called out a heavily bearded man at the bar. "You got that part in for my hog?"

"Not yet, Bubba." Jake forced himself to speak normally despite his urgency to find Emily. "We'll give you a call when it comes in."

"Thanks, man." Bubba turned back to his drink.

Scanning the room, Jake ignored the leather-clad, heavily pierced crowd seething to the throbbing music. Then, far to the left, he saw her.

Emily sat at a table in the corner, her newly cut hair caressing her cheek while her teeth worried at her full lower lip.

Wasting no time, Jake crossed the distance, threading his way through the tables to where she sat.

"Come on, Emily. Let's go."

She started, glancing up at him in surprise, a faint anxiety in her luminous eyes. "Jake! What are you doing here?"

"Taking you home," he said, his voice uncompromising.

Her expression turned mutinous. "You're not my keeper. We've just been dancing and Mark is getting drinks."

"Listen," Jake said, leaning down, one hand on the table. "You have no idea of the kind of loser Mark is."

"That's a nice thing to say about one of your employees," she said, a bit primly.

"I pay him to be a mechanic, not date my sister."

"I'm not your sister," she all but snarled. "And I'm not a two-year-old."

Mark walked up then, his handsome face wary. "Hey, boss. What are you doing here?"

"Taking Emily home."

"Emily? I thought your name was McKinnon." The mechanic's gaze swung between them. "Oh. Well, we were just having some fun. No harm done."

Even with every muscle in his body tight with the effort to control himself, Jake was aware of Mark's assessment. Clearly, he thought his boss had flipped out.

"Come on, Emily," Jake commanded.

For a moment, she defied him, her glare filled with anger.

Mark broke the silence, saying uneasily, "We'll get together another time, honey."

Jake held out his hand. "Emily."

Furious, Emily still recognized Mark's position. Jake signed his paycheck.

More than anything, she wanted someone to punch Jake in the nose. No matter how responsible he felt, he *wasn't* her keeper. But she didn't want to make trouble for Mark, whose only crime was in showing his interest in her.

Slowly, she rose from her seat, ignoring the hand Jake held out to her. Ignoring the relief that flooded her. The place was a bit on the scary side. She was such a wuss . . . but she'd die before admitting it to Jake.

The walk out to Jake's truck was as silent as the drive back to his apartment. His anger filled the cab of the truck, thick as smoke, but Emily couldn't care less.

Why the heck had she let him bully her? She was just on a date, for heaven's sake, not selling herself on the corner, which wouldn't have been any of his business, either. Okay, Mark made her a little uneasy. Particularly when his eyes roved over her with a predatory gleam. Still, she was an adult. Surely, she could hold her own on a date!

She should have stayed at the bar with Mark, even though the place had startled her. But if she was looking for adventure now and trying new things, she'd have to actually do something adventurous every once in a while. And having her hair done didn't really qualify, no matter how traumatic it had been.

Jake had barely pulled the truck to a stop in front of his apartment building before Emily got out, slamming the door. She stalked up the walk to his apartment, hating the childish helplessness that cloaked her.

She'd let him order her around. He'd snapped his fingers and she'd come to attention. Emily wanted to throw up. Where was her backbone? How could she have let him march her out of the bar like a delinquent teen?

Jake unlocked the door and held it open for her. Barely able to contain her anger, Emily went in.

"How dare you?" she said, rounding on him. "Just because you happen to be my brother's best friend doesn't give you the right to order me around and threaten my dates."

"I didn't threaten anyone," Jake said, obviously annoyed.

"Of course you did. If you hadn't been his boss, Mark would have punched you in the nose before he'd let you walk out of there with me."

"If you really meant anything to him, he'd have tried anyway," Jake challenged.

Emily gasped.

"I'm sorry," he said, not sounding apologetic. "But you've got to get a clue here. Guys like Mark are great at working on Harleys, but they have no morals when it comes to women."

"This isn't about Mark," she said. "You'd say anything to keep me away from a man who might possibly find me attractive. And what if I'm not worried about his morals? Besides, I was just having a drink with him."

"Haven't you heard about the trouble women can have when they go out with men they don't know?" he demanded. "What if you'd had a few drinks and he'd suggested you go to his apartment? You'd have gone like a little lamb to the slaughter!"

"I am not totally helpless," she all but shrieked as if convincing him would settle the issue for her. "Believe it or not, I do have some judgment, some ability to figure out when people might try to hurt me. Besides, I'm here in *your* apartment. Am I in trouble? Are you going to take advantage of me?"

"What would you do if I did?" Jake asked, his eyes suddenly intent.

"If you attacked me?" she said in disbelief.

"If I tried to *persuade* you to have sex," he said, his voice low and warm as he took a step toward her.

She felt the timbre of his words like the stroke of velvet over her bare skin. Still, Emily squared her shoulders. "I'd leave, I guess."

"But what if I wouldn't let you?" Jake took a few more steps toward her, stopping only a foot away.

"I could get away," she claimed, feeling unaccountably breathless.

"You think if I tried to hold you . . ." He reached out, his hand skating over her shoulders and settling firmly on her back. ". . . you'd be able to get away?"

"Yes." The word came out with an exhalation, Emily mesmerized by the intensity in his eyes, the palm of his hand warm and disturbing on her back.

"What would you do, Emily?" he asked, drawing her closer. "How could you keep me from touching you . . ."

Emily swallowed hard, a succession of bewildering sensations rippling through her. Jake, tall and broad, beautifully muscled, moved closer, the heat of his body enveloping her.

"Uh . . ."

"I'm bigger than you, Emily," he whispered. "And you're very attractive."

"I am?" she whispered back in wonder.

"Yes," he said, bending his head, his lips close to her ear, his breath tickling her hair. "Admit it, I could take your innocence, right now, and even hurt you . . . and you couldn't stop me."

Stung, she reared her head back. "For your information, Jake Wolf, I haven't been a virgin for a long time and I'm fully capable of keeping people from hurting me. Maybe I wanted Mark to kiss me, maybe I'd like to have a man try to seduce me."

"It isn't seduction that worries me most," he said, his voice low and angry. "There are men who rape women. If I were to try to force you, you couldn't stop me."

"Yes, I could," she declared defiantly.

Jake's jaw tightened, his face dark. "Prove it."

Without warning, he lowered his mouth to hers.

Emily went still beneath his touch, stunned that Jake was actually holding her, kissing her. His mouth moved against hers, hard and demanding, his tongue playing at the seam of her lips. The arms that bracketed her tightly up against his chest were powerful and heedless.

He meant to frighten her, she knew, and she resented his manipulative determination to save her from herself, but still, Jake was kissing her.

Jake with his soft lips, his hot mouth on hers.

Emily fought to cling to her reasoning ability. She couldn't just cave in like this, stand in his arms like a frightened, overwhelmed idiot.

He'd started this, she thought, as his mouth seduced her sanity. If he wanted to fight dirty, she'd make sure he walked away wounded. She was going to take charge of her life, damn it. And right now she wanted nothing more than to kiss him back.

The smell and taste of Jake encompassed her. She opened her mouth to his assault and kissed him for all she was worth.

Emily snuggled closer, angling her neck to maintain

their kiss while pressing against his chest. In the tangle of lips and tongues, his kiss changed from brute force to aroused exploration. He nibbled at her mouth, his breathing harsh in his throat.

Heat as dark and heady as midnight swirled through her. The brush of his mouth, his breath mingling with hers. Blood pounded through Emily's body, a ragged rhythm that tangoed through her nether regions.

Her breasts felt full and tight, flattened against the wall of his chest, her heart pounding against his. Slipping her fingers into the dark curls at his nape, Emily strained up, drawing him closer. Never had a kiss pulled her into a well of sensuality, drowning her consciousness and pitching her into a world of abandon. Never before had she felt such a drive to shed her clothes and press her naked body against a man's.

She wanted his touch everywhere, wanted the palms of his hands to cup her breasts, wanted to feel the driving force of his erection hard against her. Rocking mindlessly against this evidence of his desire, Emily gave herself up to the crescendo of passion.

Heaven was the heat she felt in his arms.

Caught in the haze of sexual hunger, she didn't realize at first that he was pushing her away, his strong hands at her shoulders.

Jake tore his mouth from hers, putting the length of his arms between them, his breath coming in ragged gasps.

Blinking, Emily slowly came to consciousness, registering the shock and dismay in his face, the swift coming of his self-condemnation and, she dared to hope, a lingering amazement in his eyes.

"Ahh . . ." He let go of her, taking a step back as he

rubbed a hand at the back of his neck. "I, uh, shouldn't have done . . . that."

"Why not?" she asked, her voice husky.

"I, I need to, uh, check on some things at the shop," Jake said, without answering her. He went to the door and paused, his hand on the doorknob. Looking back at her for a moment, he drew a deep shuddering breath and then walked out.

Emily stared at the door for a long moment, still shaken by the explosion of their kiss. Slowly, a surprised smile grew on her face. Regardless of his devotion to boyhood honor, Jake wasn't immune to her.

And if his kiss was anything to go by, she wasn't just sweet little Emily anymore. She'd taken charge of the moment and been rewarded and . . . terrified by the most arousing, disturbing kiss in her entire life.

Sinking to the couch, her body still trembling with sensual aftershocks, she stared into space and tried to regroup. Tried to make sense of the longing and panic in her stomach.

She'd had sex before, but she'd never felt . . . this. Here she was meaning to teach him a lesson, to assert her independence, and she ended up shaken to the core herself. What the heck was happening to her?

"Cassie?" Emily said, gripping the phone to her ear, a few minutes later. "I think I'm in over my head."

"What do you mean?" her friend asked immediately. "Are you okay?"

Emily's laugh sounded shaky to her own ears. "I guess so. I'm just wondering if I'm an idiot for doing all this . . . coming here."

"Now, wait a minute," Cassie said. "What happened?"

"Uhhh . . ." Emily tried to find a way to put her panic into words. Jake had kissed her. She'd kissed him back. She'd wanted to make love with him. How could she admit being way in over her head when all they'd done was kiss? Surely, she wasn't that big a baby.

"Are you okay?" her friend asked again in fear-sharpened tones.

"Yes," Emily told her, drawing a deep, steadying breath. "I'm here at Jake's apartment. I'm fine."

"Jake Wolf?" Cassie sounded surprised.

"Yes, David called in the rescue squad. It's a long story." Emily wound the phone cord between her fingers. For some reason, she couldn't talk about the kiss, yet. "I guess, nothing . . . really happened. Jake's trying to get me to go home and . . . I was thinking maybe he was right. That I'm too naive and ignorant to make it in the big city."

"Don't be ridiculous," Cassie said. "I don't understand your wanting to live there, but we went over this before you left. When you finally told me how you'd been feeling about living here. Are you telling me you've changed your mind after being gone overnight? That Middleton sounds good to you now?"

"No."

"But Dallas is scary?"

Emily sighed. "A little, but nothing I can't handle. I guess I was feeling lonely and overwhelmed. I just wanted to hear a familiar, friendly voice."

"Well, that's me," Cassie declared cheerfully. "Both familiar and friendly. But I'm going to kick your tushie if you don't stick it out and follow those dreams of yours."

"You're right," Emily said, feeling stronger the longer she thought dispassionately about that kiss. "I guess I'm just tired and hungry. I'll be fine."

Three

Jake came back to the apartment an hour later, opening the door with some trepidation. He'd spent the last sixty minutes berating himself for so much as laying a finger on Emily. The whole kiss thing should never have happened, and after much thought he'd decided to play it that way.

If he could manage to forget the physical arousal that had tortured him since he'd bolted out of his apartment. That and the silky feel of her beneath his hands. The molten hunger of her mouth beneath his.

Damn, she made him hard.

Somewhere, sometime, he'd been a really bad person. Maybe this was the payback for those twins he'd dallied with several years back. Maybe his entire trouble-making, juvenile delinquent past had caught up with him. This had to be a kind of atonement for sins.

Emily sat on the couch watching television, her feet curled under her despite the fact she still wore the skimpy skirt. If it hadn't been for her provocative attire and sophisticated new hairstyle, the scene might have been plucked out of their childhood. Only then he'd come to their house as David's guest and now she was making herself at home in his apartment.

She glanced up, her face cautious and self-conscious.

"Watching anything in particular?" He dropped into a chair across from her, not letting himself notice the sweet scent of her skin, the whisper-soft corner of her mouth.

"No." Emily ran her hand nervously through her hair, ruffling then smoothing the short tresses.

The cultured tones of Channel 4's news anchor filled the awkward silence. Jake cursed himself again, silently frustrated with himself for losing control with her earlier.

Still twiddling with a strand of hair, she glued her eyes to a news report about the local school district. She might just be a responsible citizen worried about the state of the nation's education, but Jake didn't think so.

Compared with her earlier stance of "I am woman, hear me roar," Emily seemed chastened. Had their passionate moment disturbed her? Frightened her?

Damn. Jake closed his eyes. He was a world-class heel. How could he have kissed her like that? Sure, she'd responded to his kiss, but now she was probably in major regret mode. Regardless of the intentions she had claimed yesterday, he doubted Emily was the kind of woman to get physical with a man she didn't love.

Particularly with a guy her parents knew only as their son's troublemaking friend.

Maybe it wasn't such a bad thing that he'd kissed her, though. At least now she seemed to be getting a clue about the down side of being wild.

"So," Jake said, a shade too heartily. "Have you had dinner yet?"

Emily looked up. "No."

"Well, I'm not much of a cook. Maybe we could go

out somewhere? You know, just a couple of friends grabbing a burger."

"Okay," she said, giving him a long, considering look.

"Good." Jake got up, snagging his keys from the coffee table. "I know of this really good place where you can get just about anything."

They left the apartment, carefully not touching as they walked down the sidewalk to his truck. Fortunately, the restaurant was close by. Jake hoped dinner would help loosen the tension. At this rate, he would rather have her impulsive bullheadedness.

Funny, how all these years, he'd never before been annoyed by Emily's quietness. How much of the real Emily had he ever known?

The Friday night crowds were out in force, clogging the busy West End streets. Jake found a parking place near the restaurant.

After the hostess had seated them in the noisy, well-lit eatery, Jake tried to find a safe topic of conversation. "So, what do you think of Dallas?"

"I like it fine." Her sardonic glance told him what she thought of his lame attempt.

Fortunately, the waiter appeared then, taking their order before disappearing too quickly.

"Jake," she said, leaning forward, "we need to talk about what happened earlier."

"Um, earlier?"

"Yes, when you kissed me," Emily prompted, her dark hair swinging forward to caress her jaw.

"Oh, that." He tried a short laugh. "I don't really think there's anything to talk about. I shouldn't have tried to scare you."

"What?"

Jake shuffled the dessert and wine menus. "It was

stupid. I was just trying to make a point. I shouldn't have touched you. It's my fault."

"What about the kiss, the way we . . ." she faltered.

"What about it?" Jake repeated, hoping she'd let the matter drop. It was bad enough to have kissed his best friend's little sister like she was the only woman on earth. Dissecting it afterward would only make him feel more like a heel.

Emily was going through a difficult period. It would be easy for an unscrupulous guy to take advantage of her determination to wallow in the flesh pots. Jake was bent on avoiding temptation. And she represented a bigger enticement at this point than he'd ever thought possible.

"What about it?" Emily echoed with disbelief. *"What about it?"*

"This is a nice place, don't you think?" Jake said heartily.

She just looked at him, her lip curling in disgust.

"Hey, here's our food already," he said with relief a few minutes later.

The silence was tense as the waiter positioned their plates and deposited condiments in the middle of the small table. Jake glanced across at Emily's face, baffled by the indignation he saw in her hazel eyes.

The woman continued to confound him. Sure, he'd overstepped his bounds and done a macho he-man thing with the kiss. *Me, Tarzan. You, Jane.* But he'd told her he regretted it.

Jake closed his eyes in realization as his own thought echoed in his head. How stupid could he get? She made herself over into a sex goddess and then he'd been insensitive enough to tell her he shouldn't have kissed her. What an idiot.

"Listen, Emily. You kiss great. I just meant that I was wrong to—"

"I'm sure your burger is getting cold," she interrupted, her voice very cool.

Jake gave up after that, allowing her to finish her meal in near silence. She asked him to pass the salt once. But pleasant dinner conversation was apparently not going to happen.

After signing the credit card receipt and leaving the waiter a tip, Jake followed her out of the restaurant.

Friday night revelers crowded the sidewalk, a combination of tourists and ultracool locals dressed in clunky shoes and black lipstick. Even some of the men.

Jake paused a moment, looking for an opening in the flow of bodies. Emily stood beside him.

"Oh, look," she announced with the first real enthusiasm he'd heard all evening. "There's a tattoo parlor. I've always thought tattoos were interesting."

"Emily," he said with exasperation, diving into the sidewalk traffic to follow her.

Making a beeline for the neon-lit tattoo parlor half a block up the street, she strode ahead of him, her hips swaying seductively in the tiny skirt.

He should have asked her to change the damned skirt.

"Emily," Jake called out again, catching up with her.

She wheeled around. "I've decided only to answer to McKinnon. And don't even think about trying to stop me from getting a tattoo."

"Are you nuts?" he asked as she once again headed down the street. "You know this is the real thing. It doesn't wash off."

"You are so patronizing," Emily declared, not looking up at him as her long legs carried her closer to her goal.

"You know. You're just doing this to punish me for

kissing you," he informed her, hoping the insight would penetrate and stop her crazy notion.

"Arrgh!" she growled, walking faster.

"You're acting like a two-year-old," he shouted after her, appalled by the idea of her deliberately marking her creamy flesh for life.

Emily McKinnon Loughlin stopped at the doorway to the tattoo parlor, turning to glare at him, her hands on her shapely hips.

"Take a good long look at me, Jake. Do I look like a two-year-old?"

If she'd been anybody but Emily, she'd have embodied some of his favorite fantasies. Long, slender legs straddling him, full breasts bouncing while their cries of passion rose.

God, what was the matter with him? He had to stop thinking of her like that.

"You're not getting a tattoo," Jake declared, knowing it was the worst thing to say, but unable to get beyond the horror of some cheesy cartoon burned into her perfect flesh.

"I get to decide that," Emily snapped, nearly flinging herself through the open door.

Jake followed her, reminding himself to count to ten before he succumbed to the urge to turn her over his knee. No telling where *that* could lead to.

"Don't do this, Emily. You'll regret it. Your hair can grow out, you can always go back to your old wardrobe, but this is *permanent*."

"I'm not going back to anything. When are you going to get that and just go away?" she said distinctly before turning to the pasty-skinned guy behind the counter. "I'd like to look at some of your designs."

"Sure, over here," he said, ambling over to a wall covered in drawings. "Take your pick."

"If you think tattoos are so attractive, why don't you take a good look at him?" Jake recommended, keeping his voice low as he eyed the tattoo artist. The skin revealed by the man's sleeveless shirt sported imprints of dragons, naked women, and improbably, several renditions of the Road Runner.

"I'm not considering forty tattoos," she said, as if she were speaking to an incredibly dense child.

"You're not getting *any*," Jake said again. The guy's skinny body and unfocused eyes shrieked of a more than passing acquaintance with recreational drug use. "He looks like one of the walking dead."

"They have to be licensed," Emily said. She continued to peruse the drawings as if he weren't there.

"I don't care if they have rabies tags," he retorted. "I am not letting you do this."

"You can't stop me," she asserted. "Listen, Jake. Your loyalty to David is admirable, but I'm grown up. I'm going to do what I want."

Loyalty to David had nothing to do with it, oddly enough. Jake would take on every zombie in the joint before he'd let Emily do this. No way he was letting this guy lay a needle or a finger on her.

She turned to the tattoo guy. "Would this one take long to do? Maybe just a small heart on my left breast."

"What!"

"Not long," the tattoo artist said, ignoring Jake's exclamation, "If you're ready, just go in that booth, take your shirt and bra off, and I'll be there in a minute."

"That's it," Jake said, taking hold of her arm with resolution as Emily turned toward the booth. "We're leaving."

"No, we're not," she said, trying to pull free. "I'm an adult and you can't—"

Bending down, Jake hoisted her onto his shoulder in a fireman's hold and headed out the door as the tattoo guy watched with disinterest.

"Call the police," Emily shrieked, beating her fists on Jake's back. "I'm being kidnapped!"

Jake stalked down the sidewalk, hoping the guy in the tattoo shop was too stoned to intervene. At this point, he was doing all he could to hold on to his prize. Who'd have thought such a slender woman would have so much fight in her?

With her every twist and wiggle, he'd swear her skirt rose higher. Aware of the amused attention they were attracting, Jake forged onward down the street, trying to ignore the feel of her bare thighs beneath the palm of his hand, her firm hip snug up against his cheek. Damn, she smelled good.

"Put me down," she yelled, thumping him on the back. "You dirty, rotten—"

He bounced her on his shoulder, knocking the wind out of her. "Now, now, Emily McKinnon. Don't say anything you'll regret."

"Atta boy!" called out a man walking past, earning himself a slap on the shoulder from the woman at his side.

"I'll teach you to regret," Emily croaked a minute later. "Put me *down*."

"No. You'd just run back," he said, having a good idea of her determination by now. How could he have thought her shy and sweet. The woman was a hellion, albeit a damned sexy one.

"Arrgh!"

"I know you're not very comfortable," Jake said, readjusting his grip on her disturbingly curvaceous fanny. "But we'll be at the truck in no time."

"What are you going to do, Jake, handcuff me in the truck?" she asked sarcastically as they neared the parking lot.

"No," he retorted. "I'll just kiss you again. That's the only thing that seems to scare you."

For the life of her, Emily couldn't think of a single satisfactory reply. The thought of kissing him again did things to her that she couldn't even explain. The word "scare" fit pretty well, but didn't really cover the range of emotion his touch wrought in her. Was it normal to have a panicky fear the first time a woman came close to drowning in hunger for a man?

Drawing in a shuddering breath when he finally set her on her feet, she just leaned against the truck, adjusting to an upright position while he unlocked the door.

"Get in." He walked around to the driver's side without another word.

Her hackles raising again at his autocratic tone, she considered bolting but decided against it. He'd probably come after her. And what would she do if she managed to give him the slip? Going back to the tattoo parlor didn't have much appeal at this point. If she were honest, she had to admit to herself that the thought of needles injecting permanent dye into her skin wasn't all that attractive. She'd just been *considering* a tattoo, for heaven's sake, until his arrogance egged her into making a stand.

Still, if she'd really wanted to get one, Jake had no right to act like he was her keeper.

Emily hunched in the seat, pointedly ignoring him as he drove back to the apartment. Some way, some how, she'd show him he couldn't treat her like an infant.

Sure, she'd let her self-doubt overtake her after their kiss this afternoon, but Cassie was right. This was her chance, her big moment to make of her life what she wanted. She couldn't let her fear and uncertainty take over, couldn't go back to being little Emily of the mayoral Loughlins.

When they reached the apartment, Emily got out of the truck and went up the walkway, still ignoring Jake as he unlocked the door and mockingly held it open for her.

Glaring at him, she swept past, stalking straight into his bedroom and slamming the door behind her. Truth be told, she *felt* like a frustrated teenager at that moment.

Waking around ten the next morning, she peeked out of the bedroom door and discovered the couch empty. Great, Jake had already left for the cycle shop. She had the whole day to herself. Maybe she'd look for an inexpensive apartment.

Gathering up her toiletries, Emily headed for the bathroom, only to come to a halt when she rounded the hallway corner.

Jake stood in the small bathroom, naked from the waist up, his dark hair gleaming wetly. A white towel, tucked at his waist, clung snugly to his narrow, muscular hips. Silhouetted against the white tile, the skin of his back was smoothly tanned, rippling over muscular shoulders.

Emily swallowed hard. She remembered the feel of him as she'd clung to those shoulders, awash in his passionate kiss.

Here he was, the most profound example of animal magnetism she'd ever run across, and he was bound and determined to save her from herself regardless of her desire to the contrary.

Jake turned slightly, catching sight of her in the mirror. "Good morning," he said, his grin seeming smug with his victory last night.

Emily stared at him.

There on Jake's smooth tanned bicep was a small image of a seductive, naked woman in a red hood and cape.

Riveted to the floor, Emily couldn't believe her eyes. Realization flashed all over her in a second. Jake Wolf had a tattoo of a naked Red Riding Hood on his arm.

Jake had a tattoo!

Mr. High-and-Mighty with all his talk of how *permanent* it was had a tattoo of his own. At that moment, it was all Emily could do to keep from throwing something at him.

"You hypocrite!" Whirling around, she dashed back into the bedroom and slammed the door again.

It seemed like an hour before she heard him walk past the door. Relieved to finally be able to answer nature's call, Emily whisked herself into the bathroom, muttering beneath her breath, still unable to believe what she'd seen.

All the while he'd protested about her "marring" her flesh, he'd sported a provocative little insignia of his own.

Emily ground her teeth, envisioning the buxom Red Riding Hood on his smooth bicep. The nerve of him!

Surely, he'd be gone by the time she was through with her shower. Weren't Saturdays big retail days?

But he was still there, sitting on the couch with an

array of papers spread across the coffee table when she came out later.

Emily retreated to the bedroom once more, her frustration growing. She could just leave, regardless of the fact that he'd apparently ensconced himself on the couch for the duration, but she suspected Jake would somehow try and interfere with her plans, whatever they may be.

And she didn't want to get into a tussle with him. As rebellious as she felt sometimes, her new life wasn't about fighting with Jake.

He had to go to work sometime. She'd just wait him out, although she hated having to. The day was ticking away and she had things to do. . . .

Emily stopped in the act of combing her hair, remembering all at once that she didn't have "things to do." Not in the way she'd used to. In one fell swoop, she'd wiped her life clean of any expectations and demands except her own.

Just for a moment, she felt a sense of loss, almost as if she were adrift. What did people do all day when they didn't have to go to work? Her job and family obligations, as burdensome as they'd been, had always defined her. Now, she had to find her own rhythm somehow.

"Emily?" Jake tapped at the door. "I've got some muffins and coffee out here. Aren't you hungry? It's almost lunchtime."

"Go away." She snapped the comb down on the dresser and dropped onto the unmade bed, hearing his footsteps recede.

Never had time passed more slowly. Emily lay back on the bed for a while, perversely determined to outwait him, but boredom soon set in. After an hour, she found herself making the bed she'd so determinedly left rumpled that morning. By two, she'd refolded all the clothes in her suitcase and thought about rinsing out her soiled lingerie in the bathroom sink. But she didn't go out of the bedroom, not wanting to give him the satisfaction. Maybe it was childish, but she couldn't forget what a jerk he'd been last night.

Every thirty minutes, she ever-so-carefully cracked the door to check on her guard. He still sat on the couch, shuffling his papers.

A standoff. She and Jake were in a battle and she was determined to win. He wasn't going to treat her like a child to be baby-sat. One way or the other, she'd outlast him. For some reason, doing so had become terribly important.

Minutes ticked past like a film in slow motion. By the time she'd read the few magazines she'd brought with her, including every ad, Emily knew how it felt to be a criminal in a standoff with the cops.

Around seven that evening, her stomach seriously growling, she first got the idea. While idly examining the bedroom for the zillionth time, her gaze wandered to the darkening window and the grassy verge between the building and sidewalk.

They were on the first floor. All she had to do was open the window, slip the screen loose, and she'd be gone.

Emily leaned back on the bed, suppressing her laughter at the thought of Jake coming to the door later that night, opening it, and finding her long gone. Oh, the perfection of it.

She'd never snuck out as a teenager, never been sneaky at all. Suddenly, the whole idea seemed deliciously exciting. She'd slip out the window, no harm done.

Quickly changing into one of her new outfits, this one with a fuller, although equally short skirt, Emily grabbed her purse and eased the window open. Unlatching the screen took some doing. She had to wrestle with it for several minutes, her knee thumping painfully against the wall at one point.

At last, it gave and she eased her leg over the window sill and dropped to the ground outside. Freedom! And one large victory over Jake.

Jake heard the thump over the low tones of the television. What on earth was she doing? The whole day had been weird. Who'd have thought a grown woman could sulk so long?

He went to the bedroom door. "Emily? Are you all right?"

No answer. That in itself wasn't a shock. She hadn't answered him all day, but he didn't hear any other noises either. No sounds of movement.

Tired of playing games, Jake opened the door. The room was empty and the window gaping wide.

"Damn her." Jake spun around and went out the front door of the apartment.

He spotted her immediately, standing beside her compact car wearing another indecent outfit with black spiked heels and too much skin.

Wasting no time, he reached the car just as she opened the door. "You snuck out the window because you don't want to be treated like a rebellious teenager?"

Emily jumped. "Don't try to stop me."

"Going back to see our friendly neighborhood tattoo junkie?"

"No—not that you have any right to say anything," she said with a defiant toss of her head. "I'm going out."

"By yourself?"

A taunting smile curved her lips. "I hope I won't be alone for long."

Jake could feel his temper rising. "You're going to a bar? Dressed like that?"

"Not just any bar," she declared. "That biker bar you dragged me out of."

"There is no way—" He started toward her.

Emily took a step back, holding out a hand to stop him. "Lay one finger on me, Jake, and I swear I'll go back to that motel."

"What?" He'd half expected her to threaten to call the police. Hauling her away last night was one thing, but keeping her a prisoner in his apartment was something else.

And truthfully, using brute force on a woman wasn't his favorite option, even when her life was on the line.

"I swear, Jake. I'll move back there in an instant."

"Okay," he said, stepping back, his hands raised.

"Okay?"

"I won't try to stop you from going to the bar," he said, "but I'm going with you."

She looked startled. "What? No way."

"It's a public place," he reminded her.

Emily sighed, clearly angry. "And you won't get in my way? Won't try to scare other guys off?"

"No," he promised through clenched teeth.

* * *

The action apparently started early on Saturday night. Jake could hardly find a parking place in the crowded lot and the biker revelers spilled out into the doorway much like the smoke and loud pounding music.

He followed Emily into the bar, wondering for the first time if he ought to buy a gun. Guarding Emily tonight was going to take all his wits, if not firepower.

She looked like innocence personified amid the denizens of hell. Even in her flirty black skirt and the snug knit shirt that skimmed her body, stopping just above her waist, she didn't look like the other hard-fisted women in the bar.

As he steered her to a table by the door, Jake couldn't help hoping that most of the men in the place would mistake her for jailbait.

"How about getting me a drink?" she said, sitting down.

"Okay." He had to stifle the urge to ask her just how much drinking she'd done and if she was sure she wanted to start now.

Jake flagged down a waitress and ordered two beers.

"Nothing stronger?" Emily challenged him as the woman left.

"Why don't we start with this," Jake said, leaning closer. "If you want to work your way up to tequila, I'm sure they have that, too."

"I just might." She lifted her chin, not breaking his stare.

"Fine," he said, unable to resist adding, "I hadn't realized booze was part of your life-enhancement plan."

"I want to try new things," she declared, defiance in every line of her body. "How many adults do you know who've never had tequila?"

"A few. Here, start with this," Jake said as the waitress approached with their beers. With any luck, the alcohol in the beer would knock her inexperienced body for a loop and he could haul her out of there before any real damage was done.

Emily raised her glass and drained it.

Jake watched her with trepidation. "Hey, you haven't had anything to eat today. Slow down."

"I don't want to go slow," she said, wiping her mouth with the back of her hand. "I want to go very, very fast."

When she drank her beer and his in less than fifteen minutes, Jake was seriously regretting his earlier wish that the alcohol would rush to her head.

Emily stood beside the table, swaying seductively as she watched the heaving, seething crowd moving to the throbbing beat.

"I like this place," she said, her head dropping to one side as she rolled her hips to the beat.

"Sit down, Emily," Jake said, feeling more than a little tense. Who'd have thought two beers would have loosened her up so quickly?

And she loosened up in a most attractive way. Emily had garnered a certain amount of interest when they walked in, but now, moving sensuously to the music, Jake could all but feel the temperature rising around him.

He couldn't blame them. If he hadn't been in the position of protecting her from these guys, he'd be drooling, too. Hell, even being the one responsible for her, he still wanted to kiss her again, to hear her hungry sighs and feel her curvy body against his.

Jake yanked his attention away from Emily's rear. He had to keep his wits about him.

A brawny guy in a leather vest and worn jeans walked over, stopping in front of Emily. "Wanna dance, babe?"

Jake started to rise when Emily swung around and stabbed him with a defiant stare. "You promised. Remember the deal."

Reluctantly, he subsided into his chair, frustration practically choking him.

He watched her join the throng, clenching his fist when the brawny guy reached out, taking her arm to draw her closer.

Emily kept pace with the music, smiling at the guy in a vaguely unfocused way. The music went on forever, one pounding rhythm sliding into another. Jake sat at the table, every muscle coiled, his heart thundering in his chest.

Surely, she'd pass out soon. The small amount of alcohol she'd consumed had acted swiftly. Although not yet in the way he'd hoped.

He didn't know what he'd do if Emily tried to leave with one of these beefy bikers. Letting her go home with a total stranger was beyond him, impossible to conceive. So Jake watched and prayed.

Emily's partner had pulled her closer, his hand now on her shoulder. He swayed and rocked suggestively, his gaze hot on her face.

Jake watched, acid rising up in his stomach as the guy's hand slid slowly lower and lower.

"Hey, honey."

Jake looked up, surprised. A skinny woman with peroxide hair and improbably large breasts stood beside him, bending down to display her cleavage.

"Wanna dance? Or whatever?"

Hell. He smiled at the woman in what he hoped she'd take as a regretful way. "Sorry. I've got a bum leg."

The woman looked him up and down. "I bet the rest of you is just fine. We don't have to dance. We could go to my place."

"Ahh. No, thanks. Another time maybe."

"Too bad." She shrugged and walked away.

He turned quickly back to search for Emily among the crowd and nearly shot out of his chair.

There on the dance floor, the beefy biker held her plastered to his chest, one thick hand cupping her rear.

On his feet in a flash, Jake jostled his way to where Emily and her dance partner stood. Restraining himself with effort, he tapped the biker on the shoulder.

"I'm cutting in."

"What?" The other guy glared at Jake.

"I'm cutting in," Jake repeated with a tight smile and menacing eyes, ready to beat his opponent to a pulp if necessary.

Apparently, his intent showed. The leather-vested biker took a last reluctant look at Emily, still swaying to the music. "Sure, whatever."

"Hi, Jake," Emily sighed, coming into his arms without resistance.

He enfolded her, deeply relieved that he'd avoided a fight that could have been ugly and conceivably involved both of them ending up in jail. Fights at this particular bar usually became a community matter with the entire crowd joining in.

"I'm having a good time," Emily said, her smile both welcoming and seductive. "Don't you like this music?"

He'd like it a lot better if she weren't dressed like that, her sexy body swinging in rhythm. Just looking at her made him hot. Emily leaned closer, her body just brushing his as she stared into his eyes.

"Are you having a good time?" she asked huskily, her breasts soft against his chest for a fleeting instant.

"Yeah," he managed with a strangled voice.

"I like dancing with you better than that other guy."

Jake couldn't help appreciating her preference, even if he shouldn't care.

"I, uh, don't guess you're ready to go or anything," he asked, unable to keep from responding physically to her closeness. Wondering what he'd do with her when he got her home.

Emily shook her head, that honey-sweet smile still curving her lips.

"Hey!" a woman's coarse voice called from behind him. "I thought you had a bum leg."

Jake cringed, turning around just as Emily did.

"Are you talking to Jake?" Emily asked the woman, a frown replacing her smile.

"If he's Jake, yeah, I'm talking to him," the other woman said, her hands on her skinny hips.

"Jake's dancing with me," Emily declared. "He likes me."

"I don't see why," the woman said insolently. "But he looks like he's man enough to handle us both."

"You stay away from him," Emily said, her eyes narrowing. Her threatening stance was marred only by the fact that she swayed a little. "He doesn't want to handle anyone like you."

"Why, you little—"

Jake groaned, barely managing to grab Emily out of the way of the biker woman's fist.

Within minutes, the entire bar had exploded into a melee of punches and shoves. Sweet Emily Loughlin was locked in a hair-pulling clinch with his skinny admirer. Trying to contain Emily enough to push her protectively behind him, Jake dodged a burly man bearing down on him at ten o'clock.

Ducking down to grab Emily by the waist to pull her out of the fight, Jake saw her arm swing back too late. Her elbow caught him on the cheekbone with a jarring blow. Stunned for a second, Jake recovered just in time to thrust Emily out of the way of the chair her opponent swung.

Oh, yeah. He'd handled this real well.

Jake's bruised jaw and swollen eye were the first things Emily saw when she woke.

"Oh, I don't feel so well," she whispered, head pounding.

"Tell me about it," he said, slumped in the chair next to the bed.

"My head hurts," she managed as she hoisted herself slowly into a sitting position. "Actually . . . everything hurts."

Jake smiled, the effort crooked.

"Your eye looks terrible," she said after a moment. "Does it hurt really bad?"

"I'll live," Jake assured her.

Emily felt awful. Unfortunately, she remembered every detail of the previous night with excruciating clarity. *She'd* started the fight, insulting that bimbo and cracking Jake in the face with her elbow. And he'd had to punch his way out of the bar, keeping her behind him and managing to get them both safely away before the police came.

"I'm very sorry," she said, feeling two inches tall. To

be the one who sparked trouble after she'd told him over and over she could take care of herself.

She'd definitely let her temper get out of hand, insisting on returning to that bar, then drinking so much on an empty stomach. The bar frightened her, so of course, that was part of why she'd had to go back. To face her fear. Only she'd never meant to get tipsy, certainly hadn't intended to start a brawl.

"It's all right, Emily," he said, his voice level.

"Thanks." Still wearing her clothes from last night, she sat on the edge of the bed, resolved to avoid beer the rest of her life. There had to be better ways to assert her independence.

"So, are you ready to go home?" Jake asked gently.

She lifted her head too quickly, the movement blurring her vision for a moment.

He met her gaze, his face somber.

"No, Jake," she said after a moment. "I came here for a reason. I have to stay."

"I thought you'd say that." He looked at her for another long moment, contemplation in his battered face. "So I have an offer for you."

"An offer?"

"Yeah," he said. "If you're determined to walk on the wild side, I'll be your guide."

Four

He'd guide her all right, guide her straight back home to Middleton where she'd be safe and happy, once this rebellious phase was past. If he had to be deceitful to protect her, he'd lie to her without the slightest qualm.

Just the memory of last night's bar fight made Jake shudder. If he hadn't managed to get her out of the place before the cops came, Emily would have had a real introduction to the seamier side of life. Saturday night in a Dallas jail.

He threw a couple of pieces of bread in the toaster, listening for the sound of the shower cutting off. She'd looked tired this morning, no more than was to be expected, but still the sight of her pale complexion and red eyes got to him.

She deserved worse, he thought savagely, but it was his job to make sure she didn't get it.

Last night had proven more than ever, he had to convince her to go home while making it look like he was leading her into the ways of temptation.

Jake shook his head. What had he done to deserve this?

Mixing up a pitcher of frozen orange juice, he heard the water turn off in the bathroom. Ignoring the slight swelling around his eye and the soreness in his cheek, he reflected that she'd taken his offer with a surprising lack of suspicion. Now he just had to come up with some activities that would seem exciting and daring to Emily without actually putting her at risk.

And he had to keep his hands off her while convincing her to go home, as difficult as it would be. She'd come here for a wild time, and if he were the same kid who left Middleton all those years ago, he'd have given her a hell of a ride. But he'd grown up and left his wild times. Now he just had to make sure Emily didn't take the same road.

Bending to scrounge some margarine and jelly for the toast, Jake heard a soft footstep behind him. He whipped around to face her, his good intentions taking a powerful blow.

Huddled in his old bathrobe, her short dark hair wet from the shower, she looked sexy as hell. Clean and damp, as freshly scrubbed as a baby, there was nothing about the woman that should send his pulse ricocheting.

He was scum.

He wanted to press her up against the kitchen cabinet and bury his face in her neck, slide his hands down her body till she moaned and melted in his arms again. Just the thought made him hard.

His soap had never smelled so enticing before, the scruffy material of his robe never clung so faithfully to him, he was sure. On Emily, the terry cloth seemed to have found its natural element. Why hadn't he noticed her curves back in Middleton?

Had he been so blinded by the fact that she was David's sister? Too bad he wasn't blinded by that now.

"Oh, Jake, your eye looks terrible," she said softly, coming to stand next to him. Before he'd realized her intent, he felt the brush of a cool finger against his bruised cheek.

"It's nothing." He should have pulled back, but the sweet concern in her eyes held him still as much as the sensual stroke of her finger against his skin.

"Should we put some ice on it or something?" Her voice, gentle and soft, mesmerized him. Jake struggled to get himself under control.

"I'm fine, but you need some breakfast," he said gruffly, turning back to search for a glass in the cabinet.

"No, thanks," she said, her voice faint now. "My stomach isn't very happy."

"Food will help to settle it," he told her, taking refuge in his supposed role of mentor.

"Okay," she sighed compliantly, sliding onto a bar stool.

Why hadn't she been that agreeable last night?

Jake found a glass and poured her some juice, putting the toast on a plate in front of her. "Just take your time."

To keep himself from staring at her, he bent to empty the dishwasher, thinking of all the reasons why he shouldn't want his best friend's sister, damp and naked, in his bed.

That, of course, was one reason. She was David's sister and even in the "love 'em and leave 'em" ethics of some men, sisters were off-limits. But David wasn't the biggest reason he had to keep his mind and his hands off Emily.

No amount of success altered the truth that, according to Middleton history, he was from the wrong side of the tracks. He'd long ago come to terms with his unfortunate parentage. Thousands of kids grew up in alcoholic homes. He bore no responsibility for that. But while he wasn't ashamed of himself, he suspected Emily eventually would be if they succumbed to the heat that hummed between them.

Good girls might like to play with bad boys, but they usually married men like their fathers. Jake wasn't in the mood to be Miss Emily's big-city fling.

He didn't fool himself. She might look at him at times like he was the only man on earth, but he was simply forbidden fruit, a potential accessory to her rebellion. The thought of being left behind for an accountant-type when she'd had her fun made his stomach turn.

"I appreciate your making me breakfast," Emily said shyly, breaking the silence. "I know I'm a big nuisance to you. You have a business to run, after all."

"Don't worry about it," he said. "The shop's closed on Sunday."

"Oh." She chewed a bite of toast in silence, her gaze seeming to rest on him speculatively.

In a flash, Jake pictured the day ahead. The two of them alone in the apartment. Reading the newspaper, watching movies on cable. She'd get dressed, wouldn't she?

He'd be hard all day. Her smell, her curvaceous body so close to his. Women thought men wanted slinky dresses and stiletto heels, but this kind of intimacy was sexy enough to raise his blood pressure fifty points.

Casual clothes were so easy to take off. All he'd have to do was slide his hand inside the robe and cup her bare breast. Jake turned away, blocking her view of his stiffening anatomy. How the hell was he going to get through the morning without kissing her? Nothing in the apartment provided a distraction, either. It seemed as if the only movies on cable pictured men and women rolling on sweat-slicked sheets.

God, he had to get them out of here. Where could

they go? His mind clicking, Jake suddenly remembered what Emily had said about wanting to restore a historic house. That was it. He had the perfect distraction for her. At least for the day.

Thank heavens for friends who were realtors.

"Listen," he said, "why don't I take you to this great place I know for lunch."

"Okay."

"Don't dress up," he said, digging his keys out of his pocket. "Wear pants. I've got to run to the shop for a little while—some paperwork I can never get done when we're open and people are in and out. When I get back, we'll go."

"I just had breakfast," she reminded him, a twinkle in her eyes.

"That was more of a snack," Jake retorted. "I promise you'll be ready for lunch when we get there."

Emily barely had time to slide off the stool before he was gone. Shaking her head at his air of mystery, she went into the bedroom to dress. After her crazy impulse to raise hell and rile Jake's temper last night, she couldn't help feeling like an idiot. He could have been really hurt. Truthfully, she was appalled at herself. Yes, she needed to change her life, but her behavior in the biker bar last night had been driven by her anger toward Jake.

Here she was proclaiming her ability to take care of herself and she'd let her temper lead her into outright danger. That was the drawback to never having taken risks. Her judgment couldn't help but be faulty when she'd never strayed from the safe path her parents had defined for her.

But that didn't mean she should go home with her

tail between her legs. She'd just be more careful from now on.

Climbing into a pair of blue jeans, she made herself a solemn promise. There was a difference between taking charge of her life and putting her life in peril.

Jake's turnaround was surprising, considering the ammunition last night gave him. She'd have expected him to use the episode as proof that she couldn't be trusted outside her parents' house, much less her hometown.

Still, she didn't mind the truce. Fighting with him had never been her intention. She hadn't come here to succumb to Jake's charms either, although just being near him tended to raise her temperature ten degrees.

It was amazing how natural their sparring felt, but she had to remember why she'd left Middleton. She had a new life to create. Fears to face. Twenty-six was a little late to try her wings, but she was determined to break out of her too-safe, too-small world.

An hour later, she heard the roar of an engine outside. Glancing out the window, Emily saw Jake getting off a sleek motorcycle, a helmet in his hand.

In his snug T-shirt and tight jeans, he looked like the tough boy she'd had a crush on in Middleton. Only Jake wasn't a boy anymore. There was something about the way he carried himself, his athletic, confident stride, that had nothing to do with adolescence and everything to do with pure sex appeal.

Emily let herself watch him, her feminine sensors going off like an air raid siren. In an instant, she could imagine riding off with him into the sunset, her body clinging to his as they roared away on his Harley.

Somewhere down the road, they'd get off the cycle and make hungry, earth-shattering love in a thicket beside the road, only a blanket beneath them.

She shivered pleasurably at the image.

Jake's footsteps on the steps outside jolted Emily out of her erotic daydream. Geez, she had to get a grip. Jake had made his position clear. She was off-limits.

His refusal to talk about their kiss made that clear enough.

Emily went to unlock the apartment door. He stood on the porch, looking like every woman's fantasy with a hint of sensual awareness lurking behind the challenge in his dark eyes.

"Ready?"

He'd never know how ready, she thought ruefully. She managed to croak one word past her paralyzed vocal cords: "Sure."

"Great," he said, locking the door and pulling it shut as she slipped past him. "I thought we'd take my cycle."

"Sounds like fun," Emily said as they went down the walk. If he stopped beside a thicket, she'd fall over in a faint.

In less than a minute, they were at the curb, Jake handing her a helmet. He climbed astride the gleaming motorcycle, balancing its weight and power easily as he slipped his own helmet into place.

She'd been on a cycle before, that once at his shop, but getting on this one offered entirely new possibilities along with an enticing proximity to Jake.

He glanced over his shoulder as she hesitated.

"Get on."

Emily got on, resisting the urge to search for a seat belt.

He held the thing easily, and in an instant the engine roared to life, throbbing and vibrating beneath them. Oh, yes. This was different, she thought again as he casually rolled the cycle back and turned, heading for the street.

Clinging on for dear life, she registered a hundred impressions as they accelerated. Wind and speed, the pavement rushing past her feet at an alarming rate. Her arms locked around Jake as if on autopilot, his body hard and masculine against hers.

Her breasts pressed against his wide back, Emily drew in a shuddering breath and tried to ease herself away from him. Impossible. She dare not wiggle around too much.

The shift and acceleration of the engine beneath them was smooth and powerful. She felt the thrust every time he took off from a traffic light or stop sign. When they hit the freeway, the world became a blur.

Mostly, she registered the beautiful balance of man and machine, how gracefully he handled the Harley, as if he were part of the thing. In time, she began to feel the subtle shifting of weight herself, the lean into corners, the natural straightening.

The roar of the wind mingled with the noise of the engine seemed to isolate them, the two of them locked together in a world of sensory overload.

"So, how do you like it?" Jake's voice sounded softly in her ear.

Emily started. "What?"

"I said, how do you like it?"

"The helmets have walkie-talkies in them?" she asked in astonishment, coming to the only conclusion that made sense.

"Something like that." His voice held amusement.

"Wow. I guess it's practical." God, had she said anything aloud? Any small murmur of erotic pleasure as they'd flown down the road with her body plastered against his back?

"It's necessary, too," Jake said, apparently oblivious

to her sudden embarrassment. "If you're on a cross-country trip, communication might be required and motorcycles demand total attention. Trying to hear what your passenger is yelling at you could cost you your life."

"That's comforting," she said, remembering all the experts who claimed motorcycles were primarily useful in creating organ donors.

"You wanted to live on the wild side," Jake reminded her as he sped up to pass a slower car.

Emily stuck her tongue out at the back of his head. His immediate chuckle told her he had better use of his mirrors than she'd supposed.

Within minutes they left the highway, driving down the quiet streets of an older neighborhood, the homes beautiful and varied. It was the kind of place that spoke of moderate prosperity and established values. Mature oaks and pecans shaded lush green lawns that looked well kept but didn't have the aggressively manicured appearance that abounded in some of the newer housing additions.

Jake slowed, turning in at an overgrown drive. The house bore all the signs of a home that hadn't been occupied in some time. In fact, only the glimpse of a rooftop showed from the street.

He killed the engine, the sudden silence of the place seeming right. Despite wild, shaggy shrubs that clustered around the outline and even obscured the view of the street, Emily made out the shape of a very unusual house.

She clambered off the cycle, feeling almost mesmerized. The house was built of some sort of stone, darkened with age. Bigger than its neighbors, it seemed to sprawl over several lots, surrounded by what must have been beautiful gardens.

"What is this place?"

Jake smiled. "A realtor friend of mine is listing it for sale. It's a haunted house."

She turned to stare at him. "You've got to be kidding."

"Nope." He stashed his helmet over one of the cycle's mirrors. "This place has a tragic history. A man built it for his wife in the 1920s. It was the most lavish, most expensive house in the area at the time. Two years after they moved in, the wife ran away with the gardener."

"Are you putting me on?" Emily asked with deep suspicion. She loved this sort of story, but the twinkle in Jake's eye made her doubt his sincerity.

"Of course not." He leaned the Harley on its kickstand.

"So she ran off and died, coming back here to haunt the place?" Emily asked skeptically.

"The wife was never heard from again," Jake said. "I guess she and the gardener were a perfect match, but the husband became a recluse for a while and then he just disappeared. After several decades, his heirs had him declared legally dead, but no one did anything with the house."

"He's haunting the place?" Emily asked, walking down the cracked cement path to the front door.

Jake laughed. "Well, the haunted part comes from a local legend that the wife never really ran away. Some folks think the husband found her in bed with the gardener and killed them both, burying them in either the garden or the basement."

Now on the broad, flagged porch, Emily turned to

him. "That's a great story. Are you sure you aren't making it up?"

"Positive. I'm telling the truth, Scout's honor."

"You were never a Scout," she reminded him.

"True," he said with a chuckle, "but I've always believed in their motto."

With a flourish, he pulled a key out of his pocket. "I got the key from my friend, the realtor. Want to see inside?"

"You mean we don't have to break in?" Emily exclaimed, grabbing the key from him.

"No," Jake said, clearly amused by her enthusiasm, "but we can if you want to."

"This will be fine," she said, wrestling with the ancient lock on the massive front door. "Here, you try."

Stepping back, she was almost dancing with excitement. She'd always loved unusual homes, the more character the better. Her latent interior design instincts were on full alert now.

With a loud creak, the bolt finally yielded to Jake's persuasion. He turned the knob and pushed the heavy door open.

Emily crossed the threshold feeling as if she'd stepped back in time. To her amazement, the house was still fully furnished. Dust-laden curtains shrouded the windows and a thick film of grime lay over everything. The silence was deafening.

The exterior gave no indication of the riches within. The entry had a vaulted, mosaic-lined ceiling and three arched doorways that led off from it. To one side was a large dining room, complete with a massive table and chairs and a glass chandelier, now dull with decades of neglect.

The opposite door led to a large living area with dark

paneled walls and big, heavy couches placed before a large fireplace. The floor was stone, the ceiling timbered with yellowed plaster panels between.

Emily caught herself holding her breath. "This is amazing."

"Yes," Jake agreed, his voice echoing in the space. "Which way do we go first?"

"Living room," she said decisively, heading left.

They wandered through the cavernous space, one room leading into another. Beyond the living room was a glassed-in room with a stone floor and a now-dry fountain, a stone fish perched to spew water long absent. Three bedrooms were beyond that, lined up behind the living room.

Walking through the silent, dusty rooms, she kept seeing the house as it might be, filled with light and layered with soft textures. It was a beautiful, romantic place with a sad, melancholy air and she felt an overwhelming urge to make her vision of it come true.

A hall divided the house, running from the front door to a back entrance. On the other side of the hall, in the area behind the dining room, was what appeared to be a master suite—two bedrooms and a shared bath. The bedrooms opened onto a courtyard that could be crossed to reach the dining room and a small library. The kitchen was close to the dining room and beyond that stood a big dome-shaped conservatory with a tangle of weedy plants still growing in the raised beds.

Emily could only suppose that rain fell through the many missing panes of glass.

She drew a deep, shaky breath. "I think I'm in love."

Jake laughed. "You're kidding. Most women would find this place spooky in the extreme."

"It's terrific," she protested. "It just needs someone to bring it back to life."

"What would you do if you were the someone?" he asked, watching her.

"Besides trimming the shrubs and scrubbing everything?"

"Yeah, besides that."

"Mmmm. I'd put in area rugs and lots of color to warm the place up, maximize the light. But everything would have to be in keeping with the period. This house could probably qualify as a historic landmark. It's a tremendous example of the Arts and Crafts period with some Spanish touches thrown in."

Jake glanced at her in surprise. "You sound like you know what you're talking about."

Shaking her head, she ran a hand along the mantel. "Not according to Mrs. Campbell of the Middleton Historic Society."

"Who?" He turned to stare at her.

"No one," Emily laughed, the sound hollow. "It's just that people seem to forget I graduated from college with a fine arts degree in interior design."

"Well, you have been working as a paralegal."

"Yes," she said, frustrated at herself as much as the situation. "I actually graduated with honors from a very demanding program."

"So why have you been doing paralegal work?" he asked as they left the conservatory, heading for the foyer where the front door stood open.

"I needed a job after school. There aren't many openings for beginning designers in a town the size of Middleton."

"You didn't want to go into business for yourself?" He pulled the door shut, locking it. "I'd have thought your parents' friends would have given you commissions."

"Thanks," she said, her tone dry.

"I didn't mean it that way," Jake said, starting down the steps. "Just that building your own clientele seems like an option if you really wanted to be a designer."

"I love design work," she said firmly, "but I needed to support myself and my parents weren't particularly concerned about helping me set up a business. Their plans for me included a few years of work, then marriage to the right man and grandchildren."

Jake cocked an eyebrow at her as he bent down to lift the flap on the motorcycle's leather saddlebag. "You didn't like that plan."

"No," she said. She'd been smart enough not to let Daddy set her up in an apartment while she dabbled in her art. That would have made the last four years even more pathetic, but she couldn't tell Jake that. "I'm all in favor of a husband and kids at some point in my life, but I've never seen that as my only contribution to the world. I want to do creative things and support myself."

Jake heard the wistful note in her voice and found himself wondering why he'd never had a real conversation with Emily until she ran away from her life. Had he ever really known her? As a child, she'd been quiet and intelligent, always hiding in unexpected places. He remembered her smiling at him a lot. Back then, very few people had smiled at him.

Grabbing several paper bags and a blanket, Jake straightened. "Feel like having a picnic?"

"Sure," she said, the pensive expression still on her face as she turned toward the wilderness garden.

They spread the blanket and Emily got out the sandwiches, chips, and drinks he'd bought from a sandwich shop.

Above them, the sound of bird song rang out, the overgrown garden secluding them from the sight of any of the nearby houses. Stretched out here on the blanket, they could have been miles away from anyone.

"Just what do you want to do, Emily? How do you want to leave your mark on the world?" he asked abruptly, his half-eaten sandwich laid aside.

She looked at him for a long moment, her eyes seeming to question whether she should reveal her secret dreams. "You mean, other than not going back to Middleton to wait for my mother's idea of Mr. Right?"

"I mean, if you could do anything with your life, what would it be?"

A smile curled her lips. "I think . . . I'd like to redo this house."

Jake straightened. "I'm serious. What would you really like to do?"

"I really would like to do this house," she said, her voice low. "Once I'm through with it, though, I'd like to be in the design business full-time. Last fall, I applied for a design internship in London."

She shook her head. "It was a crazy dream really. I haven't had any experience since college and these kind of internships are very competitive. But I had to give it a shot. I couldn't just go on the way I was."

"So changing jobs is what this whole thing is about? You left Middleton because you couldn't be a designer there?"

"No," she sighed. "I've told you why I left. My frustrated dreams of creativity are just part of it."

Jake sat up, crumpling his sandwich wrapping. "You'd

have actually moved to London if you'd gotten the intern thing?"

Emily stared at a bee plundering a blossom on a rambling rosebush. "I'd like to think I would have gone back then. Now I'd do it in an instant. I couldn't live with myself if I didn't."

"I thought you worked as a paralegal because you liked it." Now that he realized it, his image of the grown-up Emily had always been a little vague. She'd never been loud about her ideas and dreams. His memories were of a mostly compliant dark-haired girl who only rarely displayed a stubborn side.

"Not only do I hate the legal field," she said, "I despised my boss. He didn't care about his clients. He was slimy in his negotiating tactics. He treated his employees like dirt and he cheated on his wife every chance he got."

Jake got a sudden image of Emily with a philandering boss. Had he messed with her, seduced her into thinking she was in love with him? Her current hatred of him could be the feelings of a woman who'd been used and dumped.

It had been a long time since Jake had the urge to beat the crap out of a man.

"Did he hurt you, Emily? Is that why you left town so suddenly?" Jake asked softly.

She glanced up. "I told you why I left Middleton. Why is it so hard for you to believe that I need to stretch out, to do new things, take charge of my life?"

"It's not," he said quickly, hoping his question wouldn't jeopardize the tentative rapport building between them. "I just thought that might be part of why you wanted to try new things *now.*"

"I've known I needed to change my life for a long

time," she said, lying back on the blanket, her curved body lovingly molded by the thin material of her shirt. "I finally worked up the courage, that's all. So, this morning when you said you would be my 'guide,' what exactly did you mean?"

A small, challenging smile hovered on her very kissable mouth, and for an instant, he thought of all the ways he'd like to guide her.

God.

"Well, I—" Jake cleared his throat. "I thought I'd point out some of the pitfalls and make some suggestions. I've made a lot of mistakes in my life, Emily. You don't have to do the same things."

"What do you mean?" Her gaze was serious.

He looked down. Not an overly reflective man by nature, he'd still found the time to review his life a few years back. "I've done some stupid things, got involved with dangerous people. I'm really lucky I didn't get killed several times over."

Emily shook her head, a smile curling the corner of her mouth. "If you hope to convince me, I'll need specifics."

He paused, reflecting on which of his various missteps would help her see his point. There was a long list of things he wasn't proud of.

"I was a wild kid," he said finally, finding the words difficult. "You were right about that. I didn't have adult supervision, no reason to want to go home. Kids can easily get into trouble that way."

"But you never did anything illegal," she said, an unconscious compassion in her eyes.

"Not really," Jake agreed, warmed by her soft words. "A couple of times joy-riding in someone's car, maybe.

Underage drinking. I didn't really hurt other people as much as I put myself at risk."

He paused, continuing with effort. "I always knew how the good people of Middleton viewed me. A bad kid from the wrong side of town. I didn't do anything to change their minds."

Emily's gaze was steady on his face.

"I took every chance that came along," he said, meeting her eyes. "Most kids don't have much sense of self-preservation, but . . . I look back now and wonder if I didn't have some kind of death wish."

A small laugh escaped her. "I can't see that. I used to think that no one in town was as full of life as you."

Jake shook his head. "I'd take any dare, go to any lengths to prove how tough I was. I once drove dead-man's curve with my cycle flat out. Fought every guy who ever called me a name, back-talked every teacher and cop in town. Made a general terror of myself."

Compelled to be brutally honest, he went on, "I asked out every pretty girl in school and slept with as many of them as I could. I know I hurt a bunch of girls who hadn't done anything to deserve it. I had a lot to prove, Emily, and I tried doing it in the stupidest ways."

Emily sat on the blanket, eyes down, her finger worrying a worn spot in the fabric.

"I woke up a few years ago and realized none of it mattered. Sleeping around didn't make me a better man, more respected. So what if I could beat someone up or risk my life ten different ways? Being wild doesn't make you happy," he finished, his voice husky.

She looked up at him. "We come from very different backgrounds, don't we?"

"Yes," he said, aware of a sense of sadness. She'd put her finger on the crux of the problem. Different backgrounds, different lives. In another situation, with other circumstances, he'd have gone after her in a minute. As it was, just her presence reminded him of who he used to be. His reckless youth had left him with an indelible image, as far as anyone from Middleton knew. And Emily was definitely from his old hometown.

She believed him to be the wild boy he was then; he knew it every time she referred to his being different from her. He wasn't afraid, she said, but what she meant was that he was still the crazy kid she'd seen growing up.

"Everyone has to make their own way in life," he said, feeling awkward and ready to shift the focus from his past, "but you don't want to act like a little kid. That's something a lot of people do when they're busting out from their parents' way of life."

He could see by the look in her eyes that she was considering this, seeming not sure whether to take offense or to agree with him.

"I don't feel like I'm *rebelling*," Emily said, stressing the word. "It's just that I've never made my own way before, done the experimenting that a lot of people do when they're younger. I've always been a good girl, too afraid to upset people."

"You're in that adolescent, 'finding yourself' stage," he said helpfully.

"No." She glared at him, straightening up. "I'm just finally doing the things I've always wanted to do, but didn't because my parents would have been hurt and I couldn't do those things in Middleton, anyway. I've been afraid too long."

"Sure," he nodded as if her garbled expression made perfect sense. "The thing is, you have to make sure you're doing what you want to do, not just doing the opposite of what everyone else wants you to do."

Jake fished a potato chip out of the bag, noting the thoughtful look on her face out of the corner of his eye. He had no doubt that down deep Emily was a warm, level-headed woman. She may not be acting tremendously mature and reasonable now, but he knew she would revert to normal soon. He just had to keep her out of trouble in the meantime . . . and keep his hands to himself so she didn't hate him when her sanity returned.

She sat up suddenly. "What I want to do now is ride on your Harley. Let's get on it and drive."

Before he'd done more than recognize her swing from pensive woman-child to biker babe, she was up and packing their picnic away. Within minutes, Emily had the blanket folded and the food and wrappers stashed in their bags.

This time she climbed on the Harley behind him without hesitation, and Jake found himself straining not to notice the cuddle of her legs around his backside. He pushed the starter button and the engine kicked in. Backing out of the driveway, he tried to convince himself that he'd made some impact on her with his comments about rebellion. Maybe now that he'd stopped trying to openly convince her to go back to Middleton, she wouldn't be so determined to do crazy things.

Maybe she'd been reacting to him like he was a strict parent.

Unfortunately, the woman didn't make him feel parental, he acknowledged to himself as he nudged the bike into gear. Even when she wasn't acting the hellion, he couldn't quite think of her as David's sweet little sister anymore.

Tempted as he was to think of her only as a beautiful, sensitive woman, he had to remember their respective places or he'd end up being badly hurt.

People could change. Jake knew that more than anyone. But Emily's sudden breaking with her old patterns seemed too abrupt to be long term. Though she denied any desire to go back to being Middleton's favorite girl, the role of a lifetime wouldn't be easy to shed.

And why would she want to shed it for more than a few weeks?

Disturbed by the question, Jake did what he often did when troubled. He rode, following the road aimlessly. Only this time, trouble sat behind him, her arms wrapped around his waist, her firm breasts against his back.

What was he going to do with Emily and the urges she roused in him? Their conversation today had made him realize it wasn't as simple as putting her on the next bus home. She'd left because of some problem, even if he couldn't figure out what it was. Still, somehow he had to help her solve it before she hit real trouble. Before he created another problem with his growing desire for her.

They drove the loop around the city, 635 not as clogged with traffic since it was Sunday. But eventually, he headed south, seeking country roads, air with no exhaust in it.

She sat behind him as if she'd ridden a cycle all her life, not fighting the tilt of the bike, leaning gracefully into the corners. He'd taken a lot of people for rides in his hog-riding career. Few adapted to the rhythm so quickly.

Dallas behind them, they didn't talk. With no landmarks to point out, Jake let himself lapse into silence.

But he felt her presence, a tenuous new awareness of connection and confusion, warm and cautious, all at once.

She puzzled him.

Fields whipped past, interrupted by dirt roads and an occasional farmhouse. The sameness was mesmerizing, tranquil. Circling around to the east, Jake turned back to the city, eventually crossing Lake Ray Hubbard, the bisecting highway seeming to skim the surface of the water.

With the sun riding low in the western sky, he pulled onto his street, turning in to park at the curb in front of his apartment.

He killed the engine and sat there without speaking, waiting for Emily to get off. After a moment, she did, leaning forward, her body brushing against his.

Jake got off the hog, leaning it on the kickstand. He followed her up the sidewalk, the helmets in his hand, his eyes following the sway of her walk, knowing he shouldn't.

Fumbling with the helmets, he finally unlocked the door and they went in. The apartment was dark, shadowy with the approaching night.

Emily stopped just inside the door, facing him, her eyes dark with something he knew he shouldn't want. Turning to set their helmets down, he couldn't seem to dispel the charged emotions between them. Awareness, longing, need.

"Jake?" she said softly.

He swung back to face her, his pulse pounding in his ears.

"Thank you for a lovely day."

Turning away from her right then would have been a good idea. But he couldn't do it. He couldn't even claim ignorance. He saw the kiss coming. Saw it and wanted it so bad he hurt.

She lifted up, sliding her arms around his neck. He felt the smooth, firm weight of her arms on his shoulders, registered her warmth as she drew near. Still, he didn't turn away, didn't push her away. He couldn't.

Kissing Emily was the only good idea at this moment.

She leaned into him, her breasts against his chest. Jake closed his eyes then, his arms going around her, his mouth urgently seeking hers.

Screw doing what he should. This was too much, the heat of her mouth beneath his, the feel of her in his arms. He drew her up tight against him, his tongue slipping between her lips. The tangle of breath and need, lips meeting and parting, meeting again.

He was hard against her, he knew. Every stolen breath held her scent, every layered kiss, her taste. It had to stop. He knew that, too, but he couldn't.

She'd hurt him if he let her. Innocently and without consciousness, but she'd leave him crippled when she eventually got tired of the city and decided to head back home to Mama and Daddy.

They had to stop, Jake thought again, plundering her sweet mouth with his own.

Sex didn't just happen. Somewhere between the blistering sizzle of a kiss and the first slide of a zipper, a choice was made. He'd already made his. He wasn't screwing Emily just for the hell of it.

She was too special. Too temporary.

He'd just kiss her a fraction of a second more and then he'd let go. Because he had to, because even a man trying to do the right thing had his limits.

Emily was pushing every single one of his.

Slowly, using more willpower than he knew he possessed, Jake cooled the kiss down, pulling back from her soft, deliciously responsive mouth.

"You're welcome, Emily McKinnon Loughlin," he whispered, setting her back on her feet.

Trying to ignore her dazed eyes and her kiss-swollen lips, Jake turned toward the door. He had a lot more riding to do before he could go to sleep within a few feet of this much temptation.

Five

Emily sat on Jake's big bed, her legs curled under her, the pounding of her heart settling down to a sultry, languorous rhythm. Even after an hour, his kiss left her body humming with urges she hadn't known before.

He'd come back in a few minutes ago and was out there beyond the bedroom door, his sexy, powerful body stretched out on the couch. Yes, they'd slept this close before, but tonight felt different. She had the sense that he'd seen the true Emily today for the first time. Not just David's sister or her parents' daughter.

At some point in the afternoon, she'd glanced over and realized she had his complete attention. She hadn't talked about her dreams to anyone in recent years, not even Cassie that much. Cassie's dreams were so different, all centered there in Middleton, Emily hadn't felt like she could talk about how much the place stifled her.

The design internship application had been sent in almost total secrecy. Having the truth out in the open felt good. Jake had listened as if he were really interested.

She'd loved it, feeling stronger and more sure of herself in talking with him about her personal transition.

His comments about his own youth were the most interesting, of course. It almost seemed as if he understood some of what she was wrestling with, not all of it, but some. He'd rebelled against the world at a young age because no one had cared what he'd done. She, on the other hand, had had too much intervention. His concern for her was touching. Yes, he'd first gotten involved with her new life due to his friendship with David, but today as he'd talked, Emily had realized he really cared about what happened to her. He wouldn't have talked about his own past choices with such honesty, otherwise.

She'd sat there listening to him, an overwhelming tenderness flooding through her as he talked. Even his pauses, the occasional hesitation, made him seem more vulnerable . . . and even more attractive.

Then, of course, there was the motorcycle ride. How could perching on the back of a loud, dangerous machine as they hurtled along the pavement at high speeds foster the feeling of unspoken connection? Perhaps clinging to him was part of the equation.

That and the kiss that followed.

Emily leaned back on the bed, feeling her smile grow as memory heated her body. She'd started the embrace because it felt right and she was determined now to give rein to her cravings when doing so seemed right. For the first time ever, she was listening to the voice inside.

At least with him, going with her instincts had been very rewarding. When she kissed him, she'd felt the sizzle of something warmer than lust. Even more exciting, she'd felt it from him.

She smiled at the ceiling. Even though he'd pulled back eventually, he hadn't been kissing David's sister. That much was for sure.

He wanted her as much as she wanted him. But how

to get him past that "little Emily" thing? That was the puzzle.

Emily had never deliberately set out to seduce a man before. Chewing on her lower lip, she studied the lighted mall map in the middle of the concourse and fought back the butterflies in her stomach.

There on the lower level to the right, beyond two major department stores, was the lingerie store she sought.

Starting off in that direction, she walked slowly, her head full of images and anxiety.

Her plan made real sense. She knew that and yet it required the greatest risk of her new life. She had to give herself a big pep talk to get this far.

Somehow, she had to seduce Jake into forgetting his old image of her. She had to make him want her so badly he threw caution aside and made hot, sweet love to her.

That kiss yesterday, just inside the entry to his living room, had left her feeling as if her clothes were melted to her body. Never had her heart thundered against her ribs so desperately, never had she wanted a man more.

But Jake had stopped and walked away.

Still, she was aware enough through her own fog of passion that he'd had a difficult time stopping. He'd wanted more, just as she had. So here she was at the mall, specifically to find the tools for seduction.

After all, she'd left Middleton to make an exciting new life for herself. What could be more exciting than embarking on a sexual adventure with the sexiest man she'd ever known?

It was the ultimate fantasy, the most erotic daydream she could conjure—Jake so consumed in passion for her that he forgot everything else. No thought of David or Middleton. Not seeing her as little Emily anymore. Lusting for her, only her, needing her so badly he hurt. Craving her like an addict.

She just had to get him there. That's why she was here. Ammunition.

Emily stopped in front of the lingerie store, eyeing the polished woodwork and silk-draped windows with trepidation. Through the open doors, she saw racks and racks of fluttering silk and satin, headless torsos covered only in sheer negligees. On the far wall, something that looked like pasties with tassels was stuck above a pair of crotchless panties.

Good grief! There was nothing like this in Middleton.

Of course, that was the point, she reminded herself, moving toward the shop door with determination. No sense in standing there staring like a country bumpkin. Women bought things like this every day to wear for their men, didn't they? She just needed to go in, pick out something gaudy and revealing, and buy it. Nothing to it.

From things she'd overheard, she knew that men uniformly responded to suggestive lingerie. Her own brother leered at the nightgowns in the window of Babcock's back in Middleton, and her boyfriend in college had always wanted her to wear weird things like brief French maid costumes and feather boas. Not that she'd ever worked up the courage to do so back then.

But this was different. It was now and it was . . . Jake.

Gathering her courage now, Emily walked into the crowded, artistically lit shop trying to look as if she made this kind of purchase every day. Well, she amended, suddenly hearing her own thoughts with a spurt of amusement, maybe not *every* day.

The place was amazing. Carpeted in plush mauve with deep upholstered chairs placed here and there, the lingerie shop obviously catered to the sensuous. In the background played a subdued recording of a string quartet. Small tables scattered around held artfully arranged candles and body scents.

Emily paused next to one of these, shocked to see that the entire display was made up of edible underwear and something referred to as "flavored lubricants."

Okay, she thought, swinging away from the table, *I'm obviously not in the right section.*

There was a limit as to how far and fast she could push herself.

Emily stood in the middle of all the satin and velvet, trying to get her bearings. To the back of the store were racks of plush velour robes in jewel tones and granny gowns in flowered cotton.

Nope, definitely not going there, she vowed.

"Can I help you find something?"

Emily turned around, finding herself being addressed by a thin, excruciatingly hip salesgirl several years out of high school.

"Are you looking for something specific?" the girl asked, running her gaze up and down Emily in a dispassionate manner as if she could guess her bra size. "Something for a special evening?"

"N-no," Emily stuttered, feeling stupidly intimidated and furious with herself for it. "I'll just look around."

"Of course," the girl said with an automatic smile and a shrug that nearly brought her thin shoulders up to meet her white-blond bob. "Just let me know if I can help."

"Thanks," Emily murmured, turning away with relief.

The girl looked bored and jaded, as if she wore crotch-less, edible panties and used "flavored" lubricants all the time with a variety of edible and flavored men.

Working to assume a similar air of nonchalance, Emily pushed through the crowded racks, finding a room off to the side that held row after row of bras.

Okay, this she could deal with. Bras were familiar.

Scooping up a collection of styles in various colors, Emily turned toward the dressing rooms lining the far wall. On her way to the one on the far end, she passed a rack of teddies in vivid, rich colors. Snagging several of these as well, she went into the dressing room and took off her clothes, deliberately not looking at her na-ked self in the floor-length mirror.

She was such a wuss. Still, this was a big step for someone who'd always worn plain white bras from Bab-cock's. Garments chosen more for their supportive ca-pacity than for style.

And the mirrors at Babcock's were from the waist up, as if the women didn't need to see any more of their seminaked bodies than absolutely necessary.

Fifteen minutes later, she'd tried on and discarded half her stash. The push-up bras made her breasts spill out like a hooker's, and the pastel ones left her feeling like an Easter model in a porno magazine.

Working her way through the teddies, Emily finally tried on the one she'd selected last. A fragile champagne color, it nipped in at her waist and skimmed low on her breasts. The material was so sheer, it left her nipples visible.

She studied herself in the mirror, deciding the color worked better on her than either scarlet or black and, since it blended with her own skin tones, left her looking almost nude, while still artfully concealing the important parts.

This was it. Not gaudy, but definitely seductive. Jake Wolf wouldn't know what hit him.

Jake knew something was up as soon as he opened the apartment door. Shutting it behind him, he surveyed the darkened room, the only light spilling from a cluster of fat candles on a low table.

Their dancing light played over a large vase of creamy white tulips, the heavy blossoms thick and luxuriant in the fragile candle glow.

Damn.

He didn't need the low, throbbing music in the background to figure out what Emily had in mind.

Damn it to hell.

He'd left early this morning to avoid her. But he hadn't been able to avoid thinking about her. About how good she felt in his arms, her mouth open beneath his. About how perfectly her body meshed with his. About how she was going to rip out his heart and stomp on it.

He'd been so good at protecting that vital organ all this time. Why couldn't he safeguard himself against Emily Loughlin?

The memory of their kiss had haunted him all day, pushing him into working later than usual rather than come home and look into her beautiful face, smell her fresh, sexy scent.

Emily. This was *Emily,* who'd grown up in security and wealth. Emily who had position in the select, secure town of Middleton.

He was trying so damned hard to be a decent guy about this. Trying to be smart, but she wanted trouble and wanted to drag him into it with her. And looking around him at the scented, candle-lit room with the erotic music in the background, he figured they were both in big trouble.

As if on cue, the bedroom door opened and she appeared in the doorway. Her short, dark hair caressing her jaw line, her hazel eyes wide, she stood there, the faint light from his bedside lamp outlining her body.

Jake closed his eyes for a second. God, what was she wearing? Some sort of thin, silky robe clung to her curves. With wide generous sleeves, it fell to mid-thigh, gaping open in front to reveal a hell of a lot of Emily.

Silky, almost-naked, sexy as sin Emily.

Damn, he swore to himself again, his instantaneous erection straining at his zipper.

"Hello," she purred. "I'm glad you're home."

"Ah, good," he said warily, taking off his jacket and throwing it on a chair. "Um, what have you been . . . uh, doing today?"

Keep it light. Keep it normal.

Emily shrugged, the movement making her robe part further. "Just relaxing."

She sank onto the couch, her smile inviting. "You look like you could use some . . . relaxation. Sit down and tell me about your day."

Oh, sure. Tell her I've been thinking about her *all day, that I've been hard for her all day.*

Jake wrestled with himself, wrestled with the overpowering urge to throw caution aside and give her what she thought she wanted. Wasn't this what *he* wanted? To come home at night to this kind of erotic vision? To kiss her till she was hot and wet and so crazy for him that she begged him to take her up against the wall? Even if she was Emily Loughlin.

He could have her. He could do it.

But how would she feel afterward? He'd had enough experience to know she'd enjoy herself while he was slaking his hunger in her silky, slender body. But what about afterward, when she came to her senses and remembered who she was? Remembered who *he* was.

"Sit down," Emily said again, patting the couch next to her.

"Okay." He sank onto the couch, everything in him warring.

"Did you have a good day?" Tilting her head, she smiled at him, her silky robe sliding off one shoulder.

"Uh, yeah. I guess so." Jake stared at her, struggling to keep his tongue from hanging out. That . . . thing she was wearing. It was practically see-through. Even in the dim candlelight, he could see the dusky shape of her areola, the puckered thrust of her nipple against the fabric.

He sat back in the corner of the couch, wondering if she could see the sweat on his brow, wondering when the room had suddenly become a furnace.

"I've been thinking about you," Emily said, scooting closer as she shrugged her other shoulder out of her robe so that it fell down to her elbows, the wide sleeves falling in folds to her slender wrists.

"Oh?" he said with a hint of bravado. Hell, he'd slept with more women than he could remember. Surely, he could handle this one inexperienced girl. Er, *not* handle her.

Couldn't he? She might not have had much experience, but she sure as hell had him in knots.

"Yes, I have," she said, the tip of her pink tongue flickering over her lower lip as she moved even closer.

Jake bit back a groan. The candles on the table behind

him cast a shimmering light over her. He could see the outline of her breasts, the rounded curves, her taut nipples clearly visible now.

He stared at the creamy slope of her bare shoulders, the delicate crest of her ear. God, he wanted her. Wanted to lick her there on her ear and lower, where her breasts thrust against the teddy she wore.

"I've been . . . thinking about you," she said, her voice low, her gaze luminous on his face, "about the way . . . we kissed . . . last night."

"Mmphhf." His tongue felt thick in his mouth as he pressed himself further into the corner of the couch. He wondered how it would feel in hers.

Emily leaned closer, the soft fabric at her breast whispering against his arm. He bit back a groan as she reached up, her fingers sliding through the hair brushing the nape of his neck.

The warmth of the candles on the table behind him was nothing to the heat she was building in him.

"I'd like you to . . . kiss me like that . . . again."

She threw her arm over his shoulder, falling against him, and pressed her lips to his.

Jake held still, absorbing the softness of her mouth on his, the scent and taste of her. With the blood thundering in his head, he strained backward against the arm of the couch to keep himself from reaching out to cup her delicious breast. It was right there, cuddled against his arm while her sweet little mouth sent his soul straight to hell.

What had ever made him think he knew anything about kissing a woman? With Emily's tongue flirting uncertainly against his lips, he strove to contain the lust roaring through him. Fiercer and more glittering than anything he'd ever known, desire raged in his chest, gripping him in a crushing hold.

Don't touch her breast. Don't throw her back against the couch and drive into her soft flesh.

She moaned against his mouth, stretching her hand up to stroke his hair.

Jake heard a soft *hiss,* combined with the faintest hint of a crackle, and smelled the acrid scent of smoke. In a flash, he remembered the candles on the table just behind him.

Leaping up from the couch as a startled Emily fell forward, Jake saw the flame licking at the dangling fabric of her sleeve where it must have hovered over the candle flame.

She jumped up from the couch with a shriek, flapping her arm in a desperate, awkward attempt to put out the fire.

Adrenaline pumping through his already rushing blood, Jake found the closest water source. Picking up the large vase of tulips that sat on the table near the candles, he yanked the flowers out, dropping them onto the floor, and heaved the water over the still-flapping, shrieking Emily.

Drenched from neck to knees, she stood gasping, blinking scattered drops of tulip water out of her eyes.

The burning sleeve, Jake noted with satisfaction, had gotten a straight shot of the water and now hung down, a pathetic, blackened mess. To make sure no remaining ember would burn her, he reached out and stripped the soaked outer garment off her as she stood there in apparent shock.

To his horror, as he stood balling up the flimsy, soaked fabric in his hands, Emily began to cry.

Trying not to notice how the wet, sheer fabric of her teddy clung to her body like a second skin, he held up the sodden ball, assuring her, "It's okay."

But she only sobbed louder. Then it occurred to Jake that the flame may have burned her before he'd managed to get it out.

Reaching out, he took her hand and scanned the creamy flesh for any sign of scorching.

"I don't see any burn," he muttered. "Is it tender?" Emily wailed.

Not knowing what else to do, Jake patted her shoulder awkwardly. "It's all right, honey."

"No," she sobbed, between hiccups. "It isn't all right."

Miserably aware of her drenched, nearly naked body and his own regrettable state of lingering arousal, he let his hand drop back to his side. Better if he didn't touch her now.

Even wet, crying, and smelling faintly of smoke, she still looked too damn good to him. He was a pervert, Jake decided with disgust.

"Shhh," he said without thinking, his instinct to comfort her winning out over other baser desires. "You can get another robe-thing. It's really all right."

Emily gulped back a sob, opened her damp hazel eyes, and declared passionately, *"Nothing* is all right."

To his surprise, she turned then and fled back into his bedroom, slamming the door shut behind her.

"Cassie!" Emily wailed softly into the phone, not wanting Jake to hear her. "I made a fool of myself!"

"Are you okay?" her friend asked urgently.

"Yes," Emily replied, "but I don't know what I'm do-ing here. Nothing is going right. I keep trying to be different, to be a whole new me, but I keep screwing up! I have to break out of the fear and be different, but Jake doesn't see me as sexy!"

Moving the receiver away from her mouth, she sobbed into a pillow, too ashamed to let Jake hear her distress. She must have looked like an idiot! Dressed up like a slut and begging for his attention before setting fire to herself!

"He was the one who was supposed to go up in flames!" she sobbed into the phone.

"What?" Cassie said in a bewildered tone. "Are you talking about Jake Wolf?"

"Yes!"

"Listen, kid," Cassie said, her voice worried. "From what I hear, that guy is tough as nails. I know I only moved to town a few years ago and you've known him all your life, but you have to be careful."

"H-he doesn't want me!" Emily wailed softly.

There was a pause at the other end of the phone.

"You know," Cassie said, the words bracing, "you can come stay with me while you're looking for a job in Dallas. We'll get the Dallas papers and you can send them your résumé—"

Emily heard the worry in her friend's voice and sat up straight on the bed. She had to get a grip. "No, Cassie. I'm all right. I'll get a job. I'll be fine."

"Are you sure?" her friend began. "Because it's no problem, you staying here. We'll call it a visit. No one has to know about anything you don't want them to—"

A firm knock sounded on the bedroom door.

Emily twisted around, staring at the wooden rectangle. "I have to go, Cass. Don't worry. I'll call you later."

"Okay. Make sure you do—"

She hung up the phone and brushed the tears off her face before turning toward the door.

* * *

Jake knew he should have waited till morning to talk to her. She'd showered and gone back into the bedroom a half hour before. He knew she'd be dressed for bed, although, thank God, not in that delicate nightie thing.

Still, they'd had too close a call tonight. He had to act quickly or lose the little integrity he'd won for himself in the past few years. Not to mention both David and Emily's friendship.

He knocked on the bedroom door and waited.

"Yes," she said quietly, her gaze not meeting his.

Despite his determination not to let his gaze drop below her nose, his peripheral vision reported the way the wide neck of her soft, snug T-shirt revealed a tempting expanse of bare shoulder. The damned shirt clung to her firm, rounded breasts with loving faithfulness. He could even see the flare of her delectable hips outlined by the boxers she wore.

Not much better than the sheer nightie-thing.

Nose, he thought. Focus on the nose.

"Uhh." He cleared his throat and started again. "I had an idea. Maybe you'd like to take a little trip. We could, uhh, take a few days and go somewhere tropical."

"A trip?" she said, the surprised lilt in her voice making it even sexier, despite the smudges of tears on her cheeks.

"Yeah," he said, dropping his eyes to his feet. When was the last time he'd had to do that with a woman? "Cancun, maybe, or the Virgin Islands."

"Just . . . go somewhere?"

"Sure," he said more heartily than he intended. "Why not?"

"Okay," Emily said, giving an excited little bounce.

Jake barely managed not to groan. She had no idea

what happened when she moved like that. He was probably going to be strangled in these jeans. Thank God, he'd pulled his shirt loose.

"We could probably get a flight out tomorrow," he said, keeping his own sense of urgency out of his voice. It wouldn't help his game plan to let her know how desperate he was to speed things up, to get her back home.

He *had* to get her back home.

For his well-being as well as her own.

"That would be great!" she said, anticipation banishing the clouds in her eyes.

He shifted his weight from one foot to the other. In the last half hour, he'd given the situation some furious thought.

It was clear that Emily needed a change, needed to try her wings a little, needed to find a little sense of excitement. Vacations could do that. He was betting that her need for a break from her old life would be satisfied after a few days in the Caribbean sun.

After all, he wanted her to be happy.

"I'll call the airlines tonight. Do you have a preference as to where we go?"

"Surprise me," she said, a mischievous smile lilting at the corner of her mouth.

"Okay," Jake said, turning away. "Get a good night's sleep."

"You, too, Jake," she said, warmth in her voice as she shut the bedroom door.

He went back to the couch, picking up the telephone receiver. Tonight hadn't really changed anything. Or yesterday either, despite the new side of her he'd seen. Despite the fact that he'd bared more of his soul with her on their picnic than with all the women he'd casually slept with.

Middleton was still the best place for a sexy, single woman like Emily. She had ties there. Family. He couldn't believe her folks wouldn't help her get started in business. Emily had to be mistaken about that.

He could call David and ask his help in getting her started, but Emily wanted to make her own way, and Jake could understand the feeling.

She just needed to talk to her parents. Unquestionably, it was best for her to go home. Her staying in Dallas was a bad idea, even if she did the reasonable thing and applied for a design job. If she stayed in town, he'd end up seeing her again and that wouldn't be good.

They'd both grown up since the days when he'd been Middleton's bad boy and she the closest thing to the local princess. But some things never really changed.

If her attempt at seduction tonight was any indication, Emily would continue to see him as the wild kid from Middleton as long as she saw herself as the mayor's daughter. If she stayed locked in her past, how could she let him out of his?

Jake punched in the airlines number, trying not to notice that his thoughts were repetitive. It didn't matter how horny the woman made him, or even that other emotions besides irritation and responsibility were starting to creep in. He didn't even want to think about Emily in emotional terms.

He had to keep things in perspective. Yes, Emily was a beautiful, alluring, desirable woman who brought out the beast in him. He still couldn't nail her. That part wasn't even open for debate, no matter how hard she made him.

The other stuff, though, was beginning to worry him.

He liked her. Liked her enthusiastic determination to embrace life. Liked the opinionated jut of her chin when she talked about how the old house should be decorated. Liked the way her eyes softened when she listened to him say things he'd never said before.

She was an intelligent, charming woman. And if she were in a different place in her life, from a different place, he'd have asked her out. Hell, he'd have asked her to have his baby.

But she was Emily, not just David's sister. Emily, who was confused about her life, who swung from crazy idea to crazy idea.

If she looked at him with hunger in her eyes, how could he know the truth of it? She'd kissed him with passion and unconscious sweetness, but he knew whatever interest she had in him was due to the situation rather than any real compatibility. Certainly nothing that would last.

He had to get her over this bad spell before she managed to damage his heart.

"Listen," Jake said, a faintly desperate note in his voice, "we can just stay on this part of the beach by the condo."

Obviously, he didn't want her to go topless on the beach, no matter what he'd said about guiding her to the wild side. Apparently, he hadn't envisioned nudity as a part of the bargain.

Emily stared at the sign on the fence that divided the beach, trying to ignore the panicked fluttering in her stomach. "It's a topless beach beyond the fence."

"I know." He seemed to bite back further comment, a scowl growing on his face. Tension rolled off him.

She forced herself to disregard his turmoil, determined to listen to her own inclinations. Too much of her life had been governed by worry about what other people wanted her to do. She frowned at the sign, trying to analyze the feelings bouncing around in her head.

Fear and panic, definitely. A faint sense of thrill at the thought of doing something so daring as going topless in public.

More fear.

It wasn't that she was ashamed of her body, Emily realized. Outside that television show where the surgically enhanced lifeguards bounced down the beach, her body would stand up against most women. She had her flaws, but so did most people.

Jake cleared his throat, still standing beside her on the hot sand. "We don't really need to go there. We can stay here and have lots of fun."

She glanced at him, noting he didn't meet her gaze. He looked very reluctant, almost angry. Would he have hesitated to go to the topless beach if she weren't with him? Not the Jake she'd known.

Turning back to glance at the privacy fence that separated the two beaches, Emily could almost hear her mother's scandalized reaction in her head. *Try to remember you're a Loughlin. What will people think?*

She felt herself recoil inside. People would be upset. Images of the shocked faces of her grade school teacher, the pastor's wife, the president of the garden club. People she'd known and respected all her life.

They'd be shocked if they knew she'd even considered going topless on a public beach. Emily felt herself shrinking back at the thought. She'd never wanted to distress the people who cared about her. Never liked stirring up talk.

Maybe she should just walk by this particular opportunity. She didn't have to do it just because it was shocking. That kind of thinking was childishly rebellious, as Jake had pointed out.

"Come on," Jake urged. "I see a couple of beach chairs. Maybe we can get a game of volleyball going."

"Volleyball?" she echoed in disbelief. "You'd rather play volleyball than sunbathe on a topless beach."

"Well, uh, sure." Jake shrugged, obviously off-balance. "It's not like I haven't seen it before."

The evasive look on his face kicked up a response in her. She had to ask the question, even though she knew the answer. "You've *been* to a topless beach?"

"Yes," he mumbled, still not meeting her eyes.

Frustration spilled through Emily, not at Jake's acknowledgment, but at her own incredible cowardice. She was considering a stroll across the beach with bare breasts, nothing more. What was so terrible about that? It was nudity, for heaven's sake, not some federal offense.

How could she face herself if she didn't do it? Held back out of fear and prudishness?

What should the new Emily do? Would she be afraid to try something daring and different? Of course not!

"Well, then," Emily said decisively as she hoisted her towel over her shoulder, "I see no reason why we shouldn't do it now."

"Emily," Jake protested, following her to the gate. "Why don't you think about this?"

"No," she said, wrestling with the gate latch.

"Does it matter so much that *I've* been to a topless beach?" he asked.

"No." The gate swung open. "I just realized it's something I've always wanted to do. Coming?"

"Yes," he said after a second's hesitation, grim determination in the one word.

The beach beyond the privacy fence was surprisingly crowded. Typical resort-style, there were chairs with umbrellas and people stretched out on beach towels while others cavorted in the surf.

Bare-breasted women roamed everywhere.

Emily stopped just beyond the gate, feeling the need to get her bearings. Boobs. Small ones, bigger ones. Rounded, saggy. Every shape imaginable. And no one seemed to even notice.

A quick scan of the beach didn't reveal even one man gaping at a woman. There was, however, an incredible range of body shapes and sizes. Clearly, this wasn't television land.

For one strange moment, Emily felt out of place, almost overdressed.

She couldn't fool herself, though. Stripping off her bikini top with abandon was totally new to her and not without anxiety. Terror, actually.

Pushing aside a spurt of annoyance with herself, Emily made her way to a nearby lounge chair and dropped her beach bag and towel.

It had to be done. She was determined not to stay proper, frightened, little Emily Loughlin, shut up in a small, safe world.

Reaching around, she found the clasp on her bikini top and unfastened it, letting the fabric cups fall free.

Jake felt like he'd swallowed his tongue.

He knew he shouldn't look, but he couldn't help it. Emily's breasts were staring him right in the face, this time with no gauzy nightie obscuring his view.

Full, smooth, and pale in the bright sunlight, they

looked incredibly beautiful and kissable. Her brown-pink nipples were firm and sweetly tilted.

He turned to stare at the ocean, the vision of her glorious, half-naked body emblazoned on his mind. Thank God he wasn't wearing one of those small, stretchy swim trucks. As it was, he probably still needed to find a seat and drop a beach towel in his lap.

"This is great," Emily said, her voice faintly strained as she still stood beside the beach chair. "Very freeing."

"Mmmfple," was all Jake could manage.

"Why don't we take a walk along the water?" she suggested, glancing over at him for the first time.

"Sure," he agreed, schooling his face not to show *any* emotion lest all his inappropriate hungers become visible. He followed her, threading their way through the people stretched out on the sand.

The fact that they were all half-naked hardly impinged on his awareness.

It wasn't until they'd reached the damp sand where the waves played that Jake realized walking along the water meant even more exposure for his luscious companion. Logically, everyone was facing the ocean and therefore, looking their way.

Jake positioned himself to walk between Emily and the beach. He couldn't totally block the view of her, but at least he could limit her visibility some.

He didn't want any of those other guys looking at her breasts. Just the thought made his fists tighten. Thankfully, if anyone was looking, they did it discreetly. Jake only wished he had the willpower to keep his eyes from straying.

And it wasn't just her breasts. Other than her small bikini bottoms, she was as naked as she'd been in all his fantasies. Emily had beautiful shoulders, a graceful back, and a tiny tuck of a tummy.

Why the heck had she cut her hair? The long dark tresses would have at least given her some coverage.

To distract himself, Jake deliberately focused on the mammary glands of the stream of women approaching them, also walking along the water. In doing this, he knew he ran the risk of upsetting their various escorts, but a fight actually sounded good right about now.

Anything to take his mind off Emily's naked body.

A tall blond woman came toward them, with smallish, attractive breasts. She was followed by a black woman who'd clearly nursed a child or two. Beyond her was a gray-haired grandmother with an equally gray companion. Jake wondered what they told the grandchildren about their vacation.

After that the breasts and bodies began to blur together. They walked down the length of the beach and turned back again, Jake all the while so conscious of Emily that he hardly spoke at all.

She, on the other hand, seemed in very good spirits.

"I can't believe I'm actually doing this." Her excitement added a little extra bounce to her walk.

Jake concentrated on the brunette coming toward them. Implants. Had to be because they didn't move.

"You know, this is the most daring thing I've ever done. I'm really proud of myself. Look at all these people. Everyone's enjoying the sun. No one's hitting on anyone. This place is less sexually oriented than your average bar."

"Uh-huh," Jake responded, mentally noting how quickly they would reach the end of the beach.

"I mean, I understand what nudists say about it not being a sexual thing," Emily said.

He was a pervert, Jake admitted to himself. For him, Emily's bare breasts were completely sexual. The others now, them he could take or leave.

Finally, the fence loomed up in front of them. Jake headed back to where their towels waited on the beach chair.

"Umm. Maybe we should go in now," he suggested.

"Why?" She looked at him with such innocently unaware inquiry that he wanted to kiss the woman silly just to give her a clue.

"You don't have any sunscreen on," Jake said, feeling brilliant. "You wouldn't want to get . . . yourself burned."

Emily glanced down at herself. "Umm, you're right. Okay, I guess we can go."

She retrieved her bikini top and turned her back to him to put it on. The belated modesty of it almost made him want to smile. He knew this was the real Emily, despite her recent outbreak of social defiance.

Jake followed her across the sand to the fence with an overwhelming sense of relief. Emily fairly skipped through the gate, as excited as a child who's beaten the class bully.

"I actually did it!" Her laugh was exultant. "I've never done anything like that in my life. Do you know what the people in Middleton would say if they knew? They probably wouldn't believe it."

"You could take out an ad in the paper," he suggested, able to grin now that she had her clothes on again. Not that the bikini covered much, but every little bit helped. At least, now that she was covered, he just needed to squelch his highly vivid memory of her beautiful half-naked body.

Fat chance.

"And run a photo," Emily said, giggling. "My parents would leave town."

"Yes, but you'd have a bunch of new men friends," he pointed out, the impossibility of the situation making it easier to talk about.

"I can't believe I did that." She crossed the condo beach with him, her head thrown up triumphantly. "It was strange, of course, but I did it."

Jake threw his towel down over a lounge chair when she came to a stop. "Let's sit. All that nudity is exhausting."

Emily chuckled again, clearly still in the adrenalin thrill.

Leaning back, he looked at the ocean, conscious of the tension in his muscles. Just walking down that beach with her had tightened him up like a drum. Jake glanced over at her, noticing how her dark hair, secured on the top of her head in a Pebbles Flintstone imitation, contrasted with the hectic pink of her fair skin.

A delectable, beautiful woman. Sitting there looking at her, he realized part of the problem with her being bare-breasted on that beach was that he didn't want anyone else seeing her breasts. Just him.

Damn. When had he started feeling possessive of Emily? He usually congratulated himself on his liberal approach to relationships. He'd dated quite a few women in the past, had even been with one of them when he'd first gone to a topless beach. Not a single one of his previous experiences had prepared him for this emotion.

And here he was feeling possessive of Emily's breasts and her sweet little curved fanny and the slope of her neck.

Geez. This was turning into one hell of an experience.

Six

"Jake!" Emily bolted upright in her lounge chair, her hand gripping his arm.

"What?" He looked in the direction she was staring.

"That tall frame thing over there is a bungee jump place. See that person getting ready to go?"

"Yes." A deep sense of foreboding crawled up his spine. She wouldn't.

Emily jumped up. "I'm going to try it."

"Why?" Jake hit the sand, walking fast to keep up with her. The woman was wearing him out.

Emily threw him a mischievous glance over her shoulder. "Because I've never done it before. Because I'm feeling invincible!"

She skidded to a stop beside the big air cushion beneath the V-shaped crane. A weathered, forty-something beach boy in a Hawaiian shirt came over.

Jake heard her ask about the cost as he watched a vacationer dive off the platform overhead.

Okay, he had to admit to himself that he wasn't much more thrilled with this idea than with the nude beach thing. But he knew the sport was safer than most people thought. Heck, he'd jumped himself a few times, just for the hell of it. Yes, he'd done this, too.

Of course, now that Emily was digging in her beach

THE PUBLISHERS OF ZEBRA BOUQUET

are making this special offer to lovers of contemporary romances to introduce this exciting new line of novels. Zebra Bouquet Romances have been praised by critics and authors alike as being of the highest quality and best written romantic fiction available today.

EACH FULL-LENGTH NOVEL

has been written by authors you know and love as well as by up-and-coming writers that you'll only find with Zebra Bouquet. We'll bring you the newest novels by world famous authors like Vanessa Grant, Judy Gill, Ann Josephson and award winning Suzanne Barrett and Leigh Greenwood—to name just a few. Zebra Bouquet's editors have selected only the very best and highest quality romances for up-and-coming publications under the Bouquet banner.

YOU'LL BE TREATED

to tales of star-crossed lovers in glamourous settings that are sure to captivate you. These stories will keep you enthralled to the very happy end.

4 FREE NOVELS
As a way to introduce you to these terrific romances, the publishers of Bouquet are offering Zebra Romance readers Four Free Bouquet novels. They are yours for the asking with no obligation to buy a single book. Read them at your leisure. We are sure that after you've read these introductory books you'll want more! (If you do not wish to receive any further Bouquet novels, simply write "cancel" on the invoice and return to us within 10 days.)

SAVE 20% WITH HOME DELIVERY
Each month you'll receive four just-published Bouquet romances. We'll ship them to you as soon as they are printed (you may even get them before the bookstores). You'll have 10 days to preview these exciting novels for Free. If you decide to keep them, you'll be billed the special preferred home subscription price of just $3.20 per book; a total of just $12.80 — that's a savings of 20% off the publisher's price. If for any reason you are not satisfied simply return the novels for full credit, no questions asked. You'll never have to purchase a minimum number of books and you may cancel your subscription at any time.

GET STARTED TODAY –
NO RISK AND NO OBLIGATION

To get your introductory gift of 4 Free Bouquet Romances fill out and mail the enclosed Free Book Certificate today. We'll ship your free books as soon as we receive this information. Remember that you are under no obligation. This is a risk-free offer from the publishers of Zebra Bouquet Romances.

Call us TOLL FREE at 1-888-345-BOOK
Visit our website at www.kensingtonbooks.com

FREE BOOK CERTIFICATE

YES! I would like to take you up on your offer. Please send me 4 Free Bouquet Romance Novels as my introductory gift. I understand that unless I tell you otherwise, I will then receive the 4 newest Bouquet novels to preview each month FREE for 10 days. If I decide to keep them I'll pay the preferred home subscriber's price of just $3.20 each (a total of only $12.80) plus $1.50 for shipping and handling. That's a 20% savings off the publisher's price. I understand that I may return any shipment for full credit-no questions asked-and I may cancel this subscription at any time with no obligation. Regardless of what I decide to do, the 4 Free Introductory Novels are mine to keep as Bouquet's gift.

BN090A

Name _____

Address _____

City _____ State _____ Zip _____

Telephone ( ) _____

Signature _____

(If under 18, parent or guardian must sign.)

Orders subject to acceptance by Zebra Home Subscription Service. Terms and Prices subject to change.

Order valid only in the U.S.

If this response card is missing,
call us at 1-888-345-BOOK.

Be sure to visit our website at
www.kensingtonbooks.com

BOUQUET ROMANCES
Zebra Home Subscription Service, Inc.
P.O. Box 5214
Clifton NJ 07015-5214

PLACE
STAMP
HERE

bag to pay the pervert leering at her butt, the whole situation looked different. Suddenly, all Jake could think about were the live-action videos he'd seen on television. People who'd plummeted to their deaths when the bungee cord broke.

Damn.

He couldn't protest, couldn't try to stop her. He'd gotten through the topless beach thing without her calling him on his obvious reluctance. Some "guide" to wild living he was proving to be. At this rate, she'd fire him.

Then again, would that be a bad thing?

Standing there staring at the flushed guy dangling from the bungee as they lowered him to the air cushion, Jake tried to reassure himself that she'd be okay. He had to let her do it. She had a point about being cosseted and protected all her life. The woman had a right to a life of her own, particularly if she kept her clothes on.

He just couldn't stand the thought of watching.

Emily pranced up beside him. "Isn't this great? I can't believe we didn't notice this before. Don't you want to do it?"

Quickly scanning the possibilities, he realized that being up there on the platform with her wouldn't enable him to help her if something did go wrong. "No. I'm just not in the mood."

"Well, I can hardly wait," she said, energy bouncing off her.

He had an overwhelming urge to kiss her, to snatch her up and run, but he couldn't. So while she pulled a T-shirt and some shorts over her bikini, Jake dutifully accepted custody of her beach bag. He watched her climb onto the platform, feeling his stomach sink as the thing rose high above him.

Feeling helpless and hating it, all he could do was clutch her tote bag and pray.

High above the beach, the platform stopped.

Emily clutched the railing, suddenly wondering what she was doing. The guy beside her on the platform was strapping her into the ankle harness and would soon attach the bungee. He was blond, fairly attractive, and in his mid-twenties, and he seemed inclined to flirt with her. She should have been gratified, but all she could think of was how far away the ground looked, the beach and ocean a lovely, far-off view.

Jake stood down there. She could see him off to the side, his face tilted toward her, her pink beach bag in his hand.

"Stand here," the bungee guy directed. "You're all set. Just dive off when you're ready."

Emily stood in the open gap, holding onto the sides with both hands. She felt paralyzed with fear. How come she'd never realized she hated heights?

This was insane! Why was he letting her do this?

Far below, she could see Jake watching her, too distant to be able to save her from herself as he had that night in the bar.

The echo of her own whimpering thoughts slammed into Emily's consciousness. It wasn't Jake's job to *keep her safe*. She was responsible for herself. To her dismay, she realized down deep she really was a wuss! Hundreds and thousands of people had done this. Only a few had died.

"And this is perfectly safe?" she asked the blond guy.

"Perfectly," he answered, grinning. "We've only lost a few jumpers, but none of the pretty ones. Go on. You'll be hooked for life. It's a major rush."

"Yeah," she muttered. "Okay."

Quitting was not an option. It was cowardly even to consider wimping out. She couldn't back down!

"Listen, could you just push me," she asked finally, gritting her teeth.

"No problem. I do it all the time," he said from behind her.

"Okay, any*tiiiiiimmmmmmmeeee.*" The word ended in a shriek as a firm hand thrust in the middle of her back.

Emily dove forward off the platform, aware of the sudden rush of sky, ocean, and sand, the blur of the world around her. Falling, falling into nothing. She heard herself screaming and felt her heart actually stop.

She was going to die. There was no escaping it.

With the ground rushing at her, her circulatory system kicked back in with a double-time rhythm. Then there was a jerk at her feet and she felt herself bouncing back up, limp as a ragdoll on a string.

Thank God, the bungee cord held.

Springing up several more times, she felt the slam of nausea as the crane lowered her to the air cushion.

Landing into the billowy, bouncy thing didn't help her stomach. She struggled to sit up, conscious that the guy in the Hawaiian shirt was on the bag with her, dragging her feet loose from the bindings and giving her a shove to stagger toward the edge of the cushion.

She reached the side as her stomach clenched again. Half climbing, half falling, only partly aware of Jake's concerned face as he offered his hand, Emily ran to the slight privacy allowed by the base of the crane and lost her breakfast.

Jake guided Emily off the elevator, glancing down with concern at her pale, distressed face.

"Here we are," he said. "Do you feel like you're going to be sick again?"

"I don't know." She seemed almost listless as he urged her into the condo's living room.

He tossed her beach bag into a chair, glad he'd been able to arrange the two-bedroom condo at the last minute. This way, he'd be close enough to help her if she started feeling really unwell.

Emily stood next to the couch, huddled in a beach towel, looking more miserable by the minute.

"I need a shower," she mumbled, turning toward the bathroom.

Looking up from where he was peering into the stocked refrigerator, Jake saw the door close behind her.

"Emily," he called out. "Would you like some club soda or something? We don't have any here, but it won't take a minute for me to get some from the bar."

An indistinct response drifted through the bathroom door. He stood staring at the door, knowing she felt embarrassed and upset, even though she'd just done an amazingly brave thing.

Needing to do something to help, he called out, "I'll be right back."

Jake left the condo and made his way down to the bar. Making his request, he stood waiting, thinking about the woman up in the room. He couldn't help but feel a reluctant admiration for her.

Bungee jumping took courage. Seeing her do it might have taken ten years off his life, but he had to give her credit for her determination.

Emily was certainly making up for all her timid years. It wouldn't be a good idea for him to tell her, of course, but he found himself liking her way more than he should. Maybe he didn't see what was so bad about her former life, but he had to give her credit for doing something about the problem she saw in it.

Some people lived their lives in fear, always bemoaning their chains, but never leaving them. Emily, however misguided she was, was trying to change the things she didn't like about her life.

Armed with a bottle of club soda, some ice, and several glasses, Jake went back up the elevator and let himself into the condo. He'd only been gone fifteen or twenty minutes, but the bathroom door was open. Emily must have finished her shower.

In the small kitchen area, he opened the soda and poured some into a glass. Crossing the living room, headed toward her bedroom, he heard the sound of muffled sobs.

Jake stopped outside her door, the glass of soda in his hand. What the hell did he do now?

She was obviously upset. About what he couldn't be sure. Maybe she was suffering from a delayed reaction. He'd seen grown men shriek like babies after bungee jumping.

He grabbed his bag and headed for the bathroom. She was probably suffering from a temporary reaction to the risk of the jump. Letting her get herself together was probably the most respectful thing he could do.

Hurrying through a shower, Jake pulled on his jeans and went back out into the main room.

Minutes later, standing at her bedroom door, he listened to the continued sobbing. Damn, she was still upset. She claimed she hated being cosseted, though. Maybe he should let her tough it out, but he couldn't. Couldn't hear her suffer and not at least attempt to comfort her.

Tapping gently on the door, Jake called her name softly. "Emily. Em, are you all right?"

The sobs suddenly quietened, as if she didn't want to be heard.

"Emily, I know you're upset. Please, can I come in?"

A renewed burst of weeping greeted this. Not waiting for an invitation, Jake turned the knob and pushed the door open.

She lay sprawled on the bed, clad in his old bathrobe, her hair still wet from the shower, her face buried in the pillows. Jake hovered beside the bed indecisively for a moment, not sure what the hell to do.

Then a visible shudder ran through her and he winced at the sound of her tears.

"Come on, Emily," he said, crawling onto the bed to gather her into his arms. "It's all right now. You're okay. It was scary, but it's over."

She let him roll her over to face him, the dark tangle of her damp hair all in her face. Scooting down on the bed, he drew her closer. "It'll be all right."

Emily's sobs slowed beneath his hand, soothing her back. He cradled her, offering comfort even though he wasn't exactly sure what caused her distress.

Her body was warm beneath the terry cloth, warm and curved and so very female. She snuffled back her tears, her head buried against his shoulder. An overwhelming sense of tenderness, of rightness bolted through him.

"You're okay," he murmured against her cheek, brushing back the silky strands of her hair. "I'm here. Everything is okay."

"I'm such a coward," she said suddenly, the words muffled.

"A coward?" he repeated in surprise, giving in to the

urge to smooth his hand again over her beautiful hair. "Honey, you did an amazing thing."

"I had to ask the guy to push me off!" she wailed softly. "Then I barfed. I got off the air cushion and tossed my cookies. I'm hopeless. I'll never be the kind of person who can do things and really live life."

Jake laughed gently, looking down into her beautiful hazel eyes, surrounded by wet spiky lashes. "Don't be silly. It doesn't matter that he pushed you or that you threw up. You did the jump. That's what counts."

"Really?" She sniffed, looking up at him with a mixture of hopefulness and doubt.

A bolt of tenderness rushed through him.

"Really," he said, bending down to brush his lips against her cheek. Her skin was impossibly soft. She smelled faintly of soap and tears and sex.

Jake pulled back a fraction, meeting her eyes, knowing she felt the same sizzle of lightning. Awareness, tight and thick, ran between them. He felt it in her body, so soft against his, saw it in her eyes.

Without thinking, he bent, taking her mouth with the hunger of a starving man. She was beautiful and special, precious and perfect. Everything he needed. Never had a kiss felt so right, the softness of her mouth, opening beneath his, the straining of her body against his.

Jake pulled Emily up against him, plundering with a heedless need. He'd fought against her pull, tried to walk the straight and narrow, but he couldn't resist any longer.

He needed her with every part of him and he knew, beyond reason, that she needed him at this moment, too.

Heat and hunger swept through Emily's body, sudden and startling. Locked in his arms, pressed against Jake's powerful body, she trembled beneath his softly persuasive kiss. He wooed her with his mouth, slow and wanton, as if he were memorizing the shape and texture of her lips. As if kissing her would satisfy a lifetime of need.

When had she ever felt so cherished? Not as a perfect child or a demure woman, but as a person in her own right.

Here was what *she* needed, craved. His touch, the drugging wonder of his kiss. Conscious only of the need for more, she clung to him, her hands slipping beneath his shirt to stroke his muscled back.

The misery of moments before evaporated in the heat of their bodies, locked together on the bed. Despair and utter failure giving way to a blazing fire in her bones.

She dimly realized he kissed her like a man starved, like her mouth was a marvel of nature to explore. Tongues met, lips and breath mating. Jake urged her closer till they lay entangled on the mattress, her leg wedged between his, hard against the evidence of his desire.

Emily squirmed against him automatically, drawing forth a groan from deep in his throat. Urgently she pressed closer, her body aflame, a heady sense of feminine power raging through her veins.

Aching for him in places that had never actually ached before, she rocked her hips. Jake groaned again, hurriedly brushing her robe open, his hand finding her naked breast. She arched into him, breaking their kiss. He bent to her neck, his mouth hot and urgent, his hand deft and thorough on her sun-pink breast.

Writhing against him in mindless urgency, Emily pulled at his shirt, managing to free several buttons. She wanted him inside her, wanted to know him completely. Nothing felt more right, more completely perfect than this moment.

To her shock, Jake pulled back, his eyes dark with hunger. He stood. Then to her sobbing relief, he took off his jeans with swift efficiency before climbing back onto the bed with her. Until that moment, she'd wondered if he would stop. Would Jake really make love to her, to Emily Loughlin?

She knew he wanted her. That much had been obvious on several occasions, but until he stood beside the bed and stripped, she hadn't been sure he would choose her, the woman she was now, over the image he'd held of her so long.

God, he was beautiful. Strong and muscular, the hair on his chest sprinkled over toned skin, narrowing as it reached his waist. She ran her hands up his chest as he tugged at the tie holding her robe together. Cooler air caressed her skin as he pulled it free, baring her to his hungry gaze.

Emily felt a flush of embarrassment. Never had a man so avidly gazed on her nakedness, never had she known lust in full daylight.

Had she ever felt anything remotely like this hunger?

Nudging her to lie flat on the bed, Jake crawled between her legs. With almost reverent hands, he stroked her from breast to belly, his touch leaving a hot, shivery trail of sensation. Bending to suckle her breasts, he gentled his hands over her thighs, moving ever closer to their juncture.

Emily lay in a state of shocked sensation, overwhelmed and aroused beyond belief. Lifting her hands, she touched him, gliding her fingers over shoulders, powerful arms, torso. Glancing down, she saw his erection, smooth and hard, so close to her portal, so ready to fill her.

His ministrations at her breasts left her squirming, her

breath short and hard in her throat. Moaning as his fingers delved and teased, she arched to him, reaching down to stroke his thigh, her fingers restless and urgent.

When Jake licked her nipple and straightened, she reached for him, seeking union. But he sat back, rolling over to lie on his back next to her. Retrieving a foil packet from his pants pocket, he readied himself for her.

"Come here," he said, his voice low and urgent as he guided her over him.

Dazed, Emily allowed him to position her astride his hard thighs. He cupped and gently squeezed her breasts in his hands, drawing her forward till she hovered over his erection. Unable to wait any longer, she reached down and guided him into her, sinking slowly over his shaft with a long gasp of pleasure.

Glory flooded her, spinning out from every point of contact. Jake rocked with her, filling her until she felt nothing but the bliss of his touch. Stroke after stroke, he built the fire between them, his hands eager at her breasts, gentle on her face.

"God . . . you're beautiful," he gasped in a soft, husky voice. "Perfect."

His hands settled on her hips, driving deeper with every thrust. Hard against her, inside her, each stroke a revelation, driving her need higher and tighter.

She heard herself draw a sobbing breath as her world exploded. So intense were the sensations that she held her breath as wave after wave rolled through her, precious and soul-shattering.

Dazed, Emily collapsed on his chest, conscious of him still strong within her. He cradled her to him, brushing kisses against her hot skin, his hands eager and questing.

Bracing her to him, Jake rolled on top of her. She felt the warmth of the mattress against her flushed skin, the length of him, hot and hard within her, and she adjusted herself beneath him, spreading her bent knees wide. Holding his weight off her, he leaned forward, taking her mouth in a sensual kiss, his tongue finding hers.

Emily writhed beneath him, hunger and need rising again from smoldering ashes.

Never had she felt so alive, so powerful.

Kneeling between her spread legs, he began moving, the hard, driving rhythm ceaseless and wonderful. She clutched at his shoulders, thrilling to his touch and the ragged, labored sound of his breathing. They rode the storm together, locked in their own universe, sufficient and enthralled.

When he stiffened, his muffled cry triumphant as he emptied himself into her, Emily tumbled over the rainbow again, shattering into a thousand pieces, each of them soul-deep in love with Jake.

Emily snuggled into the pillow, only half awake. More content than ever before in her life, she knew she'd had a smile on her face all night. With Jake beside her, his even breathing close to her ear, she'd slept wrapped in the conviction that she'd finally found her place in the world. Here, in his arms. Unafraid to take the risk of loving him.

It was the bravest thing she'd ever done, offering her inexperienced self to a man who'd made an art of experiencing life.

She was alone in the bed now, lying cuddled beneath the covers, half listening to the cozy sounds of Jake moving around in the bathroom. The shower had stopped a few minutes before. Still smiling, she rolled over in the bed, imagining licking droplets of water off his beautiful body.

He'd made love to her, responded to her as a woman last night, a person who could meet his needs. She hadn't been Emily of Middleton, the sister of his childhood friend. He'd seen her only as herself, a woman who'd wanted him, needed him.

Awash in a deep sense of excitement and contentment, Emily looked up eagerly as the bathroom door opened.

Jake came into the room, a towel thrown around his bare shoulders, jeans slung low on his hips. Crossing the room without looking at the bed, he rummaged in his bag, finally pulling out a shirt. Since they'd been scheduled to sleep in separate rooms and he'd ended up in hers, he must have retrieved his luggage when he'd gotten up.

"Good morning," she said, a hint of a purr in her voice.

"Good morning." Jake didn't look at her as he started to pull on his shirt.

Watching him search through the bag again, it hit Emily that he hadn't glanced in her direction since he'd left the bathroom. A shiver of unease ran down her spine.

Ignoring it, she scooted up in the bed, reclining against the pillows, the covers falling loosely over her lap. "So what shall we do today?"

"I don't know," he replied, sitting in a chair to put on his socks, still not glancing her way. "I think there are several excursion tours, if you're interested."

"What I'm interested in touring," she said seductively, "is right here in this room."

Jake looked up, his expression serious. "Listen, Emily . . . we need to talk."

"Okay." The shiver of unease shifted into a wave of anxiety. Beneath his troubled gaze, she felt the urge to tug the covers up to her chin, but she didn't.

They'd made love last night, shared something real and true. Somehow they'd deal with whatever was bothering him, and recapture the magic.

He looked down again, as if he didn't know what to say, where to start. "Maybe you'd like to get dressed first."

She'd heard that husky sound in his voice before. The faint echo sent a quiver through her. Maybe staying naked was a good idea. "No, thanks."

He glanced at her again, his frown deepening. "Whatever. Look, I just wanted to . . ."

Getting up from the chair, Jake went to the window, his back to her. "I want to say I'm sorry. I shouldn't have let things get so out of hand last night. You were upset. . . . I don't know what to say. Usually, I have better self-control."

Emily sat in the bed, staring at his back, feeling as if a dagger had sliced through her heart.

He was *apologizing* for making love to her?

Sudden, jolting pain shook her, sending a spiral of nausea through her midsection.

"I know you're going through a rough time," he said, "trying to figure out a lot of things in your life. I shouldn't have . . . taken advantage of you."

She stared at him, as disoriented as if she'd been ripped from a beautiful dream and thrown into a cold, bitter reality. Only last night had been real and *this* seemed more of a nightmare.

It didn't make any sense. Only hours before he'd held her as if she were his lifeline, as if she mattered more than his next breath . . . and now he was . . . apologiz-

ing for it. As if they'd had some sort of drunken, casual
interlude?

A slow, furious sizzle joined the nausea in her gut.

"Oh, is *that* what happened last night?" The angry,
flippant words slipped out of her before she knew it.
Clearly, he saw last night very differently than she did.

A mistake. A moment of unguarded lust?

"What?" Jake turned to look at her.

"I've never been 'taken advantage of' before," Emily
said, her smile feeling brittle on her face. *He must not
know she was dying inside.* "I thought we were having
great, fabulous sex."

He turned back to the window.

"But maybe I was wrong about that," she forced herself to say, bitter hurt and anger warring inside her.
"With my limited experience, I might have been mistaken. *You* know all about these kind of nights. Was it
typical? Or maybe even sub par?"

Jerking around to glare at her, Jake's expression was
dark with emotion. She couldn't reliably read it, but
she'd be damned if she'd give him a clue as to her own
silly hope that she meant something special to him. He
obviously had more regret than tenderness.

"It shouldn't have happened," he said, his words as
stony as his face. "You're not the kind of woman to
sleep with guys just because they're there."

Emily made herself shrug. What did he know about
the kind of woman she was? Obviously, he still clung
to the old image. Last night had been an aberration on
his part, an error due to his loss of "control."

"Too late to undo it," she said, tossing back the covers. She'd chew glass before she'd let him see how much
he'd hurt her. Anger would be her shield. "Console yourself that I'm changing the kind of woman I am. Sleeping

around was never my goal, but last night was totally in line with your offering to be my 'guide.' I can't imagine a wilder ride."

Jake winced.

"Listen," he said awkwardly. "We used protection, so you're safe. But I just want you to know you don't have to worry."

"Worry?"

"Yeah." He looked down. "Because of my . . . past. I had myself tested six months back and got a clean bill of health."

"Well, that's good to know," Emily said cheerfully. "I'm glad you mentioned it. Next time I'll have to remember to ask the guy first."

She heard the sharp intake of his breath.

Reveling in the pitifully small victory, Emily got out of the bed just as he glanced at her. A bittersweet awareness of her tender spots, the sensitivity of a body that had never been so well loved, accompanied her desire to punish him. Knowing his eyes were unwillingly drawn to her, she stretched her arms above her head, bare breasts thrust forward.

Even from across the room, she felt the change in his temperature. For a long moment, his eyes fastened on her naked body hungrily.

"I'm going to get a newspaper," Jake said abruptly, heading for the door.

Emily watched him go, aware of the perverse satisfaction of arousing him even as he crushed her heart. Bitterness and a corrosive sense of bleakness crashed in on her with the shutting of the bedroom door.

For one night she'd thought she'd found a man who could appreciate her for herself, regardless of her family or even her failure to succeed as an adventurous babe.

Just for her, Emily who was determined to test out life, even if she messed up once in a while.

This experience, anyway, was a complete loss. She wouldn't let herself regret sleeping with him, but she couldn't rejoice in the crack he'd left in her heart.

She couldn't let this sink her, couldn't let her pain overwhelm her, no matter how much she wanted to drop to the floor and cry her heart out.

There was still the world to be conquered and all her "little Emily" inhibitions to be overcome. She wouldn't let Jake keep her down, no matter how much his desertion made her want to bawl like a baby. Or put a bullet through his heart.

Jake picked up their bags, following Emily to their departure gate. He'd come back to the room with the newspaper only to discover her dressed and packed to go home. His first reaction had been relief, of course. If he'd come back to find her still naked in the tumbled bed they'd shared last night, he'd have thrown his scruples out the window again. The woman tempted him like no one before.

And that was saying a lot.

But he couldn't hurt her again, couldn't steal her innocent caresses like a thief. She deserved better, deserved a man with a clean past, one with fewer apologies to make.

Someone she could be proud to take home to her parents.

And he deserved a woman proud to be with him, not one who took notes on what to "remember to ask the guy next time." In her determination to change her life, she was riding roughshod over his. . . . What, he asked himself. His heart?

No, he couldn't let her touch his heart. She'd shown him that this morning. She was experimenting; he was the subject. But that didn't stop him from bursting into flames at the thought of making love to her again.

So he'd been relieved to see her dressed when he returned to their room. That she'd wanted to fly back to Dallas this morning had surprised him, however.

As she made her way through the airport now, he walked a step behind her. It kept conversation at a minimum, but the view was killing him.

Still, he'd suffer in silence rather than try to carry on a conversation. She was in a weird mood. Even though she was only using him in her rebellious phase, he'd overstepped the bounds of her trust in making love with her last night, without a doubt. Maybe that was why she'd talked so dismissively of their encounter.

Shock, embarrassment, even anger wouldn't have surprised him. He deserved all that from her. But this strange mix of seduction and coolness baffled him.

Jake couldn't believe how stupid he'd been, allowing himself to act on his baser urges with Emily, of all women. There was no excuse for it, no matter how sexy she was. No matter how crazy she made him. He was supposed to be the responsible one here, the one David had called to talk some sense into his sister. Of all the regrettable things he'd done in his life, this ranked at the top of the list.

He'd have thought his own sense of self-preservation was strong enough to avoid this, even if his conscience hadn't been.

She'd seduced him, not with her curvaceous body and come-hither eyes, but with the raw battle she fought to conquer her fears. He'd never known a woman as courageous as Emily. Somehow she had to recognize that about herself before she jumped off a cliff into even more troubled waters.

Certainly, she had to go home before she managed to steal his heart.

To make matters even worse, he remembered every nuance of their lovemaking, every stroke and whisper, with piercing intensity. When was the last time a woman had touched him with such pleasure and appreciation? She'd been as responsive as a racing cycle on a five-mile open stretch, thrilling to his touch. He'd felt ten feet tall, triumphant and omnipotent, lost in her magic.

Stupidly, he longed to touch her again.

Still trailing her down the airport concourse, Jake told himself he was crazy to think of it. Remembering her innocent sensuality, her uninhibited enthusiasm, and the way she'd snuggled against him in the night would only make it harder to walk in these jeans.

Scum. He was scum. He deserved every insult she could hand out.

He'd betrayed her in the most intimate way. Last night, he'd kissed her, touched her body, with no thought of her confusion. Selfishly, he'd made love to her to fill his own need, used her to soothe the ache only she built in him.

To his disgust, it had been the most satisfying sex of his entire life. Somehow, he had to make it up to her without ever putting himself in so much danger again.

A few steps ahead of him, Emily felt his brooding gaze on her back. Their gate was just ahead, thank goodness. With him watching her, she was sure she'd stumble or trip.

Somehow make a further fool of herself.

Not doing that was her goal at this point. To no one but herself would she admit how easily she'd slipped into beginning to believe herself in love with him. The lingering influence of her girlhood crush, perhaps, but still unacceptable. For Jake, last night had been about lust. She knew that now.

In her determination to change her life, she hadn't been interested in changing her values. Whatever she may have said to Jake on that first night when he'd retrieved her from the motel, sex without love had never sounded appealing. She wanted to start taking risks in her life, in her career even, not in her sexual conduct.

Somehow last night had felt different, had felt as if he knew her and treasured her as she'd never been treasured.

Pushing the painful thought aside, Emily stopped at the airport counter, handing over her ticket.

Jake reached from behind her and gave his ticket to the attendant. Just having him close like this, an inch or two behind her, made her breath feel tight in her throat.

She inched a step to the left.

"We're boarding now," the airline employee said, nodding toward the gate.

"Thanks," Emily said when their tickets were finally handed back, boarding passes stapled in place. She let Jake take the lead this time, following him to the gate.

They found their seats, buckling in without much conversation. She sat next to him, finding herself remembering their arrival at the resort only two days before. In the space of twenty-four hours, she'd gone to a topless beach, bungee-jumped, and had incredible sex with a man who now seemed like a stranger.

She felt as wrung out as an old sponge. If this was infatuation, true love must be hell.

Leaning her head back on the seat, Emily closed her eyes and pretended to sleep.

For the entire duration of the short flight, the previous night played over and over in her head. She feigned sleep through the snacks and lunch, unable to open her eyes and make casual conversation with the man sitting next to her.

It finally occurred to her that she was angry with him for multiple offenses.

The whole "guide" thing was a farce. Emily felt her teeth clench. His apology for having sex with her made that clear, not to mention his obvious reluctance to have her do a little topless sunbathing. Jake was still humoring little Emily.

She wanted to break every bone in his body. So much for believing in her as a strong person.

He'd lied to her. That was bad enough, but the hypocrisy was what made her really mad. He thought she was an innocent girl who needed to be protected, but he'd made love to her as if she were a siren from sin city. The guy needed to pick an angle and stay with it.

Logically, she knew she shouldn't go back to the apartment with him. He had no intention of helping her free up her inhibitions, despite the wild ride he'd taken her for last night. She should get out and stay out, but for once in her good-little-girl life, Emily wanted to make someone suffer.

Jake.

She wanted him to hurt as much as she did right now. Even half as much as she did.

Her eyes still closed as the plane started its final descent, she decided to go with her gut. She'd go back to his apartment for a day or two while she found herself a place. And if during that time, she found the opportunity to use the weapon he'd given her, then so be it.

Unquestionably, he felt remorse for making love to her. Just as obvious was his response to her physically. She could make his life hell if she wanted.

There would be no repeat of the night before, however. Whatever she'd thought she felt for him this morning, he'd killed it. No, she wouldn't have sex with him again. But since he was the one who'd declared their coupling a crime, she'd help him drown in his regret.

Seven

He had to get her back to Middleton, no matter what it took. She'd lived there all her life. The town held a lifetime of memories and people she loved. All this craziness had to lose significance next to the reminders of permanence and belonging. He *had* to get her back there.

Even if he had to hijack her to do it.

He had to get her the hell away from him before he weakened, succumbing again to the lure of her soft lips and the beckoning sway of her body.

Normally, Jake figured it paid to play things straight in life, but Emily was proving to be an exception to every rule he'd learned in the past ten years.

"Hey," he said when she walked out of his bedroom the next morning looking all tousled and lethally sexy in an oversize T-shirt and flannel boxers. "I'm going for a morning ride before I go in to work. Want to come along?"

Emily brushed an errant clump of hair out of her eyes, her expression wary. "Uhh, I'm not dressed. You go ahead."

"I'll wait a few minutes while you get dressed," he offered, turning back to the kitchen. "The coffee will be ready when you're done."

Out of the corner of his eye he could see her mouth compress into a tight, straight line. No doubt about it, they were back to being enemies.

God, that was the last thing he wanted, although she had every reason to distrust him. Hadn't he taken advantage of her in a weak moment? Drawn her up against his body to soothe the ache she built in his bones.

And she had seemed to enjoy it, too, their erotic night in the tropics. But no matter how she felt about having sex with him, she had to go home, had to face herself. For some reason, it had become vitally important not to let her make a mess of her life.

Emily hovered in front of the bedroom door, uncertainty and distrust in every line of her delectable body.

"You don't have to wait for me," she said suddenly. "Go on your ride. I'll get my own coffee."

"I don't mind waiting." He didn't look at her, didn't allow himself to show any reaction to her barely hidden hostility.

He should never have touched her, he reminded himself, should never have taken the step that changed everything between them.

No matter how much she'd needed comfort, she hadn't needed to sleep with him.

"Look, Jake," she said after a moment. "I know you think I'm a twelve-year-old who can't take care of myself, but you don't have to entertain me. Just go to work. I'll look after myself."

Panic washed through him. He *had* to get her on that cycle with him if his plan was to succeed. Only strong measures would do in this situation, he knew. Still, he hesitated.

"You can't watch me twenty-four, seven," she said in a caustic tone.

Slipping into his bad-boy bravura like pulling on an old coat, Jake turned around to her, saying wearily, "You're not going to be one of *those* women, are you?"

"One of which women?" she asked, her beautiful face suspicious.

He sighed. "Women who get all weird and cranky after they've boffed a guy. Like they can't just be friends anymore because they've done the wild thing."

Emily flushed scarlet. "That has nothing to do with it!"

Leaning back on the counter, he said, "Are you sure? Because you really liked going riding before, but now, ever since we got hot and heavy in the islands, it's like you can't get over it."

"It meant *nothing* to me," she bit out nastily.

Jake turned away to get a mug from the cabinet, not sure he could trust his face not to betray the gut punch her words packed. He *knew* the truth of her statement. Sending her home made the only sense. She'd end up killing him, otherwise.

"Okay," he said, in a carefully neutral voice, "don't go all weird on me then. Get dressed and we'll go for a ride."

He waited, muscles tightening in the heavy silence.

"Fine," she snapped after a moment. "I'll be ready in five minutes."

"Good." He smiled at her, the effort costing him.

Fifteen minutes later, they stood next to his hog in the clear morning air.

"Here," Jake said, handing her a light jacket. "It's cool on the road in the morning."

"Thank you," she said, not looking at him, despite her polite words.

He handed her the helmet and tugged on his own. For

a brief moment, he regretted the helmet intercom. She was going to scream his ear off when she realized where they were headed. He could turn the thing off, but why deny her the pleasure of telling him off?

It wasn't like he hadn't heard it before.

Emily snuggled deeper into Jake's jacket, his scent filling every breath. Biting her lip, she swore at herself for being such a fool. What did it matter how he smelled or how the memories flooded back with each breath?

He'd held her tenderly that night in the condo when she'd been so miserable. Jake had kissed her as if she were the only woman on earth who touched his soul, as if she meant everything to him.

But she couldn't afford to remember, couldn't let herself be drawn into the seduction of fantastic sex. That had to be the truth of it because he sure as heck didn't act now like a man who'd found a soul mate.

He was a pig now, she thought fiercely, hearing his faint humming through the helmet intercom. The kind of guy her friends had talked about. One who went out with a woman, jumped into sex immediately, and then didn't call.

Only she happened to be living in his apartment, temporarily, she reminded herself, so instead of not calling her, he simply reverted to treating her like his best friend's kid sister. Except with less respect.

Emily pushed back an echo of her mother's long-ago advice about not letting a man think she was "easy." Heck, she'd lived with that maxim for years and ended up lonely, well protected, and so frustrated she'd practically stripped naked to get Jake's attention.

Literally setting herself on fire in the process.

Still, now that she'd made love . . . had sex . . . with him, life hadn't magically improved, either. Her long time ache for a lover's touch had shifted into an even more disturbing ache for a specific lover's touch.

Now what did she do about that? Particularly since the man she wanted gave very little indication of wanting her again. And even if he did, she wasn't inclined to slip into easy sex with a man who later acted as if she'd been a convenience.

Leaning against the backrest, the powerful motorcycle rumbling beneath them, Emily tried not to listen to the sound of Jake's breathing while she struggled with the confusion in her head.

She'd left home because she needed to take charge of her life, but so far, she hadn't done such a great job with it.

No job of her own. No place of her own. No Jake . . .

The still morning air turned cool as they sliced through the dawn, the cycle creating its own weather system. The highway pavement whizzed by, the city traffic becoming thicker as the sun rose even though it wasn't a weekday.

Her hands resting on Jake's hips, the faint sound of his breathing transmitted into her ear by the intercom, she fell into the rhythm of the ride, her thoughts circling over the same ground.

As they drove along in the morning air, time seemed to lengthen and stop. What was she to do now? Breaking out of her old patterns had seemed much simpler when she was still *in* them, still in Middleton.

As if her thoughts had conjured it up, a highway mileage sign read MIDDLETON 25 MILES.

Emily straightened, turning back to look at the sign

as if she could see through to the other side and read the words again. Had she imagined that?

Glancing around, she caught sight of the highway marker. Interstate 35E. And with the rising sun on her right, they had to be going north.

To Middleton.

Panic bolted through her, anger immediately on its heels.

"Jake Wolf, turn this thing around immediately!"

"What?"

"I said turn around!" Emily yelled, hoping it deafened him. "You are not taking me back to Middleton."

"Yes, I am," came his grim response, his gaze meeting hers briefly in the rearview mirror on the handle bars.

"No, you're not!" Sitting bolt upright behind him now, she wondered if a motorcyclist had ever been strangled by his passenger. Yes, she'd die with him, but it might be worth it.

"Emily," he said, "you have to face this."

"Face what!" she shrieked. "I've lived there all my life and I've only been gone two weeks."

"You have to face whatever it is that's bothering you," he said implacably.

"So you're just dragging me back involuntarily? Like a runaway teenager?"

She glared at his reflection in the mirror.

"Aren't you running away?" he demanded, their gazes connecting in the mirror for another fraction of an instant.

"No!" Emily denied, banishing an instantaneous mental image of her mother's disapproving face.

"Then it's not a problem to go back for a little visit, is it?" he concluded implacably.

Leaning back against the backrest, Emily averted her eyes from the mirror and said nothing.

Of course, she'd planned on going back to visit her hometown eventually. Once she was settled and successful. Christmas and Thanksgiving definitely.

Now? No.

And certainly, she hadn't planned on being tricked into returning. Damn Jake Wolf.

He'd egged her into this ride for just this purpose, she realized. Taunting her with his statement about her being one of "those women." Just to get her mad enough to get on the Harley with him so he could take her home like a lost five-year-old.

She felt like an idiot.

Another ten swift miles and they exited the highway, taking the familiar country roads back in time. Sitting balanced on the Harley, Emily drew another breath into already tight lungs. Try as she could to remember she was a grown-up, coming back to Middleton scared the hell out of her.

Twenty-six years she'd lived here, the last four spent dreaming of escape. If only she'd been beaten or abused by her parents, this would have been easier, the anger and rage would have pushed away her guilt. Wouldn't it?

Emily clung to the seat, reminding herself that all her belongings were in Dallas now. No matter how much guilt she felt, no matter how reasonably her parents argued, she had to go back.

She couldn't stay here.

In Middleton, spring Saturday mornings were assigned to gardening and mowing the lawn. As Jake drove along the main street, circling the courthouse, every other house had someone out in the yard.

The thundering cycle drew curious, censoring stares. On the corner, the white Victorian house with the lacy trim work belonged to old Dr. Bentworth, long retired. He stood on his jewel green lawn, his white hair bristling as he glared at the cycle's riders. Beyond the Bentworth house, was Linda and Ted Park's house. Linda knelt in the flower bed, her eyes widening in surprise as they passed.

With their helmets on, Emily realized, no one knew who they were. No one recognized the mayor's errant daughter and Middleton's bad boy from ten years before.

As Jake turned down the street leading into the neighborhood where she'd grown up, Emily's anxiety rose. This place was so *familiar,* so much of it beautiful to her. If she'd hated the place unequivocally, leaving would never have been so hard, she realized.

But she couldn't stay here.

When Jake pulled into the driveway of her parents' home, he killed the engine without a word.

She realized then that he hadn't said anything to her since leaving the highway and stepping back into what must have been a wealth of his own memories.

Drawing in a shaking breath, Emily made no move to get off the Harley, sitting silent behind Jake. This house with its stately trees and white-columned porch had made up her contained little childhood world.

No danger. No risk.

No chance to try her wings.

Staring at the structure with clouded eyes, she saw the filmy sheers at the front window twitch and knew they were being observed.

With cold, nervous fingers, she loosened the helmet's chin strap and took it off, running a hand through her flattened hair.

"I'll never forgive you," she said bitterly to Jake as he removed his helmet.

"I know," he said wearily, getting off the cycle. "Just add it to the list of my sins."

The front door opened and Emily's mother, looking like a throwback to Donna Reed in pearls and a cool, yellow shirtwaist dress, stepped out onto the wide front porch. "Emily?"

She got off the cycle, handing the helmet to Jake. "Yes, Mother."

"My goodness," Susan Loughlin said with sudden dismay, "you've cut your beautiful hair and have you colored it, too?"

"Yes," Emily replied, brushing a hand through the offending chin-length mass.

"Well," her mother said, eyeing her critically before hugging her. "I suppose it's not so bad. I did love it long, though. You could wear it in so many classic styles."

Emily stood on the front walk with her mother's arms around her, sadness filling her chest. She loved her mother, but when had the woman ever seen her as her own person? Susan was the one who liked "classic" French twists and chignons.

The older woman glanced over to where Jake stood next to the Harley. "Jake Wolf? I should have known it was you riding that noisy thing."

"Yes, Mrs. Loughlin."

"Well, I'm glad to see you." She reached out to shake hands with him. "I'm glad you brought our little girl home to us."

Emily's hand jerked convulsively, but she didn't pull free of her mother's hold.

"Come in. Both of you." Susan glanced across the

street to where a neighbor stood staring at them, paused in the midst of mowing. "We can't talk out here."

Following her mother into the house, Emily was acutely aware of Jake behind her as silent as when he'd been fifteen and invited into the house because he was David's friend.

"We're just setting the table for a light lunch," Susan said, always the perfect hostess. "You must both join us, of course."

"Thank you," Jake said.

"It's nothing special. We didn't know you were coming." Susan led the way into the dining room. "Would you like the chance to wash up first?"

Lunch was a stiff occasion, Emily and Jake sitting across the table from each other. The immaculate white tablecloth separated all four occupants at the table, the mayor at the head.

Emily felt her father's disapproving stare once or twice, but knew that nothing of significance would be discussed while they sat at the table. Her mother's rules of etiquette declared that dinner table conversation stay light.

"Well, Jake," George Loughlin said in hearty mayoral tones. "We appreciate your bringing our little Emily back to us."

Emily's jaw clenched while she tried to remember how much her parents loved her despite continuing to see her as a twelve-year-old.

Jake looked at his plate. "It was a nice day for a ride, sir. I thought she might want to see how everyone's doing back home."

Surprised at this noncommittal tone, Emily glanced at Jake. The way he'd been carrying on about her needing to "deal with" her situation, she'd expected him to deliver her into her father's hands with a flourish before turning around and hightailing it back to Dallas.

"Yes, well. We're glad you brought her."

"If everyone's through," Susan said gracefully, "we can go sit out on the patio."

How many times had she done this, Emily wondered, shared a perfectly orchestrated Saturday lunch with her parents, feeling as if she couldn't draw another breath. Why linen and china on a regular Saturday? Why the heck didn't they ever nuke a frozen pizza and sit in the kitchen, for heaven's sake?

Her parents were stuck fifty years back in time.

"Still riding that motorcycle of yours, I hear," George Loughlin said in a ponderous attempt at humor as he took a seat on the covered patio.

"Not the same one," Jake said with tight smile. "I sell Harleys now."

"Oh, do you?" George asked as if impressed that Jake had a job. "Been working at one of the dealerships in Dallas?"

"He *is* one of the dealerships in Dallas," Emily surprised herself by saying defensively. She wanted to strangle Jake herself, but she wouldn't tolerate her parents talking down to him.

"Really?" The mayor raised his eyebrows, obviously as surprised as he was impressed. "By heavens, that's wonderful."

"I enjoy it," Jake said.

Susan came out of the kitchen with tall glasses of iced tea on a tray. "Emily, dear, did you know that Mrs. Foster is no longer working for Jim Morris?"

"No, I hadn't heard," Emily replied, surprised. "She's been with him for years. Did she get a better job?"

"I can't say," her mother replied. "No one seems to know why she left."

"There's a rash of it going around," George Loughlin said meaningfully. "Although I'd have thought Nancy Foster had more sense than to leave a good job. *She* isn't likely to have any wild ideas about leaving town."

"Tea?" Susan said, obliviously handing out the glasses.

"Dad," Emily started, accepting the frosty glass from her mother, "I told you I wasn't happy working for Morris."

"Yes," her father agreed, "but you never told me why. It was a perfectly good job that paid you enough to support yourself as long as you stayed home with your mother and I."

"I didn't get a college degree to be a paralegal," Emily reminded him, an edge in her voice.

Her father shook his head. "It's not like you'll be needing a job forever. Just until you—"

"I don't see myself as a stay-at-home mother all my life," Emily interrupted him to say.

"Is there something wrong with being a housewife?" he demanded. "Your mother has devoted her life to us."

Emily glanced toward her mother. "I didn't say anything about Mother."

"Being a wife and mother is the most important job a woman can have," George Loughlin said with the fervor of a politician.

Emily met his stare with a stiffening backbone. "I didn't say it wasn't. I just said that *I'm* not going to be a housewife."

"If you think you can find a more *important* job—" her father began to bluster.

"If I could interrupt," Jake said suddenly, "I think

Emily has other things she wants to do with her life. She has dreams."

"Of course, we want her to have dreams," Susan said, as if puzzled how this could be misunderstood.

"She wants to be an interior designer. To use the college education you provided for her." Jake looked at Emily, the message in his eyes clear. *"Tell them."*

He didn't really understand, Emily thought, didn't see that while her parents loved her, they couldn't see her as a person beyond their own desires for her. Someone who wanted a different life.

Emily rubbed at her temples, trying to ease the pounding there. "I'm looking for a design job in Dallas."

"A design job?" Susan seemed dismayed. "Sweetheart, you don't need to do that. Running all over the place doing up other people's houses. It's not *safe*. One day, you'll have your own home to decorate. That'll occupy your time."

"No, Mother. I want to be a designer."

"But she doesn't have to do it in Dallas," Jake interjected, glancing at George Loughlin. "With all the people you know in Middleton, she could start a business here. Particularly with your backing."

Her parents exchanged a doubtful glance.

"If we thought that's what would make her happy," her father said, his words careful, "we'd do that in an instant. But running your own business is tough these days, especially for a woman. We just want what's best for you, Emily."

Emily watched the surprise flicker in Jake's eyes.

"She could start small," he said, persisting. "There wouldn't have to be a big outlay of money."

"Of course, she can do whatever she wants," her father responded doubtfully.

Jake looked at her with an encouraging smile. "You just need one or two clients. Then word will get out and you'll have other business."

He didn't really understand, Emily thought sadly.

Starting a design business here in Middleton would be an exercise in futility. Particularly if her parents were against the venture. Their negativity couldn't help but influence people.

They loved her, but they couldn't see that she was strong enough to be on her own. Couldn't see that she needed to take chances for herself.

The doorbell rang, echoing through the house.

"That will be David," Susan said brightly. "I called and told him you were here. He said he'd stop by after his golf game."

She got up to go into the house. "Silly boy. I don't know why he's ringing the doorbell instead of coming on in."

A silence fell on the group on the patio, Emily tensing herself for what she knew would be a confrontation. Her brother had been dead set against her leaving town and David rarely hesitated to express his opinion.

"So," George said heartily to Jake after a moment, "business pretty good in the big city?"

"I can't complain," Jake responded.

"I bet your taxes are sky high," the mayor said, chuckling with a certain amount of complacency.

"I manage," Jake said with a smile.

With effort, Emily repressed the urge to tell her father just how well Jake was doing.

The back door opened then and her mother stepped out, gesturing to a petite blond woman who followed her.

"It's Kristin Hanson," Susan announced with a smile.

Wearing a brief white tennis skirt and a sleeveless red knit top with a red scarf holding back her blond hair, the younger woman looked attractive and sexy in an energetic way.

"I'm sorry to burst in on you like this," Kristin said with a megawatt smile, "but I heard Jake Wolf was here and I just had to stop in and say hi."

Emily felt a sinking feeling in her midsection. Kristin Sullivan. Everybody's favorite cheerleader. Here to see Jake.

All at once, she became aware of her helmet-flattened hair and the faded sweater she'd thrown on over her jeans this morning.

Two years ahead of Emily in school, Kristin had been an icon of popularity. With her blond good looks and her feminine self-confidence, she'd always seemed to have the world by the tail.

"You remember Kristin," Susan said to Jake in her best hostess voice. "She was in the same grade as you and David. She's married to Rick Hanson now. He's a councilman, you know."

"No, I didn't know," Jake replied with a mechanical smile. "Nice to see you, Kristin."

Emily turned to look at him, her attention caught by the faintest sound of strain in his voice. He'd risen to his feet when the two women came out of the house and now he stood, the smile fading off his face as he looked at her mother, who stood next to Kristin.

"Would you like some iced tea," Susan offered, gesturing to the tray she'd brought out earlier.

"No, thank you, Mrs. Loughlin. I'm not thirsty."

"Kristin," the mayor said, "you get prettier every day."

"Why, thank you, kind sir," Kristin said, her smile flirtatious.

Feeling as if she'd suddenly grown Jake-sensitive antennas, Emily noted the hint of tension in his posture and the wariness in his eyes as he stood there listening to her father greet the other woman. Without warning, she remembered what he'd said the day they had picnicked at the haunted house. *I asked out every pretty girl in school and slept with as many of them as I could.*

Kristin had certainly been one of the prettiest girls in school.

Instantly, Emily's stomach tied itself in knots. With swift brutality, her mind's eye imagined Jake kissing Kristin as he'd kissed her that night in the islands. A younger Jake making passionate love to blond, beautiful, always-sure-of-herself Kristin.

Her knees suddenly weak, Emily sank into a wicker chair.

"Please sit down and visit with us, Kristin," Susan Loughlin said graciously, gesturing toward the wicker loveseat where Jake had been sitting. "How are those boys of yours doing?"

Susan turned to Jake, informing him, "Kristin and Rick have six-year-old twin boys. They're so cute!"

Without a doubt, Emily thought, Kristin met every expectation her mother had of a young woman. Married to a successful Middleton man, the mother of two children, undoubtedly a member of the local ladies club. How much more perfect could she be, Emily thought with disgust.

The crystal tinkle of Kristin's laugh rang out as she sat down on the wicker loveseat. "Oh, how sweet of you, Mrs. Loughlin. They are quite a handful."

Jake reluctantly sat down next to Kristin, reflecting grimly that the apples must not have fallen far from the tree.

What the hell was Kristin Sullivan Hanson thinking, coming by here today when she knew he was back in Middleton? She obviously hadn't outgrown her taste for flirting with trouble.

"So, Jake," the blonde said, glancing up at him through her eyelashes, "is that your motorcycle in the front drive?"

"Yes," he said, the word terser than he'd intended. He glanced at Emily, noting her gaze was on her lap where her fingers had knotted themselves together.

Damn. He didn't know why it bothered him. No matter how much he was aware of the gulf between them, he still hated having his disreputable past paraded by her this way.

Kristin Sullivan meant nothing to him. Nothing but a reminder of a time when he'd been good enough to provide stud service to a cheerleader who hadn't even acknowledged him at school.

Kristin sighed reminiscently. "I remember that time you took me for a ride on your motorcycle."

She laughed again, the sound setting his teeth on edge. There'd been more than one midnight ride on his hog. More than one swift, illicit coupling in the dark.

"We were such kids. Remember?" She laid her hand on his knee. "It was that night after the spring dance. My date had gotten drunk on some stuff that Clark boy brought. You were my rescuer."

"I remember," he said, acutely uncomfortable. Coming back here to Middleton, to the Loughlins' perfect house and faintly patronizing manner, was hard enough. Why the hell did he have to deal with Kristin Sullivan, too?

"How's Rick doing?" the mayor asked genially.

"Oh, he's fine. He's out playing golf today." Kristin

smiled at Jake and gestured toward the brief skirt that revealed her length of slim, tanned legs. "I was on my way home from a tennis game. I like to stay active."

He just bet she did.

No question of loyalty to her husband would stop Kristin's extracurricular habits. The last time he'd been in Middleton several years back, she'd cornered him at a Christmas party and stuck her tongue down his throat.

It had said a lot for Jake's newfound maturity that he hadn't agreed to her lascivious suggestion that they slip out and do the dirty in the backseat of her husband's car.

Then again, it said a lot about his past that she'd thought the idea would sound good to him. And it *would* have ten years ago when he'd still felt like he had payback to inflict, Jake admitted to himself with disgust.

Some choices followed a man wherever he went.

His hand clenching involuntarily, Jake grappled with the urge to once again put this town and its inhabitants far behind him. Emily belonged here. He never had.

Even if he'd changed his bad behavior, how could he expect a woman like Emily to understand the demons that drove him all those years ago?

Eight

Emily shifted in the wicker chair, trying to surreptitiously read Jake's face. It took no imagination at all to figure out why Kristin had stopped by the house today. In the adroitest manner, she was managing to convey her covert interest in Jake Wolf.

She had the hots for him, in fact. Emily repressed a sudden urge to throw her iced tea in Kristin's perfectly made-up face.

Listening to the ebb and flow of conversation, Emily studied the woman. From what she knew of Kristin Hanson, the other woman wouldn't sacrifice her position in Middleton or her small, stable family to run off with the town's bad boy. So that left sex as her only motivation for discreetly vamping Jake.

To Emily's parents, who were chronically unaware of emotional undercurrents, the conversation probably sounded like a typical high school reunion chat. Emily, as sensitive as she was to anything pertaining to Jake, knew otherwise.

Slut, Emily thought, eyeing the hand Kristin still rested on Jake's knee. Had she been one of the girls he'd run after? For the life of her, Emily couldn't remember them actually dating in high school and she'd paid attention to whom Jake Wolf dated.

Embarrassing adolescent crushes left one prone to notice things like that.

Just the thought of Jake holding the blonde, kissing her breasts and murmuring his hot hungry sexual desires into Kristin's ears, made Emily physically ill.

How could he have been with Kristin?

Jake had been the most devastatingly sexy guy in Middleton. If Kristin had liked him all those years ago, why hadn't she gone out with him? Hadn't Jake, the drunkard's son, been good enough for Kristin back then? Had she been too busy working her way through the football team?

Struggling with the catty thoughts overwhelming her brain, Emily plastered her polite smile on more firmly and tried to look as if she were following the conversation.

Jake and Kristin hadn't been a couple in high school. So maybe her antennas were wrong; maybe her own hunger for Jake had affected her judgment. Then again, instinct told Emily that Jake had seen a lot of girls who hadn't openly acknowledged going out with him.

Forcing herself to sit back in her chair, Emily repressed the urge to strangle someone. Kristin first, then Jake.

How could he have gotten involved with a woman like her? Why would he have done that to himself? She obviously didn't give a damn about him.

Just then the backyard gate creaked open, startling Emily out of her fuming reverie.

Susan Loughlin rose quickly. "David! Did you finish your golf game?"

"Come in, boy," the mayor called to his son.

Of average height and build, David had hair as brown as her own and a boyish winning smile. Something about her brother gave the impression of solidity and worth.

She'd always looked up to him and worried about disappointing him as much as her parents.

With a mixture of caution and affection, Emily got up to receive his brief hug.

"Hey, sis."

"Hey," she said, a lump in her throat.

David crossed the patio to where Jake stood. "Jake!" He grabbed Jake around the waist and playfully tried to wrestle him to the ground. "My God, you're still as tough as always, you son of a gun!"

While Jake fended off his friend's enthusiastic welcome, Emily's mother and father watched fondly from the other side of the patio. Glancing at the warmth in their faces, she tried to forgive them the satisfaction in their eyes as they gazed at David. This, at least, was one child who hadn't disappointed them.

"I can't believe you just dropped out of the sky like this!" David exclaimed, clapping a hand to Jake's back. "You could have, at least, let us know you were bringing Emily home."

Emily's teeth clenched.

On the other side of Jake, Kristin stood up, smoothing down her knit top.

"I've got to go," she said with a pretty smile toward Susan Loughlin.

"Hey, I didn't mean to run you off," David said, grinning at her. "Although I *was* wondering why you were here."

Kristin flushed, her smile becoming strained.

Emily's brother went on as if he didn't notice. "I just finished eighteen holes with that husband of yours and Rick said he had to rush home or you'd get mad at him for being late. Said something about not getting his Saturday night treat if he got you upset."

Glancing at Jake to see his reaction to this not-too-subtle reference to the couple's system of shared intimacy, Emily could read nothing but polite interest on his face.

"That's right," Kristin said to David with an arch smile. "I've been training him right."

She turned to Emily. "Well, it's been wonderful seeing you. I'm glad you're back."

Startled by the other woman's implication that she'd been the focus of Kristin's visit, Emily waved halfheartedly. "Yes. Nice to see you, too."

Sticking her hand out to Jake, Kristin said, "Glad to see you again, too, Jake."

"Sure," he said, letting go of her hand almost immediately.

To a chorus of good-byes, the blond woman hurried away, her ponytail twitching in rhythm with the sway of her hips.

"Hey," David said, punching Jake again. "I can't believe you're in town. You've got to come down and take a look at my new offices. I don't think you've been back to Middleton since I moved."

"No," Jake agreed. "But I'll come see your place another time. I have to get back to Dallas now."

Emily stood up with alacrity.

"So soon," David protested, his gaze swinging to his sister. "I hope you thanked Jake for bringing you home."

A bubble of hysterical laughter rose in her throat.

"She doesn't need to thank me," Jake said, glancing her way for what seemed like the first time since they'd come out on the patio.

"No," Emily agreed crisply. "I don't need to thank you."

She turned away to hug her mother. "I'll call you in a few days and let you know my address."

"What do you mean?" David said in astonishment.

Emily glanced at him, puzzled. "I . . . mean . . . that I'll call and give you my new address."

"Don't be a fool, girl," her father said immediately as if that covered the subject.

"Oh, Emily!" Susan said softly, tears shimmering in her eyes. "You can't mean to go away again."

Glancing at the four other people on the patio, Emily felt her backbone stiffening.

Jake stood with them, his gaze on the ground, his face stern.

Looking away from him, Emily said, "Yes, Mother, I'm going back to Dallas. I told you when I left two weeks ago that I don't want to live in Middleton. I'll be getting a job and moving into my own place."

"But you haven't even seen Cassie!" her mother protested. "How can you come all this way and not see your best friend? Just stay the weekend and we'll talk all about this."

"No, Mother. I'm going back to Dallas. Cassie spends the weekends with her boyfriend. She'll understand my not seeing her on this trip."

Emily didn't look in Jake's direction. He may have meant to leave her here today, but she wasn't about to let him.

"Are you crazy?" David said abruptly. "Hasn't Jake told you how dangerous Dallas is?"

Raising her gaze to Jake's, she wondered what he'd say if she told them who represented the greater danger to her in Dallas.

"I'm going back," she said distinctly. "Nothing's changed. I'm going back."

Only something had changed, she thought. Now, added to her memories of Jake Wolf, her sexy lover who'd been a menace to the young girls of Middleton, was the image of Jake, the outcast. The boy who might not have been good enough for some of those girls.

She'd always known the adult population looked at Jake askance. With his long hair, loud motorcycles, and bad grades, he hadn't exactly been the All-American poster boy. And there had always been that lazy sexual heat emanating from him. Parents tended to distrust that sort of animal sexuality as much as young girls craved it.

But she'd never really thought about Jake's side of it before. Had he walked on the wild side because the straight path looked dull? Or had Middleton's narrow-minded distrust and the sleazy sexual misadventures of girls like Kristin Sullivan convinced him that wildness was the only way for a boy like him?

All the way back to the city, Emily pondered the question of Jake's troubled youth. Had what she'd seen as untrammeled freedom really been a kind of acquiescence to the role the town conferred on him?

It didn't fit with her image of him, the defiant kid on the back of a Harley.

Still, she kept remembering the look in his eyes when Kristin leaned toward him, her hand on his knee. He'd gazed at the other woman with regret and resignation.

It was the resignation that bothered Emily the most. As if he knew what the town thought of him and had long since stopped fighting it.

Still, he'd tricked her into going back to her own messy family situation. She hadn't forgiven him for that, she decided as they whizzed along the highway toward Dallas. No matter what demons Middleton held for him, he still wanted her to go back there, still had apologized for sharing his body with hers in their passionate interlude.

How could she forgive him that?

He still couldn't accept her right to make her own way, couldn't see her as anything but "little Emily" who needed life decisions made for her.

Leaning back against the cycle's backrest, Emily drew in a deep breath and let it out slowly as the Dallas skyline grew larger before them. Glad that she'd asked Jake to disable the intercom, she didn't have to worry about his interpretation of her sighs.

No matter how his sexy body drew her or how she longed to erase the haunted look in his eyes, Jake Wolf wasn't on her side in this battle to reclaim her life. His actions today had proved that.

The farther into the city they drove, the warmer the day became, the pavement radiating the baking Texas sun. Noting the now familiar streets, Emily felt an odd sense of homecoming the closer they got to the apartment.

How could she feel so comfortable in *his* place when all he seemed concerned with was getting her out of his life?

Jake drove into the apartment parking lot, and after they got off, he cut the engine and leaned the hog on its kickstand. Without speaking, they walked up the steps to the apartment.

"Do you need to go into the shop this afternoon?" Emily asked when they stood before his door, her voice as casual as she could manage.

He glanced at her, turning the key in the lock. "Yeah, for a while."

"Okay," she said breezily as she headed for the bedroom. "I think I'll start looking through the paper for a job."

The sudden silence behind her was both deafening and deeply satisfying. He hadn't been expecting that from her, which was crazy. What did he expect her to do? Go on living here with him like some sort of aimless loafer?

Wake up some morning and announce she had decided to return to Middleton, after all?

She ought to feel like laughing at that image, but didn't.

Sailing into the bedroom and dropping onto the bed, Emily reminded herself that he very much wanted her to go back home. Particularly now that he'd given in to temptation and slept with her. Defiled her was probably how he thought of it. *That* was why she'd been tricked into going to Middleton today. His penance for having sex with her.

He had to pay, Emily decided, groping for anger to replace the despair in her chest.

At first she'd seen him as a bystander in her rush to change her life, called into service by his oldest friend. But now he'd sounded the battle cry. What woman could stand a man making piercingly beautiful love to her and then *apologizing* for it?

"I'll be back in a couple of hours," Jake said from the living room, his voice sounding muffled.

As the door closed behind him, Emily stretched out on the bed and started scheming. How exactly did a woman punish a man who found her physically arousing?

How did she repay an insult so profound? Collapsing

on his bed, she bent her mind on revenge. Somehow, she had to balance out the score.

Several hours later, she was ready for him, sitting in an armchair when he came through the door.

"Oh, hi," he said as if surprised to find her there.

"Hi." Emily shifted in the chair, dangling her bare legs over the arm. She'd chosen her outfit with extra care, pairing a very short black skirt with a short stretchy knit top. Leaving off her bra had taken courage, but she'd done it, remembering he seemed to like her unfettered breasts.

She wanted him to like everything he saw . . . and couldn't have.

Thank goodness he couldn't tell that the newspaper in her hand was sweaty from her palm. This femme fatale stuff took some getting used to.

Emily randomly penciled an X next to an ad for a job. To her intense satisfaction, Jake stood by the kitchen bar, staring at her in apparent helplessness. She felt his gaze sweep over her, bare feet to clingy top.

Beneath his hungry look, her nipples began to harden. It took all her willpower to pretend to ignore the changes his presence triggered in her. Determined to make him suffer at least as much as he had her, she threw her head back and smiled up at him.

Emily McKinnon Loughlin was discovering resources she'd never known she possessed.

Jake sat at his desk shuffling papers, trying not to think about the mess he'd made of things with Emily. He'd left the apartment early this morning, unable to face her after tossing and turning on the couch all night.

The memory of making love to her ate at him, but not as much as the gulf between them now.

She was upset with him for tricking her into going back to Middleton. That much he'd figured out, and he had to admit he deserved it.

He never should have given in to his hunger for her.

Making love had only complicated her confusion, he was sure. It sure as hell had complicated things for him. Like an idiot, he'd made things worse for her instead of better.

Not to mention the turmoil he'd allowed her to stir up in him. Who'd have thought that after all these years of clean living, he'd find a woman who so painfully made him regret his past?

A light tap at the door drew his glance.

To his surprise, Emily stood in his office doorway, her face hesitant, the fluorescent light shining on her short dark hair.

"Hi," she said, stuffing her hands in the pockets of her slim jeans, the movement pulling her knit top snug across her breasts. "I just stopped by to tell you something, but it can wait if you're busy."

"No, of course not." He stood up, gesturing for her to come in. She'd been in his office before, he reminded himself, acutely conscious of the clutter on his desk and the dust an inch thick on the stack of promotional fliers that occupied one of the two chairs on the opposite side of the desk.

She perched on the edge of the unoccupied chair, obviously as ill at ease as himself.

"Hey!" Jake looked at his watch, assuming as casual an air as possible. "It's almost two o'clock. Want to grab some lunch?"

Emily shook her head. "I've eaten. I had a lunch interview for a job."

"A job?" He didn't understand the streak of foreboding that ran down his spine as he slowly sank back into his desk chair. No matter what she thought, Emily really needed to return to Middleton, so her getting a job in Dallas wasn't the greatest plan. But on the other hand, finding employment was the least dangerous thing she'd done since leaving home.

At least, that would get her out of his apartment.

Not that he really wanted her out of his apartment.

Across the desk from him, she assumed a bright smile as she leaned back into the chair. "I'm thrilled about this because it's totally different from anything I've ever done."

"Really?" For the life of him, he couldn't infuse any enthusiasm into that one word. "Waitressing? Cashier at a discount store?"

"No, I'm modeling for Terrence Carr," she said in a rush, excitement sparking in her hazel eyes.

Jake stared at her. Modeling? The word conjured up a jumble of images, none of them good. Pushing aside his own, very personal concern about her displaying herself to another man, Jake shifted into his "concerned friend" mode.

"Terrence Carr? Is he some sort of photographer? Did you make sure he's legitimate? There are a lot of sleazebag guys out there claiming to need 'models.' "

Emily visibly stiffened, her gaze turning arctic. "Terrence Carr just happens to be one of the biggest up-and-coming artists in Texas. He's done one-man shows in New York and Los Angeles. He's not running some sort of massage parlor."

Trying to hide his skepticism, Jake asked, "So how did you find out about the job?"

"He ran an ad in the classifieds," she told him, her words rigid with hostility.

"Like the guys who run massage parlors," Jake murmured, not bothering to hide his smirk of satisfaction. He didn't care how big an artist this guy was, Emily didn't need to model for him. Or anyone.

Maybe modeling in the big leagues wasn't sleazy, but how often did a girl answer a classified ad and end up with a legitimate job? Didn't legitimate artists use agencies?

Jake had a sudden image of a doped-up lech chasing Emily around his studio.

"Texas Horizons did an entire story on Terrence Carr last month," she said hotly. "He's a very talented artist and I'm lucky to be able to work with someone so respected in the creative community."

Jake already hated the guy. "So what exactly will you be doing? What kind of art does this guy do? Cowboy Texas stuff?"

"No," she said with defiance, "he paints nudes."

"He what?" Jake vaulted out of his chair, glaring at her over the desk.

"He paints nudes," she repeated, straightening in her chair.

"Are you out of your mind? You can't do that," Jake said flatly, looming over her. "Why would you even want to take off your clothes and let some weird guy paint you?"

"To get out of my 'little Emily' box, that's why," she declared with passion, her cheeks flushed. "All my life I've done what I was supposed to, behaved myself, never taken chances. Do you know why?"

He just stared at her, completely aghast at what she was considering.

"Because I'm a coward," Emily declared, self-disgust dripping from every word. "Up until the last few weeks, I never wanted to upset people or shock them, but all my life I've longed to do things, go places, be someone different."

"This isn't the way to do it," Jake said more calmly, knowing he had to stay that way if he wanted to dissuade her. He looked at her, realizing again how her quest stemmed from years of bowing to others' opinions.

She needed to change her life—he saw that now. But posing nude for some leering jerk wasn't the answer.

"I know you think I've been taking unnecessary risks," she said. "You think I'm a naive, silly woman who can't be trusted off the farm. The fact that you tried to drag me back to Middleton proves that."

"That's not true. I'm just worried that you're rushing into things that are new to you. You may not see the pitfalls."

"Okay," she said, sitting back with a challenging glint in her eyes. "Tell me how anything terrible can happen if I pose for Terrence Carr. I've been naked before in public, just recently, if you remember our little vacation together."

"I remember," Jake muttered. "That was bad enough, but this is different. This guy isn't only going to paint your body, he's going to put your face on it, too. What if ten years from now, you want to run for governor of Texas? You'll be embarrassed as hell to have a nude portrait of yourself show up at auction."

"What you mean," Emily said bitterly, "is that I'll marry some guy who'll want to run for governor and *he'll* be embarrassed."

"No," protested Jake. For some reason, he couldn't picture the man she'd marry, didn't want to picture him.

"The truth is that, up until recently, I've never done anything," she said, her face filled with self-condemnation, "never really been anyone other than my parents' daughter. I need to create my own life."

"This isn't the way to do it!"

"What? There's a set of rules governing this?" she demanded. "Tell me, Jake, how can posing for Carr hurt me?"

He struggled in silence for several seconds, so frustrated he couldn't find the words to convey his concerns. No matter what he said, she couldn't seem to understand. Not that he totally understood his reaction himself. Jake just knew she couldn't do this.

Damn. The woman was driving him crazy!

"I'll tell you what," Jake said explosively, giving up on rational argument. "The guy's probably a pervert, and as soon as you're naked, he'll hit on you."

Their eyes locked, the tension between them heavy and thick with a tangle of emotion. Jake read the accusations in her gaze. *He'd* done more than hit on her. He'd taken her in heat and hunger, and he wanted to do it again and again. Right now, on top of his messy desk.

Hell, he'd wanted to drag her back to her childhood bedroom in her parents' house and lose himself in her soft, wet heat.

Just the thought made him hard for her, and he wondered if she could see his raging desire on his face.

Emily finally looked away. "Terrence isn't like that. I had lunch with him just now. He's very polite, very nice."

With nerves still jangling from feelings he didn't want

to examine, Jake snarled, "Nice guys want to get laid, too."

Her smile was cynical. She put her hands on the arms of the chair and got up. "Well, if that's true, I'll handle him. He can't be any cruder than my last boss, who assured me I'd like sex with someone richer and more powerful than my daddy."

"What?" Jake said incredulously.

"Never mind." She went to the door, determination in the tilt of her chin. "Carr wants me to start this afternoon. I might not be home till later."

Watching her go, Jake gritted his teeth, feeling both stunned and furious. She'd left her job in Middleton because a bastard had made a play for her . . . and here he'd been urging her to go back to her job!

My God. That damned lawyer had made a pass at her.

Obviously, she couldn't go back to her old job if that was the situation, but that didn't rule out going back to Middleton to work through her life crisis. It tore Jake up that he didn't know how to fix this for her. Emily needed to find her own path. He ought to be able to stand back, to let her fumble her way through the situation, but he couldn't.

What affected her, affected him.

The thought of her naked in some man's studio made Jake want to be violent, made him want to go after her. Tie her up if he had to. Take her back to Middleton where she belonged, where she would be safe . . . as long as she got a different job.

Jake wanted to take her back to his apartment where he could be indecent with her till they were both exhausted.

But he couldn't do that, either. Couldn't stop her, couldn't make love to her again no matter how much he ached to. She was confused and had to sort things out for herself.

He had to try and keep some distance from her, for both their sakes.

Jake sank into his chair, his insides feeling knotted. Nothing was simple. He couldn't make her go back to Middleton, but letting her find her own freedom was likely to kill him.

And one way or the other, he had no claim on her. How could Middleton's bad boy ever lay claim to Princess Emily?

Nine

Emily stood at Terrence Carr's door, her finger hovering above the doorbell. She was so angry with Jake, she could hardly see straight. No matter what she did or said, he persisted in seeing her as an inept, silly girl, unable to make reasonable decisions.

Well, he was wrong, she told herself, pushing the doorbell with vigor. She might be less experienced than some, but she was relatively intelligent and fully capable of creating a unique, rewarding life for herself, despite her own craven self-doubts.

Okay, the modeling thing hadn't exactly been her goal, but *Terrence Carr!* She'd be a fool to turn down such an opportunity. The man had access to the artistic communities in Dallas, Los Angeles, and New York. The contacts she'd make would be invaluable for her when she decided in what direction she wanted to take her future career.

The studio door opened just then, breaking into her reverie.

"Sorry to keep you waiting," Terrence Carr said, an attractive smile on his face.

"No problem," Emily assured him, stepping inside.

"I've just been getting the easel set up," he told her, leading the way into a large, uncluttered studio. "I was so pleased to have found you. I've been wanting to start on my new project, but none of my usual models seemed right."

"I'm glad you think I'll do," she said, pushing aside the clatter of nerves in her stomach. The fact that she'd only gotten naked with a very few men in her life couldn't be allowed to dissuade her from doing this.

Besides, Jake was wrong about Carr. He wasn't the least bit lecherous. In fact, despite his fabulous success, Terrence had none of the quirks usually associated with painters.

Although she'd had enough experience with creative people to know they didn't all wear berets and have limp wrists, she'd been surprised by Terrence herself. He actually looked more like a nice, young stockbroker than a famous artist.

With short blond hair and blue eyes behind wire-framed glasses, he was conservatively dressed in flannel gray pants and an oxford shirt. He'd have easily passed her proper mother's strict requirements for husband material. Added to that, he appeared to be in his early thirties, and had a pleasant face and a really attractive smile.

There was no reason for her to be nervous.

Emily stood awkwardly where he'd left her by the door. Jake was wrong about this situation. She'd had lunch with Terrence and he hadn't given a hint of any misplaced interest. She might be fresh from the country, but she wasn't a fool. She'd been looking for signs of lecherous interest and hadn't found any.

Modeling was all Terrence Carr wanted her to do.

Realizing she was trying to reassure herself and calm her jittery nerves, she deliberately walked around the big room, examining several works in progress. Terrence's studio was housed in a modernistic building with

huge windows and skylights flooding the room with
natural light. Cabinets ran across one wall, providing
storage and counter space, as well as a sink.

The place was amazingly neat. There was nothing
sleazy or cheap about it.

Drawing a deep breath to try and calm herself, Emily
continued skirting the edges of the studio, not looking
at the models' stand in the center of the room. She was
fine. There was nothing to be nervous about. She'd
walked down a public beach almost completely nude.
This would be a piece of cake.

But for some reason, her fluttery stomach didn't see
it that way. Nude modeling required one to be nude. In
front of a total stranger, without Jake beside her.

Not only would she be naked, but Carr would be im-
mortalizing her every curve, flaws and all.

Her stomach clenched tighter.

Emily refused to think about her mother's reaction. It
wasn't as if she would be in a porno film or even a
mainstream movie where hundreds of thousands of people would see her. This was a well-known artist.

Art. She was contributing to art.

How many people would ever see the portrait when
it was done, anyway?

She stopped, hearing her own spineless thoughts.
What she was doing was all right because no one would
know? How pitiful she was. Her choice was fine not
because she believed in it, but because no one would be
bothered. The realization of her old patterns creeping
back into her thought processes stiffened Emily's re-
solve.

"Oh, I'm sorry," Terrence said, looking up from the
canvas he was preparing. "The dressing room is right
through there. We'll start as soon as you're ready."

"Great," she said, her smile feeling stiff.

Going into the small dressing room, she slowly removed her clothes. To her relief, a robe hung on the back of the door. Slipping it on, she was conscious of how bizarre it seemed to be doing this. She was actually going to get naked in front of a total stranger. Even the robe felt foreign against her bare skin.

Disgusted at how self-conscious she felt, Emily timidly opened the dressing room door, ridiculously aware of her bare feet against the wooden floor.

Terrence stood at the easel, intent on the canvas before him.

Emily nervously cleared her throat.

Carr turned his head, smiling at her. "Great. Come on over here and we'll get started."

Conscious of the cold floor, the velvety robe brushing against her skin, she crossed the studio slowly, feeling as if an anchor held her back.

"Here," he said, pointing to the frame she was to lean against. "Let's find the best pose."

Brushing past him, Emily stepped up on the frame, feeling awkward as she leaned back, her hips braced against metal cool even through the robe.

"Oh, yes," he said, studying her face with an abstracted expression. "This is great. Your skin takes the light wonderfully."

"Thanks," she murmured, her throat feeling tight.

Terrence shifted her arm position, moving her as if she were a mannequin. In a flash, Emily remembered the last time she'd been this close to a man, wearing nothing but a robe over her naked body.

Jake.

Jake's kisses, Jake's lovemaking.

She swallowed against the tightness in her throat and

made herself focus on the attractive man in front of her.
Terrence *was* attractive. His cologne smelled expensive
and she tried to find some response in herself to his
nearness.

Dispassionately, she even acknowledged that he had
a confidence that most women would find extremely attractive. This was obviously his arena and he knew what
he was doing.

He hadn't yet told her to take off the robe, which was
fine by her.

Stepping back, Terrence scanned her position. "I'm
trying something a little different with this work."

He paused, his gaze studying structure and light.
Softly, he said, "I've mostly worked with blonde before,
but this creature I'm seeing now has a darker side. She's
lovely, perhaps too lovely for her own good. She's known
evil, seduction, and betrayal, and yet, at heart, still has
a naive sweetness."

Emily quelled a hysterical urge to laugh. Even here,
taking a huge chance, this complete stranger had assigned her a role of "sweetness." Maybe there was nothing she could do to change that part of herself.

Coming forward, Terrence shifted her arm position,
his hand lingering. Feeling the warmth of his touch
through the robe, she struggled against the urge to shudder.

It was bizarre. This was an attractive man, not Jim
Morris, her former boss. Terrence was even unattached,
according to that article she'd just read about him.

Still, the jitters in her stomach were spreading. She
could feel fine tremors in her arms, even her fingers.

"I know this is your first time," Terrence said, his
words low and smooth. "It's natural to be a little nerv-

ous, but you don't need to worry. You're very beautiful. You'll make this my most successful work."

Emily looked at him and for the first time saw both interest and attraction in his eyes. It was as if putting her in the context of his creation brought some change between them.

His smile held a warmth that made her uneasy. But it shouldn't have. She had no sense of threat or of danger, only of *wrongness*.

It seemed wrong to be here like this, wrong to stand quaking in front of him with nothing on but a light robe. *She felt completely comfortable wearing less with Jake.*

"You know," he said, a musing tone in his voice as he studied her face, "I usually make it a policy to keep my relationships with my models strictly professional. I hope you won't be insulted that I'm thinking of bending that rule with you."

"Uh . . ." She couldn't think of anything besides the intense wish that he wouldn't stand so close.

His gaze dropped to her bare throat, a distinctly unprofessional gleam in his eyes.

To her shock, Emily realized he raised no spark in her.

Why not? Why was she suddenly upset, even revolted, by the thought of having sex with him?

The strength of her own reaction baffled her. There was nothing repulsive about the man. In fact, he was the kind of guy she'd always hoped she'd find. Intelligent, artistic, polite, and very, very attractive.

Terrence smiled at her, turning to go back to the easel. "Just let me sketch some things in and then we'll take off the robe."

Why couldn't she imagine herself even kissing the guy, she asked herself in dismay.

It couldn't be that the turmoil in her life had dried up her hormones because she wanted to jump on Jake every time she saw him.

Jake.

Emily stood, feeling as if she'd turned to stone. She felt . . . something for Jake. More than interest or lust. More than she felt with anyone else.

The enormity of her realization hit her like a ton of bricks. She was hooked on Jake Wolf. Despite the fact that he'd rejected her, apologized for making love to her, lied to her to get her back to Middleton and always made it very clear that no romantic relationship could grow between them, she loved Jake.

"Oh, God," she said, straightening.

Terrence looked up from his work. "Is there a problem?"

"Yes." Emily climbed down from the model's stand, heading for the dressing room.

"Where are you going?"

"I can't do this," she said hurriedly. "I'm sorry. I just can't."

"But Emily," he called after her.

She shut the dressing room door and leaned her head against it, still staggered by the realization that she'd let Jake Wolf get under her skin so thoroughly.

Whether or not to pose in the nude was the least of her problems. She didn't want to do it, she acknowledged, quickly climbing into her clothes. Not because she was afraid or because someone would be shocked. She just didn't want to get naked and be painted in glorious living color.

"Emily," Terrence called through the door. "You don't need to be nervous."

"I'm sorry," she said, pulling her shirt over her head. "I just don't want to do it."

"Was it what I said about wanting to date you?"

"No," she assured him. "You're a very nice man."

"Then what's the problem?" he asked, his expression perplexed when she opened the door.

"I'm really sorry," Emily said, handing him the robe. "I just realized I don't want to pose. I know I've wasted your time and I feel bad about it."

"If you didn't want to pose, why did you answer my ad?" he asked with understandable annoyance.

She smiled at him ruefully. "Because I'm in the middle of a life crisis and I'm stumbling along trying to find out where I want to be. But this isn't it."

Crossing the room, she opened the door and looked back at where he stood, a surprised, chagrined expression still on his face.

"Sorry," she said with a rueful grimace, before slipping out the door.

Hurrying to her car, Emily got in and stared over the steering wheel, unseeing.

She couldn't be in love with Jake. Not really.

He wanted her body, obviously enjoyed having sex with her that night, but he'd never once responded to her as a woman, a person to have a relationship with.

Except that time in the shop when he didn't recognize you, a voice whispered in her head.

Emily started the car, automatically arguing against what she knew couldn't be true. The time in the shop had been about sex, too. Although he hadn't admitted it.

Still, the voice said, *what about the picnic by the old house?*

He'd talked about himself that day, listened to her hopes and dreams, but what did that mean?

And he'd held her, comforted her, when she'd felt so bad about losing it after she'd bungee-jumped. Yes, what happened between them afterward had been sexual, but at first, he'd held her and reassured her that she was brave.

Getting onto the freeway, Emily found herself racing back to Jake's apartment, her head so muddled with emotion and wishful thinking, she could hardly see straight.

No one but Jake had ever made her feel so much. Passion, hunger, rage. That night in his arms, she'd lost herself in him, drowned in his touch.

How could she have let this happen? Let herself care about him. She'd always found him attractive, had woken up that morning after sleeping with him and hoped, planned, to have a relationship with him. But this, this emotion now felt too strong, too overwhelming.

With the tumble of feelings inside her, all she wanted was to throw herself into his arms, to kiss him, to make love to him.

She realized she was driving into the apartment parking lot feeling dazed and lost. Wanting him was one thing, but seeking him out was impossible. He wouldn't be home now. He'd be at the shop still.

If she could just get her head straight, she'd be all right, able to see him without winding herself around him and pressing heated kisses against his flesh. He wouldn't like her touching him again, not when he felt so guilty about the last time.

She had to put him out of her mind.

Getting out of the car, she ran up the walk as if she could escape her own thoughts.

Jake thought she was a nuisance. A silly kid who needed to run home to Middleton and stay there. He didn't want her in his life, but suddenly all she could think of was staying with him forever.

Fitting her key in the lock with trembling hands, she turned it. She'd get over this. The day had just been too intense.

Jake was attracted to her physically, but couldn't bring himself to see her as a woman separate from their shared past. He refused to let her out of his fantasized image of the perfect family, the idyllic small-town girl. Clearly, he didn't see himself in that picture at all.

Somehow, she would push her longing back into the corner where it belonged. Falling in love with a man who wouldn't let himself touch her was a bad idea.

Jake sat in the armchair staring at the door to his bedroom, the room where Emily slept. He'd come home almost immediately after she'd left the shop. Unable to work, to think of anything besides her, he'd been sitting there staring into space for nearly an hour, wrestling with himself.

How could he have let her leave like that? The whole thing was intolerable. Her, sitting naked in front of some guy who'd no doubt do his best to seduce her.

Her beautiful body, full breasts and flaring hips, on display for some pervert to lust after.

It had nothing to do with David anymore, and very little to do with her place in Middleton society. All that still existed, but right now, Jake couldn't sit there knowing she was exposing her lovely body to someone else. A man other than him.

He had no right to feel possessive. In fact, it was stupid of him to do so.

There could be no future for them together. He knew that. Any doubts had been extinguished by their trip back to Middleton. Back to his rebellious, no-rules past.

Emily belonged there in Middleton with her stable family and inherited value system. He'd never fit in there, never had much of a family, and what he had hadn't imparted any values worth keeping.

Despite all the urges she roused in him, despite her stirring up more excitement than he'd felt in the last five years, there was no way in hell Jake could see a future for them.

Her continued struggle against Middleton convinced him over and over how emotionally tied she still was there. She wouldn't have to fight so hard against her hometown and her image there if it didn't mean so much to her. People moved away from hometowns all the time. Emily had dragged hers with her.

And as long as she was still caught in her past, how could he trust her to respond to him as anything more than the bad kid he'd been back then?

She wanted to do risky things, wanted to break out of her old life, and his old reputation drew her to him. Having an affair with a bad boy sounded tempting in her current state of mind.

In Middleton, Jake would always be that Wolf boy, rebellion springing from bad blood. People would always talk about his white trash roots, whisper about his daddy's weakness for whiskey. There could be no even match between them.

But that didn't mean he had to let her make this big

a mistake. They might not ever be more than acquaintances again, but he'd be damned if he let some artist try to find just the right shade of rosy brown to match the areola of her breast.

Feeling his fists tighten, Jake racked his brain. The guy's name had been Terrence something. Surely he had a phone in his studio. Somehow Jake had to find her.

Crossing the room, the telephone book his objective, Jake stopped, hearing keys in the front door.

He turned toward the entry, watching the door knob turn.

Emily pushed open the door, freezing at the sight of him. Her eyes wide with emotion, he saw her swallow hard.

Jake didn't move, didn't say anything, so filled with relief that he didn't trust himself to speak. She was here. She hadn't gone through with it, hadn't stripped naked in front of another man.

Drawing a deep breath, she stepped inside and shoved the door shut behind her.

Jake saw the faint pulse beating in her slender neck, felt the room thicken with what he saw in her wide eyes.

In that instant, he knew he had to make love to her. Damn the consequences.

"You didn't pose," he finally said, his voice low.

She shook her head, her gaze never leaving his.

Without thinking, he moved toward her, his own heart thumping hard in his chest.

She's here. She didn't go through with it.

Maybe he was stupid, risking this much hurt, but he couldn't bear it, not touching her. The longing in her eyes was so exactly like his own.

Reaching her side, he took her by the arm. She looked

up at him, eyes wide, pupils dilated. He saw desire there, hot and heedless.

Longing.

"You don't want to be 'little Emily' anymore?" he challenged suddenly. "Then I'm the man to give you the wildest ride of your life."

Jerking her against his chest, Jake kissed her, savoring the crush of her mouth beneath his own, the sweet warmth of her breath mingled with his. Instantly, her arms were around his neck, holding him tight against her.

Jake felt her catch fire in his arms. Her breasts snug against his chest, her mouth hot beneath his, Emily left no doubt as to what she wanted of him. Fool that he was, he didn't give a damn.

He'd be her big-city fling, give her the hottest, hardest sex she'd ever have in her life. And if, when she went back home, he had a gaping hole in his chest, it might just have been worth it.

Pressing her back against the wall, Jake pillaged her mouth, his hands kneading her breasts through her knit top. She squirmed against him, rocking her pelvis against his. He felt her hands at his waist, struggling with his belt buckle.

This was the Emily he'd come to know, impetuous, lost in the moment, fiercely determined. Sexy enough to make a man lose his mind for wanting her.

Sweeter to the taste than anything else on earth.

Lifting her shirt he bent, his mouth skimming her swelling breast above the line of her bra. He felt the snap of his jeans give way beneath her questing hand, felt the brush of her fingers against him through his shorts.

Fighting the urge to take her up against the wall, Jake

scooped Emily into his arms and crossed the small living area in three strides. He wanted her under him. Slamming back the bedroom door, he dropped her on his bed with a feeling of primal satisfaction.

She was his, no matter what the peripheral complications. At this moment, she was his.

Nothing else mattered. Not his bad boy past or her confused future. Just now, the two of them.

With her knit shirt rucked up on one side, the smooth naked expanse of midriff exposed, she seemed completely unself-conscious. Her eyes were dark with hunger as she watched him pull off his shirt and shed his jeans. By the time he'd found a condom and sheathed himself, she'd shimmied out of her clothes, tossing aside her bra and panties without any apparent pause.

She lay back on the bed, a feast for his eyes.

Sweetly curved and beautifully naked, she waited for him, her breath rapid, her nipples peaked. This was heaven. Jake knelt before her, spreading her legs with eager hands. She was so beautiful, so moist and eager. He bent to her, so caught up in the drumming in his head that the moment seemed unreal. Hands stroking her breasts, he surged forward. Emily was a carnal apparition, a man's fantasy come to life.

No words between them. No way to make everything right. Only this, the slide of his flesh into hers. If he couldn't make it right, at least they could be here together, locked together in an exquisite meshing that sent pleasure screaming through him. Nothing felt righter than this.

He surged against her, reveling in the eager clutching of her hands on his shoulders, the moans escaping from her sweet mouth as her legs locked around him. Slamming into her, he lost himself in her over and over as she fell apart in his arms.

She cried out once, her head thrown back. Jake pushed ahead, hearing the catch in her breathing, her thrusts meeting his.

Maybe he couldn't keep her with him, but he'd hold her now, love her now.

He felt the clench of her muscles again. This time the shudders shook them both and he knew a man's satisfaction as he collapsed against her, careful not to crush her with his weight.

Her breath was warm against his shoulder, soft sighs that matched the heavy thud of her heart beneath him. Jake felt a clog of emotion in his throat, a sudden, swift longing that pierced him.

If only she could find herself, find a way to deal with who she was and who she wanted to be.

Then, maybe, they could make it. Maybe it wouldn't matter that he was Middleton's bad boy and she its princess. If only he could hold her like this for a lifetime.

A woman like Emily deserved nothing less.

Emily cried out, locking her legs around him as Jake drove into her most sensitive flesh. He'd made love to her twice in the night and woken her just now with his mouth at her breast, his clever fingers teasing her folds.

Jake slipped his hands under her bottom, lifting her to fit against him as he knelt before her, each thrust a ripple of heaven.

Teetering on the brink, she chanted, "Yes, oh, yes."

Shattering into a thousand pieces, she heard Jake's hoarse cry, felt him stiffen in her arms.

Heart still pounding in her ears, she cradled him to

her, reveling in the completeness of the moment. He was hers, had given himself to her in so many ways. No words could convey her joy. He'd mastered his overdeveloped conscience, had come to terms with her as a person separate from her family.

She knew it because he wouldn't have made love to her again if he hadn't.

He moved off of her, turning to lie beside her, his hand gentle against her hair. Feeling she was floating in the euphoria of the moment, Emily snuggled into him, inhaling the warm, musky scent of his skin.

Maybe it was foolish, but never had she felt more contented, more sure of the future. They hadn't talked about anything. She knew there were still things to work out, her career, her ties with the past, but the connection with Jake, that was the beginning of her tomorrow.

Lost in the pleasure of being wrapped in his arms, she didn't immediately notice the pounding sound coming from the living room.

Jake stiffened, his face suddenly alert as a man's muffled voice called out at the front door.

Emily heard the voice and froze. "It sounds like David!"

Ten

"Jake! Emily!" David called again.

Jake pulled away, straightening in the bed. Even in this situation, she couldn't hold back a murmur of protest. He climbed quickly off the bed and grabbed at the jeans he'd discarded the night before, his face tense.

"Get dressed," he hissed, yanking a T-shirt out of a nearby drawer. "I'll tell him you're just waking up."

"Why don't we just tell him the truth?" she asked, feeling disoriented at the sudden change in him.

Jake flashed her a look filled with frustration and urgency. "Not a good idea. Get dressed."

She watched him thrust his arms into the shirt and fasten his jeans before pulling the bedroom door shut behind him.

Still lying on the tousled bed, Emily stared at the closed door, a jarring sense of bewilderment holding her paralyzed. One minute, she'd been in the throes of afterglow, her lover locked in her arms. The next minute, Jake, her brother's best friend, had jumped away from her and scurried out of the room.

A sinking sensation hovered in her midsection as she got up, searching for clean underwear. The shock of being jolted out of the moment mingled with embarrassment, making her hurry to get dressed.

She'd never been caught *en flagrant delicto* before. Of course, she'd never had much experience before Jake and certainly none remotely resembling the intimacy they'd shared together.

"She's just now waking up?" David's voice floated through the closed door, his question incredulous. "Emily never sleeps in. I saw your motorcycle and her car parked outside, so I knew you were both here."

Jake's deeper voice could be heard responding, but his words were too muffled to make out.

Emily thought about the way he'd shot out of bed, obviously eager to hide their activity even though they were both adults, completely free to establish an intimate relationship. While she could understand some of Jake's agitation at being so inopportunely interrupted, a part of her wondered what he'd have done if he'd been making love to some other woman when David knocked at the door.

She fought back a wave of dismay and then immediately felt guilty. Trusting the man she was in love with only made sense.

He'd come so far in accepting her as her own woman. His tenderness, his complete sensuality with her last night, told her that. Seeing David at this moment was probably a shock, but it was better to face him as a couple now. They'd have to break the news to him sometime that they were an item. Better now when they didn't have her parents to contend with.

She grabbed a comb off the dresser and smoothed her tangled hair.

"Emily!" David called, knocking on the bedroom door. "Come out of there."

Putting down the comb, she went to open the door, not relishing facing the older brother who'd always thought he knew best. It didn't matter that she hadn't given him many opportunities to rescue her from trouble. He'd always played the role of junior parent to her hapless child.

She loved him, though. That was the irony. She loved her folks, too, but she couldn't seem to be herself with any of them.

"Hello, David," she said, brushing past him to go into the living area.

Jake stood by the front window, hands shoved into his back pockets, an unreadable expression on his face.

"That's all you have to say?" her brother asked, following her into the room. "Hello? You get some crazy idea about leaving town and you just go, regardless of anything Mom and Dad or I have to say. Don't you think we're worried about you? Particularly after you show up the other day for lunch and then just leave again?"

In his Brooks Brothers sport coat and perfectly pressed slacks, he looked the same as always, except for the frown on his pleasant face. David was a genial guy, happy-go-lucky until something went wrong in his world.

"I'd been gone less than two weeks," she reminded him, her voice cool, "and you could see when I was there the other day that I'm fine."

Not moving from his position, Jake said nothing.

"Maybe so, but Mother has been worried sick," David said in obvious reproach.

"I don't know why," Emily said, rubbing at a spot between her eyebrows. Being "caught" in wrongdoing had always given her a tension headache.

Why was Jake standing so stiffly? She wished he'd come take her hand, offer some sign of his support.

"You don't know why your parents and your brother

are worried about you?" David said, incredulously. "You quit a good job for no reason, sell all your furniture, and leave town without any explanation, and you don't know why we're worried?"

"I did explain," she said with as much patience as she could muster, her uneasiness increasing as Jake's expression remained the same. "I told you all that I needed to make some changes. I wasn't happy. I've told you that several times."

David threw up his hands. *"Making some changes* can be accomplished by getting a new haircut. You packed up and left town!"

"I did get my hair cut," she shot back with sarcasm. "But the rest of my life needed work, too."

Still Jake stood, saying nothing, his hands in his pockets. Extremely conscious of his apparent removal from the scene, Emily pushed on, trying to make her brother understand.

"David, I'll tell you again. I hated my job for years. You know that because I told you several times."

"Yes," he acknowledged, grudgingly, "but there were other jobs you could have gotten in Middleton. Instead, you ran off."

"And what would have happened if I'd changed jobs," Emily asked with a tired sigh. "If I tried to start an interior design business in town?"

Her brother looked at her.

"Mother and Dad would have had hushed discussions about my poor judgment and why I can't find a good man to marry. Then, Mrs. Knight would have told Elder Brisby that she always thought I was flighty. The ladies' league would have questioned Mother *why* I can't find a man to marry. I'd have gotten phone calls from six different friends of Dad's about how important it is for his reelection that we kids look stable and reliable."

Her brother shrugged. "Middleton is a small town."

"No." She shook her head. "It's more than that. And it's not just the busybodies. Dad would have taken me to lunch and given me a lecture on the evils of dissatisfaction. Mother would have dropped hints about me dating that new salesman at the car dealership, by now desperate to see me marry anyone with a decent status, and then she would have spoken to me about not worrying Dad."

"So people would have talked to you. What's the big deal about that?" David asked impatiently.

Emily flushed, feeling stupid and wimpy. Feeling alone. "I've always done what I'm supposed to do, David. I hate seeing Mother's stiff upper lip and Dad's disappointment in me."

"Well, they don't ask much of you. All you have to do is be polite and dress properly," her brother retorted. "I've had the worst of it. Do you know how hard it is to be the mayor's son? You have to do everything well because people are watching, and then when you do achieve something, everyone thinks it's because of your dad."

"I know," she said, reaching out to him. "That's why I left."

David stared at her a moment, genuine concern in his face. "You have to come back, Em. Not just for Mom and Dad. You've never lived anywhere but Middleton except when you were at that tiny college. You're not equipped to be totally on your own."

"I'm doing fine," she retorted, fiercely conscious of her lover's aloofness across the room. Why didn't he tell David she was okay? She didn't need his support, she could stand on her own two feet, but his silence cut into her like a knife.

"Sure," David said, nodding toward Jake. "You've got someone watching over you. But Jake's got a life. You can't expect him to take on the responsibility of keeping an eye on you."

"Is that what he's been doing?" she asked coldly, throwing Jake a challenging stare.

He met her gaze with troubled eyes, his silence speaking volumes.

Nothing had changed, she realized after a stunned second. Despite the fact that he'd touched her like a lover, crooned to her about how beautiful she was, how wonderful and free, he'd only meant in bed.

Only when his lust had overruled his conscience.

She'd misjudged him, had thought him a better man than he was. How incredibly stupid of her.

Jake had had sex with her last night because he liked having sex with her, not because he'd finally come to accept her right to direct her own life.

Her right to choose with whom she fell in love.

What an idiot she'd been!

Like David, Jake thought she needed a keeper, thought she was incapable of life outside Middleton's sheltered enclave. No matter how hot the fire burned between them, she was still little Emily, the mayor's daughter.

He'd given in to the chemistry between them, nothing more.

Pain, hot and gut-wrenching, pierced her. She'd thought they'd shared incredible intimacy, but it was only another physical interlude. He still thought she was a naive girl better off at home. Better off with her family and the whole damn town to keep her safe from men like Jake Wolf.

"Tell her, Jake," David insisted, turning toward his friend. "She can't just run away from her responsibilities. Mother and Dad have some right to her respect and consideration. She has to come home and stay home."

Emily waited, steeling herself for what she knew was to come. She knew now how things stood between them, but the words would still hurt when she heard them from his lips.

He slipped his hands out of his pockets, the brooding frown still on his face. "Emily doesn't have to go home."

A foolish shiver of hope streaked through her, but she tried not to let it show on her face. He'd fooled her before.

"What?" David sputtered. "You told me yourself that she didn't know the time of day."

"He told you that?" When had the two of them discussed her?

Jake put up his hand to stop his friend's fragmented expostulations. "I know what I said when I called you after that first night. What I mean now is that Emily should live her own life. Make her own mistakes. I think she's better off in Middleton, but she doesn't and she gets to decide."

Emily stared at him, her battered heart distrustful. If he was trying to express a belief in her capability, he was doing a lousy job.

Her brother's protests were indistinct in her ears. She could only meet Jake's gaze, seeing emotion she couldn't read, feeling a wash of incredible loss.

"I think she should go back," Jake continued, still meeting her gaze, his own troubled. "Not to the same job, but back to Middleton and face what she's running away from. Family means a lot, and freedom doesn't mean throwing everything away."

That was it. Despite all she'd said about needing and wanting to leave Middleton, he still saw her as a child who was running away from home. David's sister. The mayor's daughter. A woman he'd wanted to sleep with. She meant nothing more personal to him.

Jake wanted her to go back to all the things he'd never had as a kid.

"I've got an appointment in Middleton at two o'clock," David told her, glancing at his watch. "If we're going to make it back by then, we'll have to leave now."

"You're planning on *escorting* me back?" she asked dryly, her heart breaking in two. Here was the brother she loved standing across the room from the man she'd given everything to, both of them believing her too foolish to know her own mind.

She wanted to scream, wanted to dissolve into tears.

"Well," David huffed, "I thought I'd follow you home in case you ran into car trouble."

Emily walked to the door, pulling it open for him. "I wouldn't want you to miss your appointment, David. When I come back to visit Middleton again, I'll find my own way."

Her brother looked at her, disbelief leaving his chin dropped. "Emily, you *must* come home—"

"Good-bye," she said, unyielding.

"Well," he said again, outrage in every line of his body. "Fine, that's just fine. I'm going. And I'll tell Mother and Dad that you're no longer the sister I thought I knew."

"I'm glad you've finally realized it," she said in a hard voice, sick that matters had come to this. Why was it so difficult for them to accept that she needed a life of her own?

David went to the door, glancing back to where Jake stood. "I'm relying on you to bring her to her senses."

Jake said nothing.

Closing the door behind her brother, Emily turned.

"You don't have to go home for David," Jake said, finally breaking his silence. "But what about your parents? I know you don't want them to worry about you."

"I can't do anything about that," Emily said, her voice low. "They worry because they think I can't take care of myself. If I'm in Middleton, they think they're watching over me, making sure I don't get hurt. The only way they'll be convinced I'm capable is if I stand on my own two feet."

She paused, a lump of despair in her throat. "But I don't really want to talk to you about my parents."

Jake looked puzzled.

"I want to tell you that you're the lowest scumbag I've ever run across," she said as cordially as she could manage. "If you were trying to teach me how dirty men can be in the big city, then you accomplished it."

"Wait a minute, Emily." He raised a hand to halt the flow of her words. "I've said a hundred times that you needed to go back and face things in Middleton. That's why I took you back."

"Yes," she said, strolling over to where he stood. "You also said I was so confused that you regretted sleeping with me in the Islands. But that didn't stop you from doing it again last night."

The shift in his expression would have been ludicrous if she'd had the heart to laugh about anything.

"What happened to your good intentions?" Scorn vibrated in her words. "You certainly didn't rethink your opinion about me. What a fool I was to think that's what last night meant."

Jake looked down wordlessly. His obvious chagrin fanned the fires of her anger.

"All your talk about protecting me! Why didn't you tell David who I needed protection from the most?"

He met her glare, his expression grim.

"No," she spat. "You stood there while he lectured me like a grandparent, stood there and agreed with him like you were my priest."

"Emily . . ."

"You used me, Jake," Emily said, her voice shaking. "Used me for a couple of nights of damn good sex—"

"No," he interrupted, "I never meant to . . ."

"Maybe you're right about one thing," she said when he fell silent. "I have been naive about men. There's only one reason I let you touch me. Because I thought it meant something to both of us—"

"Emily, don't," Jake said, shaking his head.

"—but I was just another roll in the hay to you. You're wild Jake Wolf. Men like you can't have serious relationships."

"Hold it just a second," he said bitterly, his head rearing up. "What do you know about 'men like me'?"

She took an involuntary step back. "I know a lot more now than I did before."

"You know nothing," he declared, his eyes boring into her. "You're too damn caught up in rebelling to see anyone else's point of view."

"I've spent my life worrying about other people!" Emily yelled. "For the first time, I have enough courage to listen to what I want. But you've taught me a lesson. Never trust a guy with notches on his bedpost. If he talks like a snake and crawls like a snake, he's a snake!"

"What the hell are you talking about?" he yelled back. "I never used you."

"No," she said with bitter sarcasm. "You wanted to have sex with me because we're so *compatible*. We have such a future together."

Jake wished with all his heart that the chance he'd thought he could see for them wasn't dwindling away. He'd hoped she was strong enough to go back to their hometown and be herself. Maybe she wouldn't eventually choose to stay there, but somehow she had to see that rebelling against the people who loved you wasn't the way to personal growth.

But he couldn't answer her now. He'd stood silent while David tried to take her back, hoping she'd be able to make her peace with her family, with herself.

Maybe then there would have been a chance for the two of them. But he doubted it.

"From the time you were in middle school, you've gone after anything in a skirt," she accused him when he remained silent. "What made me think you'd changed?"

He watched her stalk out of the room, feeling as if she'd driven a stake into his chest. She hated him, thought him as low as a man could be. Thought of him as a more heartless version of the kid he'd been ten years ago in Middleton.

Things didn't change.

He shouldn't have made love to her again, shouldn't have given in to the desperate hunger she wrought in him. She'd seemed different when she came through the door last night, stronger, more sure of herself for having walked away from the modeling job.

Stupidly, he'd thought she'd turned a corner, seen that she could be herself without doing things she'd regret. Maybe she wasn't still sneaking off to dangerous bars, but she'd turned her back on her past and her family.

Jake knew the power the past had, knew the power of family because he'd never had much of one. Nothing could be right for Emily till she made peace with her past.

He raked a hand through his hair. Hell, he'd better be done with fooling himself. Blinded by his own needs, he'd seen what he wanted to see. She was still running away. Her accusations, the hatred in her eyes, told the story of her deep-seated contempt.

Stupidly, he'd wandered into the land minefield of her self-doubts. They were both still trapped in their history, on opposite ends of the street, opposite sides of town. She had to stop reacting as "Princess Emily," stop being her old self before she could move on.

What were the chances of that, he thought wearily. And even if she were to make the transition, what made him think her attraction to him would survive?

The whole thing was a mess, and for the life of him, he didn't see how to fix it. Didn't see a way to keep the woman who held his heart hostage.

Emily shut the bedroom door with a quiet snap. She slumped onto the unmade bed, her mind spilling over with replay after replay of the confrontation with her brother . . . and everything Jake had said. Every nuance of every facial expression.

She really loved him. The kind of love that didn't fade with time. The realization had hit her again somewhere in the middle of telling him off. She'd never been so angry with anyone before, never felt so betrayed. Never felt so desperately sick with longing.

It had to be true love.

But that didn't change anything.

She couldn't stay here any longer. Doing so could only make things more uncomfortable between them, and she couldn't be absolutely sure she'd reject him if he kissed her again.

Getting up, she walked decisively over to the closet. If she was going to move out, she had to get a job. Few decent landlords would rent an apartment to someone without any visible means of support.

With dogged determination, Emily studied the outfits she'd brought with her, mentally excluding the few frisky things she'd bought most recently. Finally pulling out a short, dark green dress, she hunted for shoes and hose. How long had it been since she'd dressed for work?

Going back to work for that sleaze bag in Middleton held zero appeal, but finding a job in the design field now might give her something to distract her from her battered heart.

When she went to take a shower a few minutes later, she saw that Jake was gone. Crying her way through a fifteen-minute shower, Emily forced back the tears and dressed.

She left the apartment and drove to one of the most upscale furniture stores in Dallas. They'd placed an ad in the classifieds for a designer just a week ago. Maybe the position would still be open.

Parking her small compact, she got out and walked into the store on trembling legs, clutching her portfolio. It was pitifully thin, she knew. As she threaded her way through the beautiful displays of furniture, she almost became more convinced that her parents, David, and Jake were right. She should just go home. At least, someone there would give her some kind of a job out of pity.

What was she thinking, presuming that her degree and

the meager designs from school would earn her any respect? This was the stupidest thing she'd done since leaving home. Asking someone to actually employ her in a creative capacity felt like a bigger risk than diving head-first off the bungee platform.

Anyone could fail at bungee jumping, but designing was her secret love. Failing at this would kill her dreams, and now that her heart was dead, she desperately needed her dreams.

"May I help you?" a sleek, young saleswoman asked before Emily could turn tail and run.

Ten minutes later, she left the showroom with a scribbled address on the back of a card, unable to believe her good fortune. This job had been filled, but the head designer had a friend who was looking for a very junior designer to do legwork.

Elated to have another lead, Emily stared down at the card. Even if she had to take part-time jobs to support herself, just the chance of working in the design field was thrilling.

Climbing into her car, she drove to the address on the card. The head designer's friend, Sally, was expecting her.

The traffic in North Dallas was appalling, but she pulled up in front of the posh office complex, so nervous she was almost sorry the drive hadn't taken longer. Forcibly rejecting her own wimpy thoughts, she got out of the car and walked up to the building. After all, she was just applying for a job of running errands. Surely, even she had enough talent for that.

Glancing at the building directory, however, Emily was shocked to discover that "Sally" was actually Sarah Blair, one of the most influential designers in the Southwest.

Her work was both elegant and functional, her reputation being that she created environments that fit the client rather than seeking to impose her own taste on each home.

Giving herself a pep talk, Emily allowed her feet to carry her relentlessly down the hall until she stood in front of the desk of a very superior-looking receptionist. She cleared her throat. "I'm interested in applying for the entry-level job. I'm supposed to talk to Sally."

After all, she thought, Sally might not be Sarah. Maybe she was a designer who worked under the big name.

"Sally?" the receptionist repeated, lifting her supercilious brows.

"Yes." Emily proffered the card.

"Wait just a moment," the woman said, holding the card by a corner as she left the room.

She reappeared a moment later. "Come this way."

They walked down a hall to an office in back that was cluttered with fabric swatches and wallpaper samples. The receptionist stopped at the door. "Here she is, Sally."

A slender gray-haired woman dressed in slacks and a simple gray sweater with a red scarf at her neck glanced up and gestured for Emily to come in, her attention returning to shuffling through the items on the desktop. "I know it's right here."

Determined to do her best to get the job, Emily walked forward with confidence, stopping in front of the desk.

"Well, it's just gone," Sally Blair announced. "Hand me your portfolio, please."

"Excuse me?"

"Your portfolio," the older woman repeated, a smile quirking her mouth.

Emily handed the portfolio over, repressing the urge to confess that the majority of the projects inside were from her school days.

"Sit down." The other woman flipped through the drawings, pausing at one or two. "Mmmm. These are decent. Basic and inexperienced, but you have a good eye. Most of this is traditional and safe, but here and there . . . you throw in something unique."

"Thank you," Emily managed. She'd long admired Sarah Blair's style, making even the slightest compliment from the woman very welcome.

Sally closed the portfolio, a speculative look in her blue eyes. "I don't know what kind of money you were looking for—"

"Anything," Emily inserted promptly.

The other woman laughed, handing the portfolio back. "I need an assistant. It's more of a run-and-fetch position. But this is a successful firm and I'm sure there would be future opportunities if you work hard and show promise."

"I don't mind running and fetching," Emily told her firmly. "I'd just love a chance to work for someone of your style and experience."

"Well," Sally laughed, "if I take you on, you'll be working all right."

An hour later, after filling out the paperwork, Emily left Sarah Blair's employed. Her head spinning at her unexpected good fortune, she knew a moment's urge to call Jake and tell him her wonderful news.

She wondered what he'd say about her doing "grunt" work. Driving back to the apartment, Emily was conscious of the bitter irony of the situation. Here she had the kind of job that hundreds of beginners would kill for.

She felt good about it, but the rest of her life seemed like a black hole.

Living an unfulfilled life all these years, she'd longed to meet a man she could love. Now she stood the chance of creating a decent career for herself, but she'd lost her heart to a man who wanted her body but couldn't be less interested in her soul.

Arriving at the still-empty apartment, she went to the bedroom and started packing.

Just as she zipped her suitcase shut, Emily heard the front door open. Not allowing herself to pause, she started loading her toiletries into her overnight case. No matter what Jake had to say about it, she was leaving today.

She felt his presence in the doorway a second later, but refused to look up.

"I know you're upset," he said after a moment, "but you don't have to leave."

"Yes, I do."

"At least stay till you have a job," he suggested, his tone painfully reasonable.

"I have a job," she said with pitiful satisfaction, looking up at him at last.

He frowned, clearly doubtful of her ability to have arranged a decent job so quickly. "Doing what?"

"Working as a designer," she said, so stupidly affected by his mere presence in the room that she wanted to cry. Instead, she returned to her packing. "They've hired me at Sarah Blair's Interiors."

"Well, good," Jake said after a pause.

Struggling to ignore the awkwardness, feeling as if

her heart was failing inside her, she put the last few things into her bag.

"Do you have a place to stay?" he asked after a minute.

"Yes."

She knew it was killing him not to ask where, but she didn't volunteer an address. Tonight she'd stay in a motel, somewhere less exciting than the place he'd rescued her from.

"I know you need to be on your own," he said, breaking the silence.

Emily looked up at him. "You don't know anything about what I need, but that's okay, because I finally do."

Hoisting her bags and her flagging fortitude, she swallowed, brushed past him, and left.

Eleven

Hurrying down the corridor of the Dallas Market Center, Emily juggled two bolts of drapery fabric, a sample book, and a desk lamp.

In the two weeks since she'd been hired by Sarah Blair, she'd spent hours searching through sample books and fabric swatches when she wasn't driving from one end of Dallas to the other. Sally hadn't been kidding when she'd said this was a run-and-fetch job.

Never had Emily worked harder. She'd collapsed in bed at the end of every day exhausted, and then lie there thinking of Jake. Wondering if she should have told him how she felt. Would it have made any difference if he'd known she'd fallen in love with him?

She imagined a hundred ways to convey the truth to him, but no scenario seemed right. He'd never said he cared for her. The whole situation looked hopeless. Falling in love with a man who saw her only as his best friend's little sister had to be one of the stupidest things she'd ever done.

Stepping cautiously onto the escalator leading to the sixth floor of the massive market center complex, she resolutely turned her thoughts away from Jake and her broken heart. No matter how much she loved him, she had to go on, had to build a life for herself since he wasn't offering to share his.

Besides, she told herself, gripping the lamp more tightly as she got off the escalator, hadn't she wanted this very job all of her adult life? True, she spent each night aching for Jake, struggling to find sleep without him haunting her dreams. But in the daylight hours, her new career offered wonderful distraction.

Coming to work for Sally had been like diving head-first into a whirlwind of creativity. When she wasn't picking up small objects for the many homes on Sally's slate, she spent her time arranging for furniture deliveries and nudging suppliers to meet their deadlines.

Once in a while, Sally even asked for her opinion on something.

Stopping now in front of a showroom with a gorgeous bed linen display in its front windows, Emily readjusted her armload and went inside.

"Excuse me," she said to the woman behind the desk at the back of the showroom, "I'm here to pick up a dust ruffle for Sarah Blair. It's a special order, I think."

"Of course," the woman said with a friendly smile. "I'm sure that came in. It's the one she wanted us to check to see if it matched the comforter on display, right?"

"I believe so," Emily said, resting the desk lamp on the showroom's counter.

"Let me check the supply room." The saleswoman disappeared through a doorway.

Leaning against the tall counter to rest her arms, Emily thought about how much her life had changed in a few short weeks. She'd gone from sorting through boring legal documents to wallowing in a thousand little design opportunities. Every day another lesson met her around the corner.

Never had she felt so fulfilled . . . and so empty, at the same time.

"Cassie?" Emily said, struggling to keep the lonely quaver out of her voice. "I hope I'm not calling too late."

"Emily!" her friend squealed. "No, of course it's not too late. Good heavens, it's not even eleven o'clock. You know I'm a night owl."

"Good." Emily leaned back against the lumpy motel-provided pillow, crossing her feet under her as she sat on the bed. She'd called her friend just wanting to hear a friendly voice, hoping to stave off sleep and her tumultuous dreams.

"How are you?" Cassie asked, her tone both serious and interested.

"I'm good," Emily said, pushing aside her ever-present thoughts of Jake. "I called to hear your voice and to tell you about my new job."

"You're working with some hot-shot Dallas designer," Cassie said triumphantly. "Your mother's been bragging about you all over town."

"Mother has?" Emily echoed in surprise.

"Yes," her friend confirmed. "Proud as a peacock."

"Wow," she breathed. "I'm amazed."

"Well, I'm not," Cassie said stoutly. "Not amazed that your mother's proud and not amazed that you've landed on your feet. Your friends always knew you were going far."

Emily giggled. "Liar. My friends thought I'd stay right there in town."

"So, you showed us a thing or two," Cassie said equably. "Hey, have you heard about Nancy Foster suing Jim Morris for sexual harassment?"

"What?" Emily straightened. "You're kidding."

"Nope," her friend denied. "She's got a lawyer and everything. Believe it or not, she claims he's been grabbing at her for years and she just got fed up."

"Nancy Foster," Emily breathed in disbelief. "Wow."

"Yeah," Cassie said, "big stuff for our little town."

"I'll have to call her and volunteer to testify for her," Emily murmured, half to herself.

"What!" Cassie screeched. "He pawed you, too?"

"Mmmm, not exactly. Just made lascivious, highly illegal suggestions and threats," Emily said. "Gee, who'd have believed Mrs. Foster would turn on him?"

"I don't know," Cassie said, apparently losing interest in the scandal. "Hey, do you love your new job?"

"Yes," Emily answered simply, not having to force enthusiasm into her words. "It's terrific. Everything I've ever wanted to do."

"And . . . Jake Wolf?" Cassie's voice sharpened. "What about him?"

Emily stared at a spot on the far side of the motel room, the pain sharp in her chest. "He's . . . done his duty. I don't suppose I'll be seeing Jake anymore."

Two days later, Emily scooped up a stack of wallpaper sample books and crossed the crowded office to put them back on the shelf.

Surely, the hurt would grow easier with time, she told herself, hunting for a pen on the untidy desk she'd been assigned. The work was a hundred times more interesting than anything she'd done before. In time, her heart would heal enough for her to care. Just lately, she had a hard time getting up in the morning.

Of course, she couldn't tell Cassie that. Couldn't tell anyone that falling in love meant slicing off a piece of herself.

Living at home all her life had been misery, but she'd never known real pain till Jake had trampled on her heart. The worst of it was the arguments she had with herself. Should she give him one more chance?

Footsteps in the hall made her look up from her desk just as Candace, the receptionist, stepped into the office.

"You've got a visitor," the other woman said, lifting her brows meaningfully as she beckoned to someone in the hall.

Emily rose to her feet, wondering what vendor would seek her out. Normally, she went to the showrooms, rather than the line reps coming here.

To her shock, Jake stepped through the door, a watchful expression in his blue eyes. "Hello, Emily."

"Hello," she said after a second's pause, striving to subdue the foolish joy that sprang up in her heart at the sight of him. Stepping out from behind her desk, she fixed what she hoped was a pleasant, welcoming smile on her face, barely conscious of Candace leaving the room.

She wanted to throw herself at him, to feel him wrap his strong arms around her again, but nothing in his cautious expression encouraged her to take such a drastic step. He looked as if he were skirting a potentially angry wasp.

Emily lifted her chin. If it killed her, she wouldn't let him know how hard breathing had become since that morning when she'd discovered how easily he could use a woman.

"How have you been doing?" he asked, his searching gaze and serious expression giving the question more than casual meaning.

He was back in his protective mode, obviously. Had David been after him to get her to change her mind? Was that what brought Jake here today?

Emily forced her smile to widen. "I'm doing well. Learning a lot."

"Good." He glanced around the jumbled office, his gaze skimming the stacks of sample books, bolts of drapery fabric, and a table heaped with various decorative items.

Emily made no apology for the condition of the room. It was none of his business and she knew better than to think he really cared what she was doing, even if her crazy heart was springing into jubilant cartwheels at the sight of him.

Despite her determination not to nurture her feelings for him, she couldn't help but hungrily note how his muscular build and dark good looks contrasted with the more feminine setting of lavish colors and soft contours that abounded in the office.

He was the kind of man that drew the eye no matter where he was.

How could she have been such a fool as to fall in love with him? Hadn't he himself warned her against some men's motives?

"So what brings you here?" she asked finally, not asking him to have a seat in the only clear chair.

Jake's eyes met hers and she saw his grim understanding of her hint. "I, uh, have some mail for you. I guess David had it forwarded."

Glancing down at the envelope she hadn't before noticed in his hand, Emily fought back tears. It was dumb to feel disappointed that he hadn't sought her out on his own. If he'd have cared for her at all, he'd have found her before this. She was miserably conscious that despite his insincere denial of having used her sexually, Jake had never once said he wanted her in his life.

"Thanks," she said, trying to keep the brittle note out of her voice as she reached to take the envelope from him.

"It looked important," Jake said, "and I didn't have your home address. I hope it's not a problem for me to stop by here."

"No, of course not." Emily turned back to the desk, searching for a letter opener. Slitting open the crisp envelope, she looked down at the letter more out of a desire to seem interested than from any real curiosity. Anything to avoid looking at him.

"Oh, my God!" She sank into the chair behind her desk, staring at the letter as the typewritten words began to make sense to her. "I can't believe it."

"What?" Jake's voice sounded distant to her stunned ears.

"This cannot be for real," she whispered.

"Is it bad news?" he asked from the other side of her desk.

Emily's laugh was breathless. "No! No, it's great news. I can't believe it."

"What?" he asked again.

"I've won the internship at the British Design Institute. They'd originally awarded it to someone else, but he had to turn it down because of other commitments. I'm the next choice," Emily said, excitement spilling into her voice as she reread the letter.

"The British Design Institute? Is that the internship thing in London you told me about?"

"Yes." She looked up at him, still feeling dazed. "I applied months ago and never thought I had a chance."

Still holding the letter numbly in her hand, she was only barely aware of him staring at her across the desk, apparently as shocked at her good fortune as she was herself.

"Good grief," she said, reading the final paragraph for the first time. "This says I have to be there next week!"

"What!" Jake snapped, his expression thunderous.

"I guess the letter has been sitting in Middleton awhile. It was written three weeks ago. Geez, it's a good thing I don't have much to pack," Emily said, half to herself.

"You certainly don't mean to run off to London, do you?"

Jake's contemptuous question snapped her back to the present. She met his hard gaze, startled by the condemnation radiating from his angry expression and stiff posture.

"Exactly how far away from home do you have to go before you can act like a grown-up?" he said, his face hard.

"Jake, this is a very prestigious internship," she heard herself explain. "I still can't believe I won it. Why wouldn't I go?"

"It looks like another excuse to run away," he said in a tight voice, as if he were trying to hold his disgust on a rein. As if she were a child who needed spanking for bad behavior.

Emily stared at him, his disapproval washing over her. For one crazy moment, she wavered, wanting to slip into her old pattern, wanting to plead with him, to beg him to understand.

She loved him.

But just in time, an indignant voice in her head reminded her that accepting the internship wasn't the same thing as getting into a bar fight or choosing to stay at a disreputable motel.

This wasn't something irresponsible.

With a piercing sense of grief, she told herself Jake would never see her as adult, capable of making independent and autonomous decisions. To him, she was still the good daughter, the obedient child he'd known back in Middleton. The girl who'd had everything he never had.

In a flash, she was deeply grateful that she hadn't given in to the urge to confess her love to him. He'd only have used it against her.

"Listen, Emily," Jake said, clearly trying for a more reasonable tone. "I know you think I've been hard on you—"

"You listen, Jake," she said, bolting out of her chair. "You're not my father, my brother, or my minister. And I am hereby declining any of your so-called help in changing my life."

"I'm just trying to keep you from making a huge mistake," he insisted. "You're throwing away things some of us never had, like a real family. Maybe your folks aren't perfect, but they love you."

"Yes," she said crisply, anger lending an edge to her words, "I believe they love me enough to eventually come to terms with my new life. Even if it's in London."

Jake shook his head. "You can't build a new life by skipping out on the old one. Somehow you've got to *come to terms* with who you are, where you came from."

"And I can only do that by *staying* where I came from?" she asked incredulously.

"I don't know," he admitted. "But it seems like a good place to start."

"I'll tell you what I think," Emily said deliberately. "I think you've had a fantasy about my family, my position in Middleton. Maybe that's even why you wanted to jump in bed with me. But you don't want anything more to do with me because it would tarnish your idealized picture, the big gulf between my perfect family and the world you grew up in. It's not my past you're struggling with as much as your own."

Jake's jaw clenched. "Look, I'm sorry that I've hurt you. I never meant to do that. If I had been . . . stronger—"

"Never mind," she said, sitting down and turning away in an attempt to dismiss him. His words cut through her. He regretted being involved with her personally, regretted the most piercingly powerful hours of her life.

She just needed him to go.

"No matter what we do," Jake persisted, "the past still comes between us. You spend all your energy running away from being Middleton's favorite daughter. You're stuck in that role and, so, I'm stuck being Middleton's bad boy. Maybe that's why you responded to me—"

"I'm tired of this conversation," she interrupted, the muscles in her throat feeling stiff and hot. "Would you please go?"

She'd loved him a long time, she realized, had been drawn to him even back when she'd lacked the courage to act on her own feelings. But that didn't change anything.

Jake leaned forward, one palm braced on the desktop. "Forget about the mess between us. You need to go back to Middleton and *just be yourself.* Don't waste your life running away. Go back there and set up your design business. People will accept you."

"They probably would if I wanted to do that, but I don't. Maybe *I'm* not the one who's stuck in a past role," she shot back. "Why don't *you* go back to Middleton and sort through your past? I'm a big girl now and I'm through being afraid to take chances. I'm going to London."

He straightened, his expression bleak. "I guess you have to go your own road."

She watched him turn and walk out, her heart dying inside her. Going to London seemed like the obvious thing. She couldn't go back to her old life and Jake wasn't interested in having a place in her new one. Staying here in Dallas would be torture, wondering if she would bump into him, maybe out with another woman.

If he'd asked her to stay with him, she was miserably sure that she would have. London meant nothing to her compared to what he meant. But he didn't ask her to be with him, only to go back to Middleton.

No matter how she loved him, it seemed they couldn't triumph over the past.

Two hours later, after closing her office door and sobbing quietly into a pillow, Emily felt like a wrung-out excuse for a human being. She had to pick herself up, had to make some decisions.

The design internship she'd dreamed and longed for now seemed worthless. But she couldn't let herself cave in, she thought, pushing back a strand of hair as she wiped away the last traces of her tears.

Should she go to London even though all she wanted

to do was stay here? Stay here and pine for Jake, Emily thought angrily.

She'd be an idiot to let this chance pass her by. The British Design Institute was one of the most prestigious design schools in the world. All her life, she'd given in to others' plans for her future, let other people sway her choices. How could she turn down such a big honor?

Still, she loved the job she had, as menial as it was sometimes. She was just beginning to learn from Sarah Blair's vast experience.

Compelled to talk to someone about the dilemma, Emily crossed the office and went down the hall to see if Sally was in her airy studio.

Finding the door to her boss's lair open, Emily peeked inside. She was through letting other people decide things for her, but seeking counsel could be a good thing.

"Sally?"

The gray-haired woman looked up from her sketch pad. "Emily! Come in."

"If you have a moment," Emily said, trying to banish the timid note from her voice, "I'd like to talk with you about something."

Her boss laid aside the sketch pad. "Ask away."

Emily sank into a chair facing the other woman's desk. "Six months ago I applied for an internship at the British Design Institute. I just received a letter saying their original choice for the internship has withdrawn. I'm next in line."

"Emily!" Sally sprang up from her chair and came around the desk to bestow a warm congratulatory hug on her. "What an honor. The British Design Institute!"

"Thank you." Emily blinked back a tear. It was nice to have someone excited about her achievement. Jake's disapproval had robbed her of some of the joy she'd expected to feel when she dreamed of winning the internship.

Sally slipped behind her desk and sank into her chair. "Of course, it's a wonderful compliment. You don't really have to do an internship to be successful, but London is a big, exciting place."

"I know," Emily said firmly. "I never thought I'd get this kind of opportunity. This kind of background will really help me in my career."

"Well," Sally said, "it can't hurt. Particularly if you're interested in handling large contracts for big corporations."

Emily refolded the letter nervously. "I haven't really thought about whether I'd specialize or not."

"BDI has a strong industrial slant, although they don't advertise it," Sally told her. "Their reputation is impeccable."

Looking across the desk at the older woman, Emily felt a wave of gratitude. "I really appreciate your taking a chance and hiring me."

Sally smiled. "It wasn't such a huge leap. You obviously have talent and a determined attitude. I like that in a junior designer."

"I've loved working here," Emily said, realizing just how much she'd miss the designer's eclectic array of jobs if she left. Just for a moment, she felt a surge of resistance to the idea. Sally's design practice included a number of expensive homes that allowed a real range of creativity.

It wasn't just the work, though. Emily felt as if she'd already slipped into a niche here, working easily with the four designers who labored under Sally's supervision. Even Candace, the perfect receptionist, had grown on her.

"You said you wanted to ask me something," Sally reminded her.

"Oh?" Emily looked down. What was there to hesitate about? She'd been offered the internship and she felt she had to accept it. If she stayed in Dallas, she'd be near Jake. The thought left her torn, longing to stay near, but wanting to flee from the pain loving him brought her.

Two months ago, she'd have jumped at this chance. Now, she saw it as a way to escape her inner turmoil. Maybe London would be far enough away to help her start over again. Maybe she'd eventually stop loving Jake.

"I guess I just wanted to tell you about this," Emily said finally. "There's really no question about what I need to do. Only an idiot would turn this down."

"Mmm, maybe." Her boss sat behind her desk, a shrewd expression on her face. "I tell you what, Emily. I think it's great that you won the internship and I understand your going for it, but I want you to know you have a place here if you end up deciding to specialize in the residential market. Either after you finish at BDI or next month if you decide the food in London isn't worth eating. You just let me know."

"Thanks," Emily said, affection and appreciation choking her voice.

So that was it, she thought as she left the room. She and her broken heart were going to London.

Twelve

Maybe I'm not the one who's stuck in a past role.

Emily's words echoed in Jake's head as he pulled the Harley into a parking space in front of Middleton's old-fashioned drugstore.

He looked around, seeing the pink granite courthouse in the center of the square, the bank building with its short, heavy columns so out of place. The names of the tired little stores that rimmed the square had changed, all but one or two. Across from the drugstore, the cinema still played movies that were three months behind the new releases.

When he'd hijacked Emily, short weeks ago, he hadn't even looked at the place as he'd driven through it. Maybe there was a reason for that.

Jake leaned his cycle on its kickstand, pulling off his helmet and running a hand through his hair. It was so much the same. He couldn't help the memories that came crashing in, the images of his boyhood he'd thought so far behind him.

He'd been arrested and spent a night in jail at the age of fifteen. The unimposing building was two doors down. How many times had he been cautioned for driving too fast through the center of town?

It didn't take much to be a bad kid in Middleton fifteen years ago. He'd smoked behind the school, drove a noisy motorcycle, pulled a few pranks. Most of all he'd had a father who drank and routinely sobered up in the city jail. He'd come into the world with a bad legacy and a chip the size of Texas on his shoulder.

In the blink of an instant, he remembered going to Susan Mills's house to pick her up for a date. Blond and bubbly, she'd chased him for a year before he decided, in the arrogant way of troubled youth, to give her a tumble.

Her father had taken one look at him, James Dean reborn with an attitude, and kicked him off the front porch.

In retrospect, Jake supposed he'd deserved it. But at the time, he'd worn the town's distrust and condemnation like a badge, flaunting his bad blood and challenging every restriction.

No wonder he'd so easily succumbed to deceitful interludes with girls like Kristin Sullivan. Girls who liked the taste of the wild life he offered, but had no intention of risking their spotless reputations and more acceptable boyfriends to take on trouble in the form of Jake Wolf.

Where had Emily been back then? Safely tucked into her upper-middle-class family home, far above his touch.

Had he even seen her as a distinct person back then?

If he were honest, he had to acknowledge that sadness shaded almost all his memories of this town. Emily's life back then had seemed the direct opposite of his. Had he always just assumed that her life here couldn't have been anything but good since it was so different from his own?

On the way into town, he'd passed the cemetery where, at seventeen, he'd buried his father. In a plot next to him lay the woman who'd given birth to Jake. He could hardly remember her.

Jake slung his helmet over the cycle's mirror and stepped up onto the sidewalk, his mind full of Emily.

A week after their last conversation, he'd stopped back by the design studio where she worked, unable to bear not knowing what she had decided to do. The receptionist had told him Emily had moved overseas two days before.

In the past month since she'd left, he'd thought of her constantly, replaying their every conversation, remembering the way she smiled, the way she'd touched him.

Losing his mind.

Was he an idiot to have tried to get her to deal with her past? He could have kept her with him, warm and sweet, recklessly ignoring the reckoning that would have eventually caught up with him. Eventually, she'd have to come to terms with their differences.

Eventually, she'd have left.

He'd been with a lot of women in his wild days. Until he'd taken her, Emily had slept like an unawakened princess. Not a virgin, as she'd angrily said, but essentially innocent.

Until he betrayed her, stealing her soft caresses when he didn't have a right to them. Not because he felt condemned by where he'd come from . . . not anymore, but because he knew in his heart that she had to accept herself before she could really accept him.

Then again, had *he* truly come to accept himself?

No matter where he started, he always ended up at their last fight, hearing her words over and over again.

Ever since he'd rescued her from that hellhole of a motel, he'd been clear that she was running away from her past. No one changed completely overnight. Sure, people grew and made different choices, but huge personality changes didn't happen unless a person was on drugs or mentally imbalanced.

Emily was neither of those. He might not have known her as well as he thought back in their years of growing up in the same vicinity. But he knew she was as sane as he thought himself to be.

Walking along the sidewalk, he barely noticed the office supply and beauty parlor.

It was only after she'd hurled her last accusations at him that Jake had wondered if he'd been wrong about Emily, all along. True, she was definitely in a life crisis, but had he been way off base about her needing to come back here to Middleton to face herself?

Stopping at the corner, he waited for the light to change, aware of receiving a hard stare from the old biddy behind the wheel of the one car at the light.

He hadn't done much beyond flouting a few rules and breaking a few teenage hearts all those years ago, but Middleton apparently still remembered him. Unless he was blowing his reputation out of proportion. Maybe the old lady hadn't even recognized him.

Conscious of the sardonic smile that curled his mouth, Jake crossed the street and walked the few steps to where David's office stood. DAVID LOUGHLIN. C.P.A., the sign read.

Pushing the door open, he saw a weatherbeaten woman in her fifties pounding away at a keyboard as she scowled at the screen of an ancient computer. He glanced around, curious to see how his old friend spent his days.

The room was modestly furnished, looking a little like a page out of a Sears catalog. David could have used his sister's creative touch, Jake mused.

"Can I help you?" the woman behind the desk challenged.

"I'm Jake Wolf. I'd like to see David, if he's in."

"Jake Wolf!" The woman stared at him. "I remember you."

The bluntness of this announcement made him smile ruefully. "Do you? Well, hopefully, we've all matured."

David's secretary looked him up and down, an answering smile creasing her lined face. "Possibly, but it's not polite for you to say so."

Startled, Jake laughed.

"You stay here," she said. "I'll tell David you want to see him."

The woman disappeared into the back office.

"Jake!" he heard David's voice exclaim. "Here? Well, send him in."

Two minutes later, Jake found himself seated in his old friend's office.

". . . so my parents met her at the airport to see her off," David said. "I'd have gone myself but I couldn't reschedule things here."

Emily's brother shook his head. "She was as cool as a cucumber, not panicked at all, Mom and Dad said. Had her passport and all the necessary papers. Here she is moving to a foreign country and she's not the least scared, according to my mother."

Jake realized with a jolt that he could see Emily handling the transition. Had she grown up since she'd come to Dallas, or had her maturity been there all along, submerged in the emotion stirred up by the major changes she was initiating?

"I still don't understand her," David complained, faint frustration on his face. "Why is she doing all this? When we were growing up, she didn't say anything about wanting to move away."

"Maybe she didn't really want to move," Jake heard himself say, "maybe she had to leave to . . . disconnect. It's hard to change your image of yourself."

"Is that what you did when you moved to Dallas?" David asked with curiosity.

Jake shook his head ruefully. "No, I raised hell for a while, same as I did here. But then one day I woke up and realized no one there cared if I was a rebel or if my father was a drunk."

His friend looked down at his desk. "People here cared, didn't they?"

"Yep," Jake said, "just like they care that your daddy is the mayor."

David lifted his gaze. "It *is* hard sometimes. Do you think Emily *had* to leave Middleton?"

"I don't know." He sat in silence for a minute. "The trouble with Emily is that she has a tender heart. She could have stayed here and broke out from her old image, but your mom and dad, and the rest of the town, would have been really upset. She'd have had to tell them all to go to hell. Can you see Emily doing that?"

David paused. "No. I mean, she's never said anything like that before."

"So she left Middleton. That way, she could do what she wanted and not really worry anyone." Jake smiled. "Or it would have worked out that way if you hadn't sent the troops after her. Maybe you and I were doing the same thing as the rest of the town. Not letting her be herself."

"Maybe," her brother said with a brooding frown. "She just seems—seemed, so helpless."

Jake laughed, thinking about the chase Emily had led

him on in the past month. "Kind of reminds me of how a colt can look when they first stand up, all wobbly and unsteady. Before you know it, they're running around and nipping at you. Emily faltered a few times, but she seems to have found her feet."

"I guess so," David said doubtfully.

"I'm wondering," Jake murmured, "if she was ever really so helpless. Did you know the lawyer jerk she worked for made a pass at her?"

"What?" David straightened in his chair. "Jim Morris? I knew that idiot was being sued for sexual harassment by another woman who worked for him, but I never thought he'd dare do that to Emily! I'll kill him."

"I understand the urge," Jake said dryly, "but Emily seems to have taken care of the matter in the way she wanted to. Said she could have sued him but didn't want to waste any more time and energy on him. She turned him down flat and was glad when he fired her."

David gazed across the desk in amazement. "That's what set her off! Morris made a pass and fired her. God, she left town to get away from him?"

Jake shook his head. "No, she said she was relieved when he fired her. Apparently, she'd been unhappy for a long time."

Emily's brother didn't say anything for a long moment. "I don't want her to be unhappy, but I'm worried she won't ever come back. That we won't see much of her anymore."

"Me, too," Jake said slowly. "I'm in love with your sister."

To his surprise, David just nodded. "I wondered about that when you guys were here that afternoon . . . and when I went down to Dallas. What are you going to do?"

A ghost of a laugh escaped Jake. David didn't seem the least bit surprised or disturbed by his declaration. Jake had held back from pursuing a future with Emily because he'd been convinced that *she* still saw him as Middleton's bad boy. But somewhere in his head, he'd wondered what her family would say about the two of them.

Now he knew. David, at least, didn't seem horrified. Of course, David had accepted him when he'd been a cocky kid with a chip on his shoulder. He should have realized that if his friend saw past their class differences when they were young, he wasn't likely to be judgmental now.

Jake had left Middleton years before, determined to outrun his own unpleasant past. For a long time now, he'd felt successful at that. Starting his own business, living a clean life. He wasn't caught up in proving any-thing to anyone now. But had he really let go of all that?

Then Emily had erupted into his life and stirred everything up. Brought him alive, it seemed. Yes, she had to break out of her old patterns, but with her chal-lenge ringing in his ears, he saw now that some of his history had still echoed inside him, as well.

Sweet, innocent, determined, sexy Emily had taught him a thing or two.

Jake realized now that while he cared about David, he didn't give a damn what his old friend thought about his being in love with Emily.

He loved her like he'd never loved a woman. He just had to find a way to convince her of the fact.

Emily moved forward with the crowd of commuters as the subway train pulled into the station. She'd been in London less than a month, but she'd become accustomed to taking "the tube" to work each day.

Not finding a seat, she grasped a hanging strap and hiked the shoulder strap of her briefcase higher. The past weeks had been stressful, but not unsuccessful. She'd managed to find herself a decent place to stay, close enough to the Institute while still costing a reasonable amount. Even if the flat didn't quite feel like home, she still collapsed there every night with gratitude.

Still, her tiny rooms could barely contain her grief of loving Jake so futilely. But she craved the solitude to indulge her emotions to their maximum. Without the distraction of people around her, she could remember the exact color of his eyes, the sound of his laugh, the faintly desperate expression on his face when he was trying to keep her from taking a risk. She could remember and weep bitter tears until she fell into an exhausted sleep.

So much for distance easing the pain.

But all in all, she was surviving better than she'd expected. When she had moments like this to reflect and see the experience outside of her broken heart, she felt competent and . . . brave, very unlike the person she'd been before in Middleton.

She also felt deeply lonely. Who would have thought she would miss Jake so much after all this time? Especially as rancorous as their parting had been? How could she have become so accustomed to his presence in only a few short weeks?

Accepting the internship had been her own choice, but she'd begun to consider the basis of that choice in the last few days. She had realized late that she'd come here to lose the pain of a broken heart. How brave was that?

Emily automatically tightened her grip on the strap as the train reeled around a corner.

London was a beautiful city, rich in history. She made herself spend all her free time exploring the sights and soaking in the British culture. Coming here was a great opportunity, both career-wise and culturally. She knew that.

Still, she hated the constantly damp climate, the inedible food, and even, most of the work. Interior design had first drawn her for the opportunity to create *intimate* spaces. She'd never seen herself laboring to make intimidating official lobbies in public buildings.

The internship had already been educational, but none of the work in front of her brought her any excitement.

Involuntarily, she remembered the haunted house Jake had taken her to the day they'd picnicked. Aside from the joyful afternoon spent in his company, she'd loved the old house. She knew that places like that weren't plentiful enough to make a career of them, but she'd had enough of this soulless corporate prettifying.

She'd come all this way to find a whole heart and she wasn't happy now that she was here.

Staring blindly at the back of the commuter standing in front of her, Emily tried to imagine telling the Dean of Instruction at BDI that she'd changed her mind and didn't want the internship after all.

It was impossible, she told herself, shrinking at the thought of such a confrontation. What was the matter with her? She'd dreamed about this internship and the recognition it brought, pined for it as she sat in her paralegal job in Middleton.

But she'd accepted the job because it was far away from Dallas and Jake. Maybe she *was* running away this time.

The staff at BDI would think she was a fool if she quit now.

The commuter train braked to a halt, the doors sliding open as a herd of humanity pressed through.

Emily sank onto a vacated seat, suddenly hearing the familiarity of her own thoughts. All her life she'd based her decisions on what people would think. She'd stayed in that paralegal job in Middleton because she hadn't wanted to upset people by leaving it.

Living on her own terms, making her own choices, all that had been her goal. Now here she was afraid of leaving the internship because of the possible disapproval of a bunch of people she'd potentially never see again in her life.

Leaving Middleton to create her own life had made sense, but she'd come to Britain for all the wrong reasons. To escape being near Jake. To run away from her own feelings for him.

Here she was in a new country with a new life . . . and the same old patterns.

Involuntarily she remembered Jake's words, *You don't have to throw out everything to change your life.* She'd thrown out a few things all right, but had she really changed?

When the train braked at her stop a few minutes later, Emily got off in a daze. One thing was clear. If she was living a new life, making her own decisions, she ought to try doing things she *liked*.

Working for Sally, for instance.

Nothing drew her back to Middleton to live, but she wanted to be nearby. Her parents weren't getting any younger. Someday David would get married and have kids. Not living in Middleton didn't mean staying away from them.

As she walked the short block to the Institute building, Emily remembered her most recent phone call to her mother. There had been a sad note in the older woman's voice but, surprisingly, no criticism. They'd talked for half an hour about London and all the places she'd seen.

Finding herself standing beside the desk assigned to her in the central intern room a half hour later, Emily acknowledged to herself that she wanted to go back to Dallas. Damn the staff at BDI if they didn't understand. She wanted to work with Sally on creating beautiful homes.

More than anything, she wanted Jake, but Emily knew that possibility had little to do with where she lived. Even when they'd been in the same apartment, the past had separated them.

But she knew she was going to seek him out on her return to the States. If only to tell him how she felt, she'd see him. What good did it do to shake off her "little Emily" persona if she couldn't go after what she wanted most in all the world?

Sitting down at a vacant computer terminal, Emily wrote out her resignation.

An hour later, feeling lighter than she had in years, Emily climbed the steps from the tube to the wet street. Mentally planning her packing, she walked along through the rain, only half-conscious of the drops that plastered her hair to her head.

She'd put her foot on the first step of her apartment building before she realized a man stood at the top of the steps, his back to the door, watching her through the misty rain.

"Jake!"

"Hello, Emily." His blue eyes looked darker as he stood huddled in the doorway, his short hair wet with the rain.

Staring at him in shock, she couldn't help the joy that surged through her, making her legs weak and trembly beneath her.

"You startled me!" she said, still standing on the bottom step looking up at him. "What are you doing here?"

As soon as the words were out of her mouth, caution set in. It didn't seem likely, but had he come all this distance to chastise her, to try and convince her to return to Middleton?

"I came to see you," he said, his gaze intent on her face.

Trying to hold her tumultuous emotions in check, she dug her keys out of her pocket and climbed the rest of the steps to unlock the door. "Let's get out of the rain."

With him standing beside her, so close, so beloved, her fingers fumbled with the keys. Jake said nothing.

Finally unlocking the door, Emily led the way inside. "I'm one flight up."

His footsteps sounded loud as he climbed the stairs behind her. Why had he come?

Opening the door to her flat, she flicked on the lights and nervously dropped her keys and purse on a nearby table.

Jake closed the door behind him, glancing around at the bare, furnished room. "I guess you haven't had a chance to really settle in."

"No," she said, gesturing for him to sit down. The moment was too fraught with emotions and possibilities. She didn't have it in her to chitchat.

All she wanted to do was fling herself into his arms

and hold him forever. But she couldn't. Too much stood in the way.

He sat down on the couch, leaning forward, his posture revealing his own tension. "Emily . . ."

Jake paused as if unsure how to continue. "I had to come. There are a lot of things I need to say to you."

She held very still, afraid to interrupt him, afraid to hear what might come next.

"I keep remembering what you said that day about me using you. I can't stand you thinking that." He lifted his gaze to hers. "It's not true, Em. I made love to you because I couldn't keep my hands to myself, couldn't resist you. You mean so much more to me than just another woman."

Emily stared at him, conscious of a drumming in her ears, not sure what he meant, but pitifully hopeful.

He sat on the couch, seeming to watch for her reaction. "I've realized some things since you left Dallas and I had to see you, to talk to you."

"What have you realized?" she heard herself say through a throat that felt paralyzed.

Jake straightened, shoving a hand through his damp hair. "I went to see David last week. Went back to Middleton and took a hard look at . . . myself."

Emily waited, her heart thundering against her breastbone.

He took a deep breath. "What you said about me dealing with my past? You were right. I have a lot of history in that town, just like you do."

"So what happened when you went back?" she asked, hope flowering in her.

"I saw myself," he said with a short laugh. "I kept remembering how it was there. How I felt when I lived there as a kid. But more than that, I kept thinking about you and the weeks you were in Dallas."

Jake got up and went to the window. "I've known for a long time that I'm not still that rebellious kid from Middleton, but I didn't really see until I went back that you're not the shy little girl you were back then, either. When you came to Dallas and I found myself wanting you so bad, somehow I slipped back a little into that kid I used to be. I guess I've been doing the thing I accused you of doing—being afraid to completely let go of the past."

"Oh, Jake," she said, her voice shaking.

"I was wrong to try and get you to go back," he admitted. "I honestly thought you needed to, but I was wrong."

Jake crossed the room and came to where she sat, crouching down before her. "I never wanted you to be stifled. You have to know that. I just thought you had to deal with all that small-town stuff before you could really be free . . . to be with me."

"Really?" she asked, staring into his beautiful face, dizzy from the rushing of her blood through her veins.

He seemed to understand now what she'd been struggling with all this time, she thought, feeling dazed.

"Yes, really." Jake smiled, still crouched in front of her. "But you've proved me wrong. You got a job and then this internship thing. Here you are in London. You've taken charge of your life."

Emily shook her head, very conscious of the irony of the situation. "I've taken charge of my life all right, but I realized today that I've also taken a few missteps."

"What do you mean?" His brow knit into a puzzled frown.

She drew in a slow breath. "I took this internship to . . . put some distance between . . . us."

Jake's frown deepened. "You moved here to get away from me?"

Emily hesitated. "Yes."

He stared at her a long moment, as if uncertain what to say.

"I'm in love with you," he said at last, the words seeming to tumble out.

She could only look at him, uncertain if she'd heard him correctly. How many times had she dreamed of hearing him say those words?

"You're what?" she asked faintly.

"I think I fell in love with you that night at the ratty motel," he said with a rueful smile. "I don't know if you can believe that or if you have any serious feelings for me, but—"

Released from her paralysis, Emily sprang forward on the couch and threw herself into Jake's arms.

Caught hard against his chest as he straightened to his feet, she lifted her mouth for his kiss.

His mouth hard and desperate against hers, he kissed her. Emily felt his hand shake as he stroked her face.

"God, Emily, I love you so much," he said, his voice low and intense.

"I love you, Jake Wolf." She smiled up at him through a mist of joyful tears. "I've been in love with you since I was fourteen. When I came to Dallas, everything between us just sprang up. But you seemed so appalled to be . . . involved with me."

"I'm sorry," he whispered. "I was afraid of getting hurt. More afraid of hurting you."

"Me, too," she said, her voice low. "Afraid of being hurt, I mean. That's why I came here, to keep myself from hoping that I'd see you again if I stayed in Dallas, run into you somewhere. Maybe with someone else."

He shook his head, his face fierce. "Not a chance, honey. I love you so much I haven't been able to sleep the last month. Can't eat, can't think about anything but you."

She brushed a kiss across the strong hand that gripped hers.

"I want to be with you," he said decisively. "I've talked to some people about putting the dealership up for sale so I can move here to London to be with you. Will you marry me, Emily?"

Drawing him closer, she whispered a heartfelt "Yes."

Their lips met in a sweet, piercing kiss. She felt as if he'd given her his heart in the mingling of their breath.

"Yes, I'll marry you," she said, drawing back a fraction. "But you should keep the dealership because I resigned my internship today."

"You resigned it?"

Emily nodded, blissfully happy. "What I really want to do is work with Sally and live with you."

His laughter rumbled in his chest. "You can work anywhere you want as long as you always live with me."

Locked in his arms, Emily marveled that she'd finally found herself and the love of her life in this one man.

Epilogue

"So what's my anniversary surprise?" Emily teased, tickling her husband of two years with a long strand of grass.

He lay back on the blanket, his powerful body stretched out beside her.

"What makes you think I have a surprise for you?" Jake said, raising an eyebrow in query. If it hadn't been for the grin quirking the corner of his mouth, she might have been fooled.

"Let's see, you show up at my job, kidnap me for a picnic lunch here at this wonderful old house where you brought me when I first came to Dallas, and you look like a ten-year-old with a secret. Out with it!"

"Maybe I just thought you needed a break," he protested, looking anything but innocent. "You've been working so hard since Sally promoted you. Can't a guy take his sexy wife out for lunch?"

Emily laughed. "I know you too well. What do you have up your sleeve?"

He heaved a big fake sigh. "Not up my sleeve. In the pocket of my jacket."

Eagerly grabbing his leather jacket, she pulled out a fat envelope. "What is it?"

"Look inside," he said patiently.

She ripped it open and scanned the top page of the thick sheaf of papers.

"It's a contract on a house." Emily looked at him in surprise.

"Not just a house," Jake said softly, his gaze on her face. *"This* house."

"Jake!" she breathed in joyous disbelief. "You worked out a deal with the current owners?"

"Yes, my love," he admitted, sitting up. "I knew no one else could do justice to the place."

She threw herself into his arms. "I am the happiest woman in the world."

Jake drew her closer.

"Even without the house," she said, lifting her mouth to his.

He kissed her long and slow.

When he lifted his head, Jake smiled. "Think of it as the cherry on top."

ABOUT THE AUTHOR

Carol Rose lives in Texas with her softball-playing husband of twenty years and her two beautiful, rambunctious teenage daughters. A longtime romance reader herself, she enjoys writing realistic stories about people who could be her neighbors. Carol's always interested in hearing readers' likes and dislikes and can be contacted at:

P.O. Box 8171
Fort Worth, TX 76124

BOOK YOUR PLACE ON OUR WEBSITE AND MAKE THE READING CONNECTION!

We've created a customized website just for our very special readers, where you can get the inside scoop on everything that's going on with Zebra, Pinnacle and Kensington books.

When you come online, you'll have the exciting opportunity to:

- View covers of upcoming books
- Read sample chapters
- Learn about our future publishing schedule (listed by publication month *and author*)
- Find out when your favorite authors will be visiting a city near you
- Search for and order backlist books from our online catalog
- Check out author bios and background information
- Send e-mail to your favorite authors
- Meet the Kensington staff online
- Join us in weekly chats with authors, readers and other guests
- Get writing guidelines
- AND MUCH MORE!

Visit our website at
http://www.zebrabooks.com

COMING IN OCTOBER FROM
ZEBRA BOUQUET ROMANCES

#65 BACHELORS INC.: TEMPTING ZACK
by Colleen Faulkner

__(0-8217-6700-3, $3.99) New in town, Doctor Kayla Burns is instantly charmed by her pint-sized patient Savannah Taylor . . . and her rugged, earthy dad, Zack. But Zack wants nothing to do with career women like Kayla until an accidental kiss leads him into dangerous territory for a man determined to preserve his bachelorhood at any cost . . .

#66 THIS MAGIC MOMENT by Lynda Simmons

__(0-8217-6701-1, $3.99) After eight years of happy marriage to Reid Ferguson, his wife Viki decided that she and their two small children needed real security—security that Reid couldn't provide. Determined to win his family back, Reid invents a plan of playful seduction that just might convince Viki that happiness comes from a love that lasts forever.

#67 TWO OF A KIND by Elise Smith

__(0-8217-6686-4, $3.99) Professor Regina Sutherland is sure that she'll never find a man like the brilliant Will Creeden, the college boyfriend who broke her heart. But when he shows up as the new head of her department, his only intention is to get a second chance at his first love, and to ask her the question that can only be answered in two words: "I do . . ."

#68 SOMETHING SO RIGHT by Jane Kidder

__(0-8217-6703-8, $3.99) Caroline Sawyer is delighted that her mother is getting married—she only wishes the groom-to-be was someone besides the father of her ex-fiancé, Josh Chandler. But when the two are thrown together at the wedding, they just might be able to put the hurt and anger of the past aside long enough to rediscover each other . . .

Put a Little Romance in Your Life With
Fern Michaels

__Dear Emily	0-8217-5676-1	$6.99US/$8.50CAN
__Sara's Song	0-8217-5856-X	$6.99US/$8.50CAN
__Wish List	0-8217-5228-6	$6.99US/$7.99CAN
__Vegas Rich	0-8217-5594-3	$6.99US/$8.50CAN
__Vegas Heat	0-8217-5758-X	$6.99US/$8.50CAN
__Vegas Sunrise	1-55817-5983-3	$6.99US/$8.50CAN
__Whitefire	0-8217-5638-9	$6.99US/$8.50CAN

Call toll free **1-888-345-BOOK** to order by phone or use this coupon to order by mail.

Name_____

Address_____

City _____ State _____Zip_____

Please send me the books I have checked above.

I am enclosing	$_____
Plus postage and handling*	$_____
Sales tax (in New York and Tennessee)	$_____
Total amount enclosed	$_____

*Add $2.50 for the first book and $.50 for each additional book.

Send check or money order (no cash or CODs) to:

Kensington Publishing Corp., 850 Third Avenue, New York, NY 10022

Prices and Numbers subject to change without notice.

All orders subject to availability.

Check out our website at **www.kensingtonbooks.com**